SEARCH FOR THE LOON'S NECKLACE
Chronicles of Eirgalon: Book 2

by

Joel Kreger

ISBN 978-0-9889514-6-4

Dedication

To my students throughout the years:

May you find that which inspires you,

May you learn through your failures,

And may you always follow your heart!

Table of Contents

Prologue

By mere tendrils of thoughts do the gods shift,
ere so slightly,
the dream of a single man,
and so is altered the course of human history.

In realms which lie beyond domains of men, exist such beings called by mortal men: "the gods." Be they gods or demons in the thoughts of men matters little, for truth be told, to some they may be gods and to some they may be demons. Be that as it may, at times they touch the human world, and in their touching they move and turn that world into different outcomes and alternate timelines.

One of theses beings was known as Lox. Some claimed he was the alter image of Gluskabi, as malevolent as the former was benevolent. He saw that Gluskabi had altered human history merging Viking and Celtic settlers with the native inhabitants of the land that was now called Eirgalon. Lox determined to bend this human history his own way. In Gluskabi's altered timeline of human history, the Haudenoshonee man, Deganawida (Two River Currents Flowing Together) received a vision from the Creator. It was a vision of peace and cooperation among all the Haudenoshonee causing them to form a great lodge of the people some would call the Iroquois confederation, but the crafty Lox had different plans.

And so it was that thirty years before the Alting for the first High King of Eirgalon, Lox stepped into human time and gave to Deganawida an altered vision and so created Malsum, a human manifestation of his malevolence. His vision was to unify the land, but with terror and might against the people from the east. With determination they would drive the invaders and their collaborators from the land.

Chapter 1 – Vision

Deganawida was a young man born to the Huron people who lived in the western lands of Eirgalon. He was born west of the valley of the Mahakentuck on the northern edge of the great lake his people called Ontario, which means beautiful waters.

The vision quest is a sacred rite of passage for the young men in the land of Eirgalon. They lay themselves open to the spirit world seeking dreams to guide their lives. When it was time for young Deganawida to make the passage to manhood, his elders prepared him by guiding his fast and sending him alone to a quiet place to wait for his vision to come. None of them could know of the great vision that the Creator intended to give this talented youth. He was to be the Peacemaker, uniting the people of the region in peace and cooperation. That vision, however, was not to be, for the malevolent spirit of Lox intervened and came to Deganawida before the Creator could complete the Peacemaker vision.

Lox twisted the tendrils of this dream. It was still a dream of unity for the great people of the beautiful lakes, but this dream was twisted to become one of unity under his watchful and controlling eye as the people joined together to confront the dwellers of the lands to the east. Deganawida was to become Malsum, the incarnation of the malevolence of Lox. He would drive his people to unity against their common foe: the descendants of the European invaders.

Deganawida, now called Malsum, which means "evil wolf," returned to his village and shared the dream of his vision quest with his shaman. The old Huron shaman of his village was troubled by this vision, so he sent Malsum away from them. Malsum wandered for a time and traveled to the southern shores of Lake Ontario, where he came to live among the people of the Onondaga. There was power in the young man, for Lox dwelt within him, and in time he rose to leadership among his new people. He called them forth, and from the quarreling tribes of Mohak, Oneida, Onondaga, Cayuga, and Seneca, he formed the mighty Haudenoshonee. He united them in their hatred of the Celtic people of Eirgalon, as those people called their land.

For several years he sent agents amongst them, sowing seeds of discord and dissension among the Wabanaki and Celtic people of the lands to the east. When he heard rumors that the one who would be unifying all the people of eastern Eirgalon had been revealed by his adversary, Gluskabi, he made plans to destroy this one. Those plans had come to naught, and now Malsum was confronted by people who claimed to be one people, and who were ruled by High King Skoth.

It was an early day of summer-like weather in late May, only a few short weeks after the Alting that had proclaimed Skoth to be the High King of Eirgalon. A loyal minion of Malsum stood on the bluffs on the western shore the River Mahakentuck and watched the longships of King Duncan of Glesga returning to their port on that isle near the eastern shore. Ayenwatha was his given name, but Malsum called him simply Ayen, and he was Malsum's warchief.

Ayen had hoped to attack this Celtic stronghold before King Duncan and his men had returned, but now he must make different plans. Motioning to his men to retreat, they stepped back from the bluff and began to make their way back to camp. Ayen took one last look across the river. He cleared his throat and spat at the sight, and then followed his men.

Chapter 2 - Cats and Dogs

King Duncan of Glesga stormed out of the meeting with the new High King fuming on the inside. As he walked out the tent door where the meeting had been held he sputtered, "Some High King, I ask for help and I get told not now. "

Two steps behind him, Skoth came out of the tent exclaiming, "But I haven't given you a final answer."

Duncan, still walking away, turned his head and responded, "You've said enough. I don't know if you fear him, or what, but I go to confront Malsum. You do what you feel fit to do."

With that said, Duncan strode away from Skoth and went back down the beach toward his delegation's campsite. His people were already hard at work breaking camp and preparing to sail.

Skoth put his hands on his hips and sighed.

Behind him, he heard someone clear his throat. He turned to see Erik standing guard by the tent entrance. Erik was the grizzle-bearded (some would say elderly) warrior who had been the chief bodyguard for King Unaine of Fadis Innis. Skoth had been raised in the household of King Unaine at Dunsheelin, the capital of Fadis Innis. Somehow Erik, who had mentored the orphan boy Skoth, had simply assumed the role of being his bodyguard and advisor when Skoth became the new High King.

Skoth asked, "Do you have something you want to say?"

Erik answered with a smirk and a comment, "Looks like that didn't go so well. Maybe this High King business isn't quite what you thought it would be."

"No, Erik, it's not. He just didn't want to listen to me."

"Well, your highest majesty, I've got a thought on that one, if you'd be liking to hear it."

"I might as well. I suspect you'd tell me anyway."

"I probably would, at that," Erik said with a smile, "you see, it's sort of like the difference between cats and dogs."

Skoth gave him an incredulous look and said, "What? One of the leaders of my people storms away from me, and you start talking about cats and dogs?"

"Aye. Sometimes the simple ways of explaining are the best. You see, think about Chief Unaine, I'd say he is like a dog. You can talk with a dog. They understand reward and punishment. They are loyal and they listen. But cats - they are different. You can't really talk with them. You have to lure them in. King Duncan is a cat. Every cat thinks that it is the boss. It will pay attention to you - usually. That is, it will if you have something it wants. You see, cats don't really listen to you; they expect you to listen to them. They expect you to do things their way. King Duncan is a cat."

"What? Duncan is a cat?"

"Aye. And a right smart, high, mighty, and righteous one at that!"

"And so how does knowing this help me?"

Erik smiled, paused a moment for effect, and said, "He'll listen to you if he thinks you are telling him what he wants to hear."

"But what if I'm not really telling him exactly what he wants to hear?"

"Aye, there's the tricky part. You have to say enough his way to keep his interest, yet still be honest with yourself. Tis a king's job, to be sure."

Skoth sighed again and said a bit sarcastically, "Thanks a lot, Erik. I sure do appreciate your words of wisdom."

Erik grinned, "Nothing but the best for you, my chief."

Skoth went back into the tent thinking about what Duncan had wanted. He had pushed to have several ships of warriors immediately dispatched to his city in order to confront the gathering Haudenoshonee horde on the western shore of the Mahakentuck Bay. Skoth had listened to his impassioned plea, but then told Duncan he couldn't expect that a force would be sent immediately. Looking back on it, Skoth realized that while did he did intend to make sure help was sent to Glesga in the future, what Duncan had heard was that there were no immediate decisions made to send a fighting force to Duncan's lands. Maybe Erik was right. Maybe he could have responded in a more effective way to Duncan.

The new day that had dawned in New Caledonia, bright and full of promise, had quickly become cloudy with the departure of Duncan. Now that Skoth had been named as High King of Eirgalon in the assembly (called by the people an alting) he had to decide what action to take next. He knew the chiefs and kings of the land expected him to lead them against their common foe, the Haudenoshonee horde of Malsum, but he also knew his quest was calling him to seek the Loon's Necklace. So, before leaving the city of New Caledonia, he met with his group of close friends and advisors. This included the people who had travelled with him on the quest, as well as the certain chiefs of the people: Unaine, Tkomik, Tyg, and Gunnar (King Haggar's son).

A plan was made. The first step in that plan was for Skoth to lead a delegation to Glesga. That delegation was to include: Skoth, Evlin, Enat, Karl (placed in command of two of the Fadis Innis longships, Gunnar (in command of two longships from New Caledonia), and Padrik (Tyg's aide who would command two of the longships from Heilsand). This would be a sizeable force of several hundred men. Tyg and

Unaine would be returning to their own domains with the remainder of their men. Leesha and Tkaden would be returning with Tkomik to Wausacom, where they were to assemble a force that would head west and join in the defense of the western lands. Teite desired to go with the delegation to the west, but Skoth insisted she return with Unaine to her Fadis Innis home and continue her research at the Academy. Perhaps in some of the written records concerning the lore and legends of the land she would find more information concerning the Loon's Necklace.

It was Skoth's intention that, after a brief stay in Glesga, he would travel up the Mahakentuck in pursuit of the legend of the Loon's Necklace. How many of the rest of the western delegation that was to include was a decision he had not yet made; but as of now, he intended that on the morn of the day in two days to come, they would be heading westward to Glesga.

Chapter 3 – Departures

It was the afternoon of the day that Duncan had stormed out of Skoth's meeting with his advisors, that Evlin approached Skoth with a suggestion.

"Mayhap, my dear, we could make a small adjustment from your plan. What if Duncan is right about the dire predicament of his city? Is it possible that two days may be too late?"

Skoth looked her in the eyes, narrowed his eyes slightly, and asked, "And what would you suggest? There are still tasks to do here and ships to load. If we come ill-prepared, we court danger. Two days is but scant time to make our preparations. I don't see how we can move earlier."

"Aye, my love, tis true. But while the entire force can not, Enat and I can."

Skoth chuckled and said, "Your talents continue to amaze me, Evi, but I didn't think you could fly."

"Don't be silly. Of course, I can't fly. There is no unusual power in this. During our time here, Enat has made friends with Claire, wife of King McLean of the Drogheda domain that lies south of Glesga. They will be setting sail in short order and traveling the coast for a couple of hours before beaching for the night. They will arrive in Glesga on the morrow for a brief stop there before continuing on to Drogheda. Claire has said that they have room for us. We could get to Duncan yet tomorrow and assure him of your imminent arrival."

Skoth hesitated, "I don't know. What if something would happen?"

"Are you saying you think we can't take care of ourselves?"

He could see the ire rise in her eyes. He quickly responded.

"Oh, no. I'm not saying that. Do you really think two days will make that much of a difference?"

"I'd not be suggesting it, if I thought it didn't matter."

"Why not just send a message with McLean, and let him deliver it?"

She smiled and said, "Wouldn't you think a message delivered by two of the High King's favorite women would serve to smooth his ruffled feathers a wee bit more than some formal dispatch handed to him by a messenger boy."

Skoth couldn't help but chuckle at that as he responded, "I'm sure you're right. I give up. Go tell Enat to get ready."

"She's ready. We both are. We knew you'd say 'yes', so we got packed up and we'll be off to the Drogheda ship as soon as you can give me a worthy kiss."

He took her in his arms and said good-bye with a farewell kiss that delivered what she had asked for, and that promised more upon their reunion. If someone had been watching them, they would have thought they were embarking on a long absence instead of a separation of but a few days.

Enat said her farewells to Karl and her family, and then she was off with Evlin to board the Drogheda ship. It was less than an hour later that Skoth watched the ship as it was oared away from the docks heading south to pass the point of the headlands and then to turn west on its journey. As he waved to them from the shore, Skoth had a momentary pang of regret. He worried that it might have been a mistake to send them off by themselves.

The next morning, Tkaden and Leesha said their

farewells and made their way to the camp of Tkomik. Tkaden promised to do his best for Skoth, and Leesha good-naturedly teased him about Evlin "already chasing off after other men," but then made a point of being serious with him and warning him that he had better take care of "the best woman in the world for him."

The final day in New Caledonia was spent provisioning the ships and loading them in preparation for a military campaign. Skoth was ordering them to Glesga, but he wanted them to be prepared to make a several week run up the Mahakentuck River if needed.

That evening, he sat in conversation with Unaine. For a while they discussed elements of the campaign to the west, but then Unaine moved the discussion to personal matters.

"Skoth, you know I have always looked on you as family. Why, I even thought that one day you'd probably marry that spit-fire daughter of mine, little Leesha. Can I speak to you now, not as to my High King, but as a father might to his son?"

"Of course! I'll always want to hear what you have to say!"

Unaine smiled and said, "Well, probably not always. I'm sure you remember a few times when you were growing up, that you were less than happy to hear what I had to say to you."

Now it was Skoth's turn to smile as he remembered some of the lessons he had learned at Unaine's hand. He said, "Aye, I made my share of mistakes."

"And that is the point I want to make with you now. You will make mistakes. We all do. I made a mistake in not watching over Neal enough, and he is dead, and I am partially to blame for that. My point is that you will need to accept the fact that you will make mistakes. The real measure of you as a person, and as our High King, will be how you respond to those mistakes. Admit them. Take responsibility

---

21

for them. Do what you can to fix them. But don't let them drag you down. Use them as a way to make the future better, for yourself and for others."

Skoth was thoughtful for a moment, and then asked, "Am I doing something now that you think is a mistake?"

"It's hard to see something as a mistake with foresight. It's much easier in hindsight. You saw your words with Duncan as a mistake, and you have tried to correct it by quickly sending those two headstrong women after him. Now you worry that you have made another mistake."

"Was it a mistake?"

"I don't know. Only time will tell. But whatever happens, you can't change it now. You can only do your best in the moment. That's what I want you make sure you hear from me. Stay the man you have been raised to be. Do your best. Follow your heart. And when you make mistakes - and you will - pick yourself up, and go on."

"Thank you, Chief. You really have been like a father to me. I promise, I'll do my best."

"That's all I, or anyone, can truly ask of you. However, there is a boon I would request you consider for me."

"A boon? You know I will do whatever I can for you. All you need to do is ask. What is it that you desire of me?"

"I ask that you take Teite with you on your journey west and north."

"But she is still mourning over the loss of Neal. Don't you think it would be best for her to go back to the Academy at Dunsheelin and continue her studies and research? She is such a bookworm, I mean, she is such a scholar. Wouldn't she be more comfortable there?"

"Trust me on this, Skoth, she will grieve wherever she is. What she needs now it to be involved in something important. I know her research at the academy is has value, but others can continue what she has started. In my bones I feel it is important for her to go with you. Call it a hunch if you will, but my hunches are seldom proven wrong. This is my supplication, take her with you."

Skoth nodded and smiled. "As you wish. She comes with me."

Unaine returned the smile and said, "Thank you, my High King. Now go get some rest. You have some busy days ahead of you."

As Skoth made his way to his tent, Unaine sat there in the gathering darkness watching him walk away, and smiled to himself. There was hope for the future.

Chapter 4 – Glesga

Duncan greeted the two female emissaries of the High King in the Great Hall of his fortress in Glesga. His city was built on the island at the mouth of the Mahakentuck River. The western tip of Fadis Innis, that area they called "the broken lands", nearly touched it as well. At one time it had been the furthest outpost of the Celtic civilization in Eirgalon, but the last two centuries had seen a considerable expansion of the Celts northward up the Mahakentuck River valley and into the Haudenoshonee territories, and southwesterly down the coast into the Lenape territories.

Evlin sensed trouble the moment she entered the hall. Duncan glared down at them as he sat on his elevated throne of wood and iron, and waited for them to approach.

When they stopped before his throne, he declared in a somewhat cynical manner, "I certainly didn't expect to see either of you so soon. To what do I owe the honor of this visit?"

Enat, who was more experienced in dealing with kings and other folk who thought they were important, took the lead, "Good King Duncan, we made haste to come to you at the behest of our High King. He so regrets that in your hasty departure you were unable to hear the promise of help for Glesga."

King Duncan leaned forward on his throne. "Help? What kind of help?"

Evlin then spoke, "Duncan, you are a good man, and you know first-hand that the man I stand with, and the man whom you stood for as High King, is determined to stand by your side."

Enat continued, "Within only a couple of days High King Skoth will be arriving here with at least six longboats of the finest of Eirgalon's warriors. Your land will not be left undefended."

"And why didn't he tell me that before I left? He had his chance to speak with me about it."

Evlin was about to raise her voice in defense of Skoth, when Enat gently touched her hand, and began her response. "King Duncan, I remember you speaking at the alting and voicing some concerns about how such a position as a High King without a powerful territory and resources might operate. No doubt High King Skoth was being considerate of your concerns and was simply making sure not to infringe upon your command of this area and of your dedication to serve your people. I'm sure he was just in the process of hearing you out. And if he was a little slow, or unclear, in the manner of which he responded to you, well, you know he is a little bit new to his situation."

A trace of a smile flashed across Duncan's face, and they knew they had won him over.

Suddenly Duncan said, "Where are my manners? I shouldn't keep two beautiful women standing. Especially since you have traveled all this way to bring me such an important message. Please come join me for a light lunch. We'll go up the tower to the solarium. There is a wonderful view of the city and western bay. I'll send for my wife, Lil. I'm sure she will enjoy meeting you."

In a much less formal atmosphere, Evlin and Enat spent the afternoon with Lil in the solarium. Duncan had left their company after the lunch to go make arrangements and plans for the arrival of Skoth's fleet and subsequent campaign against the Haudenoshonee. The women had a wide-ranging and friendly conversation. They learned that Lil was the daughter of a Celtic settler from the northern reaches of the Mahakentuck River and his Wabanaki wife. She was twenty-five and had been married to Duncan for six years now, but had no children.

They left their meeting with Lil having made plans to go out early in the morning to the north end of the Glesga isle in search of some fresh local herbs. Both Evlin, the daughter of the Green Man, and Enat were skilled herbalists and always had their eyes open for local herbs. Lil was anxious to accompany them, for she also was a lover of the natural world and was proud to show them her home.

Early the next morning the three of them left the fortress of Glesga, accompanied by a guard that Duncan had assigned to watch over them, since, as he declared, "Not that I don't think you can't take care of yourselves, but it is better to be cautious, even when one is close to home."

Before long they had left the confines of the city itself. The countryside of the river isle, which was a couple of miles wide and several miles long, turned into a mixture of farm fields, prairie, and woodlands. Slowly they worked their way up the isle, heading to the north. They were a couple of miles north of the city and the terrain was becoming more wooded, when they were startled to see a fox step out from behind a tree several yards away from them. The fox stood there for several moments staring at them. Only when their guard took a step toward it, did it turn and run into the nearest bushes.

They were startled again a few moments later when a girl of about ten years came walking down the path from the north. When she greeted them, Lil didn't seem at all surprised to see her and said, "How nice to see you. You look busy today."

"Oh, but I am, Lady Lil. I'm on an errand for my master." She motioned to the basket she had slung over one arm. "I've got to deliver something for him."

Then, directing her comments to Enat and Evlin, the girl said, "I've never seen you before. Are you friends of our Lady?"

"Why, yes, I'd say we are," said Evlin as she stepped

forward to shake hands.

She felt a prick on her hand when the girl touched her, and in surprise she looked down at her hand, and then fell to the ground as if she had fainted. Enat stepped forward to help her friend, but as she did, the girl grabbed her arm and she also felt a prick, and she also slumped to the ground.

The guard, who had been standing several paces away, reacted by moving toward them, but he had only taken a stride before several arrows flew at him from the woods and sent him staggering to the ground.

Lil stood there looking at the women on the ground. Several men came running out of the nearby woods. They were Haudenoshonee warriors. The little girl then changed form before their very eyes, becoming a wiry, short, middle-aged man with a long-nosed visage.

The guard on the ground, bleeding and in pain from the several arrow wounds, saw the transformation, and uttered but one word, "limikkin" before a warrior slit his throat.

The wiry man looked at Lil and said, "You can run along now."

"But what will I tell them?"

"Tell them what you must."

"How will I explain the dead guard - with your arrows in him, and me living and walking away to tell the tale?"

"Tell him we left you live as a messenger to Skoth. Tell him Malsum and his men are to be feared. We only want what is rightfully ours. Tell him to renounce his kingship. When he does so then Malsum, perhaps, will let him have his bear-witch. Now, we must be off before others see us. Go!"

Lil ran down the path toward Glesga, while Malsum's men bound the young ladies and covered their heads with hoods. Then hefting them over their shoulders they hurried down a path, which led to their canoes hidden on the shore of the river. There they would load their precious bundles and make their way away from Glesga.

Evlin, who as a child had once been the target of evil, an evil that had cost her mother her life, was now in the hands of men who were taking her towards that evil.

Chapter 5 - Glesga in Turmoil

The arrival of the High King's fleet of longships in Glesga found the city in turmoil. King Duncan met Skoth at the docks. There was no way to avoid telling his High King what had happened and there was no point to delay, even though he hoped his men might yet rescue the women. As soon as Lil had returned with news of the frightful abduction, he had sent a troop of men in pursuit. In all actuality, he had scant hope that his men would succeed, for if their prey had crossed the river their trail would be near impossible to find.

As Skoth disembarked and came down the dock, he scanned the gathered crowd expecting to see Evlin and Enat, but he couldn't spot them. He could feel the tension in the air and knew there was something wrong as soon as he saw the faces of Duncan and those around him. Duncan, and his followers, gave Skoth a "fist to heart" salute. Then to Skoth's surprise, Duncan knelt on one knee before him. Duncan's men behind him followed his example.

Skoth spoke, "Greetings warriors of Eirgalon. Rise. We come to join you in the struggle against our adversaries."

He spoke words were which were fit and proper to the occasion, but his mind was racing as to why Evlin and Enat were absent.

Duncan responded to the greeting using the traditional Celtic words for High King "Ard Ri" which came from the Isle of Eire far across the sea to the east, "Ard Ri Skoth! Welcome you are! We are most grateful!"

Skoth nodded his acknowledgement and then said, "I sent Evlin and Enat on before me, bearing words from me, but I see them not. Did they arrive?"

"Yes, Ard Ri, they arrived with McLean of Drogheda and they shared your message with me, but they are not here. Of what has transpired since that time, I would share with you in private. Would you please accompany me to my fortress? I will explain all there. With your approval, I will leave my war captain here to arrange provisions for your men?"

Skoth assented, and with Teite, Erik, and a small contingent of guards they proceeded to the fortress. At the fortress Duncan quickly ushered Skoth, Teite, and Erik into a private conference room where he bade them to sit. Once seated, Duncan broke the bad news.

"Tis no easy way to say this, but the truth is that your Evlin and Enat have been captured by our foes."

Skoth rose in disbelief. "What say you? This can not be!"

Duncan also stood and said, "Please, please, sit. I'll tell you all the details."

But those few words had raised Skoth's ire. His eyes flashed and his voice demanded, "Tell me what has happened!"

Duncan tried to calm him by again asking him to sit, but it was Erik's comment from behind him that gave Skoth pause from his anger. Erik firmly said, "Let's give the man time to tell the details, then we'll know which way to direct our anger and what to do."

Slightly mollified, Skoth sat again and listened to Duncan tell the story of the women leaving early yesterday morning with his wife Lil and the bodyguard, and of Lil's tearful return late that morning. The rescue party had returned later that afternoon. They had found the dead guard and had followed the trail of the attackers to the river's edge, but that is where the evidence ended.

Skoth's temper was still flaring and he asked, "So you

30

just stopped searching?"

"Oh no," Duncan quickly replied, "I sent a boat of men scouting along the far shore of the river, and I sent two of my fastest longships up river to catch anyone feeling north."

"And what did they find?"

With the disappointment obvious in his voice, Duncan said, "Nothing. Not a trace. The traveled as far upriver as they could, checking all ships along the way to see if anyone had seen any likely Skraeling canoes, but they had not. With their long oars and strong arms, my ships would have outpaced any canoes going upriver. One ship stayed at Bear Mountain, in order to capture anyone who might have hidden from them as they sped northward, the other ship came back here to report. They returned just moments before you arrived. I fear there is nothing more I can do for the women."

Skoth felt his anger rising. "So that's it? You would just leave them in the hands of our enemies?"

"What would you have me do, Ard Ri? I can think of nothing else I can do. Without knowing where they are, where would I send my men? Should I scatter my warriors across the countryside and leave my city defenseless? All in the search for two women?"

At that moment, there was a pounding on the door of the room, and a voice urgently calling, "King Duncan, King Duncan, I think you should see this."

Duncan opened the door and came face to face with one of his fortress guards who said, "Please, come up to the top of the tower with me. We see smoke out west."

They quickly made their way up the stairs to the top of the tower. Looking westward, over the Mahakentuck River Bay, they could see a large column of heavy black smoke rising into the air.

The man in charge of the tower lookout told them, "We think that Inverbaile, our settlement on the banks of the West

River beyond yonder peninsula, is burning. There had been reports of a large number of Skraeling warriors in the area. Wait! Look now! The beacon fire across the bay has just been lit! That's the signal that Inverbaile has been attacked. King Duncan, what is your command?"

Duncan turned to Skoth and said, "I would send my longships across the bay and up the West River to Inverbaile to defend my lands. And I suspect if that's where the attack is, then that is where your womenfolk are captive as well. Ard Ri Skoth, what is your command?"

Skoth thought for a moment and then said, "Go, prepare your men and ships, and make sure to leave an adequate guard over your city here." Turning to Erik, he said, "Go down and tell one of your men to go and prepare the fleet to sail, and that I will meet with the Captains at the harbor in half an hour. Then return to me here." Both Duncan and Erik left, and Skoth turned to Teite, "Go find Lil. You haven't much time; you'll be sailing with us, but find out what you can from her. I think there is more to her story than what Duncan told us."

Teite left, almost flying down the stairs, and Skoth was alone on the tower with the men who were carefully scanning the western shore across the bay.

When Erik returned, Skoth bid him come over to the southeastern side of the tower so that they might talk quietly and without being overheard by the lookouts. From this position, they could look out and see their ships in the harbor spring to life as their warriors received word of their imminent departure.

Skoth said to Erik, "You haven't said anything about this yet. I'd like to hear your advice."

Erik put a hand to his chin and stroked his beard. "Well, you asked for it, so here it is. The way I look at it is that when you are fighting someone, you should figure out what they are doing, and why. It helps to think from their

———

point of view. So, if I put myself in the place of the local Haudenoshonee leader, whom Lil was told is delivering the girls to Malsum, then I want to divert my opponent's attention from what I am really doing. The safest way to get the girls to Malsum in the land of the Sunset Lakes would be to go overland from here. But that also takes the most time. The fastest way is up the Mahakentuck River, and then westward on the Mohak River. By drawing our attention to Inverbaile, our attention is drawn away from the river route. If I was him, that's what I'd be doing."

"So I have a choice. I either go to the defense of Inverbaile and confront the main force of the Haudenoshonee, or I go search the river route to rescue the women."

Erik nodded. "Tis a dilemma for a king, to be sure. You have responsibilities to both."

"And I also have responsibilities to all Eirgalon as I pursue my quest - the quest to guard our future. Of these - what takes priority?"

Nodding again, Erik declared, "I know not. I'm only a simple warrior. Follow your heart, Ard Ri, and I will follow you."

"So be it. To the harbor we go. Let's get Teite and get to the ships."

Chapter 6 – Captive

It was early in the afternoon on the day the abduction, when the women and their captors landed on the western bank of the Mahakentuck River. The warriors quickly unloaded the captives and hid their canoes in the brush that grew along the river. The women were starting to awaken but were still groggy and confused.

The wiry, fox-nosed man said, "We can't have them waking up yet. Time for another dose."

He then reached into his bag and pulled out two small vials of liquid. He took one to Evlin, quickly pulled her hood up, and forced the fluid into her mouth. She immediately went limp again. He did the same to Enat.

Then he said, "That should hold them til we get to Ayen's camp. Pick them up and let's move!"

They trudged through the woods of the narrow peninsula that ran between the West River and the Mahakentuck River. The sentries that were posted outside their camp alerted Chief Ayen to their arrival.

Ayen greeted them as they entered the camp, "Well, well, Senadondo, it looks like you were successful. Let's see what you have there."

The men dropped their burdens to the ground and Senadondo pulled the hoods from the women's heads.

Ayen asked, "Do they still live?"

Senadondo replied, "Yes, yes, of course. I only drugged them. But I must hurry and get the collar on the bear-witch before she awakens. I could keep her drugged, but too much of that might kill her. Rest assured that the spell-forged collar Malsum made for her will keep her from touching her power. But if she ever gets free, there will be a bloody mess to deal with."

"Proceed with it then. Keep them bound and call me when they are awake and can talk."

Ayen strode away and left Senadondo and his men to their task. Senadondo went to one of his packs, put on some thin leather gloves and drew out a collar constructed with links of forged iron and a lock made of silver metal. He securely fastened the collar around Evlin's neck and taking a small key from a cord around his neck closed the lock with a click. He then re-fastened the key on the cord around his neck and removed his gloves. With hoods off, but hands and feet still bound, the women were laid under a large elm tree. A single man was posted to keep watch on them and to alert Senadondo when they regained consciousness.

Later that afternoon, Enat blinked her eyes open and brought them into focus. She saw Evlin lying bound on the ground before her. Then her eyes took in the wider scene of the Haudenoshonee camp. The man on guard noticed her stirring and went to get Senadondo. While he was gone, Enat edged herself closer to Evlin and tried to wake her. Evlin was just beginning to gain consciousness when Senadondo and Ayen arrived.

Ayen drew his longknife from its sheath, held it at the ready, and said to Senadondo, "Now we'll see if Malsum's tricks are true. You better hope his magic works. If not . . . well, if she doesn't kill you, I will."

Senadondo laughed, "Oh, it will work. I can assure you it will, for I can feel its power when I touch it. You have your captives. You can do what you want with that one," he pointed at Enat, "but the bear-witch goes to Malsum."

Noticing that Enat's eyes were open and that she was alert, Ayen ordered the women to be helped to a seated position. He remained standing, with his knife ready for action, as he spoke to them.

———

"I am Ayenwatha, Warchief of the Haudenoshonee. You are my prisoners. Do not try to escape, or we will kill you. Do you understand?"

Enat glanced at Evlin, and could see that she had a pained expression on her face. Enat replied to Ayen, "We hear you. What did you do to us and what do you want of us?"

Senadondo sat down on his hunches before them and chortled, "Why I just gave you a little dose of Malsum's medicine. Feeling a mite powerless, are you?"

Evlin glared at him, but said nothing. Enat asked, "But why?"

Senadondo smirked at them and licked his lips, but said no more. It was Ayen who spoke, "You are in no position to be asking questions of us. But I do have some questions for you. I already know that your High King Skoth is bringing more warriors from the east to attack us. I would have you tell me how many men he is bringing and when he is coming."

By this time, Evlin realized that there was something around her neck. She raised her hands, still bound together in front of her, to her neck and grasped the chain collar. She tugged on it and tried to rip it from her neck, but could not.

Senadondo leaned back on his hunches, laughed loudly, and then taunted, "We won't be seeing any bears today!"

Ayen gave him a look of disdain, and then again spoke to the women, "I want to know how many men and when."

Enat replied, "What makes you think the High King would confide such information to us? We are simple women who were out for a stroll and picking some wildflowers."

"I'll not play word games with you. I know who you are, Enat, daughter of Unaine. And I know who, and what, Evlin is. Now, will you make this easy and tell me how many

---

36

men and when?"

"I can't do that."

"Why?"

"You can kill me, but I won't be disloyal to him."

"Loyalty is an admirable trait, but it won't help you earn your freedom. Would you tell me what I want to know if I would give you your freedom?"

Senadondo jerked his head upward when Ayen said that and was about to speak, but Ayen simply pointed at Senadondo with his knife. Senadondo said nothing.

Enat hesitated as if in thought, glanced again at Evlin, and answered with a question. "Are you saying that if we give you the information you want, you will let us go free?"

Senadondo was nodding his head, but Ayen said, "Ahh, no. I fear not both of you. I could allow you to leave, but not Evlin. She must go to Malsum. Will you take the offer of your freedom?"

"No. And why is it you say that she must go to Malsum?"

"In truth, I know not. I know that Malsum has commanded it. That is enough for me. As you are loyal to your leader, I am loyal to mine."

Turning his head toward Senadondo, Ayen slipped his knife back into its sheath and motioned for him to rise.

"Senadondo, you will make preparations to leave in the morning. Go get your mate and bring her to watch and tend the women overnight. In the morning, the two of you will leave with Evlin to take her to Malsum. I will send ten of our best warriors to accompany you. Take canoes up the West River as far as you can, and then portage them across the peninsula to the Mahakentuck. You will escape up the Mahakentuck. However, wait to get on the water until you see a large plume of black smoke. I will pull the attention of

---

37

the pale ones to us. When you see that smoke, you can make your escape undetected."

Looking down again to Enat and Evlin, he said, "I intend no harm to you, but I know not what Malsum intends for Evlin. Enat, you will be staying here with me. As for you, Evlin, Senadondo will be taking you to Malsum."

Both Ayen and Senadondo left to tend to other business, leaving Enat and Evlin under the watchful eye of a warrior.

Enat whispered to Evlin, "Are you well? You look so pale and weak? Is the potion he gave you still bothering you?"

"No, I don't feel at all well. And I don't think it is the potion, at all. It is this collar. There is something about it which is affecting me. There is some spell on it. It feels like there is a sort of wall in my mind, and I can't think or touch a portion of myself."

"Do you remember any of what happened?"

"The last moment that I can recall is feeling a prick on my hand when the little girl touched me."

"As soon as she touched you, you fell to the ground. I went to you and then the girl touched my arm. That's the last I remember."

"And Lil? And our guard? Do you have any idea of what happened to them?"

"Not at all. I'm not even sure of where we are; although by what Ayen has said, it appears we are somewhere west of the Mahakentuck River."

They stopped their conversation when a Haudenoshonee woman, carrying a large bundle, came up to them. She was a rather non-descript looking middle-aged woman, but she had a small hitch in her step as she walked. She dropped her bundle on the ground, and stood for a moment looking them over. Then she sat back on her haunches before them.

"My name is Gakko. It seems that I've been given charge of you. I'm going to untie both your hands and feet, so that you can visit the latrine and feed yourselves, but I want to warn you not to try to escape. There are hundreds of warriors in and around this camp, but they are not the least of your worries. I am. I always carry a knife on me, and I am good with it. There's not a man in this camp that would want to tangle with me, and I can throw a knife better than most of them can shoot an arrow. Ayen may not want to kill you, but I would have no qualms about it. Do you understand?"

Both Enat and Evlin nodded their understanding, and then they held their bound hands forward so that Gakko could untie them.

As Gakko began to untie them she said, "I could cut these off you. I do like to cut things, but why waste cord. If you give me any trouble, I may have to tie you up again."

As she was untying them Evlin was looking intently at her eyes. Then Evlin softly posed a one-word question, "Limikkim?"

Gakko looked up from her task and held Evlin's gaze, and then she smiled. "Ah, so you can see it. Yes, both Senadondo and I are limikkins."

Enat raised an eyebrow in question and Evlin answered with one word, "Shapeshifters."

Gakko laughed, "Yes, we are. That's one reason you can't escape me. I can find you wherever you are. But a better reason is my knife. Yes, I like the knife."

Chapter 7 - A Split Decision

The turmoil and activity in Glesga provided little opportunity for Teite to share her thoughts with Skoth, but she did share a few interesting bits of information with Skoth as they walked from the fortress to the harbor. Lil had been extremely startled when Teite was admitted to see her. At first Teite thought that that it might be that she shared a very close resemblance to Enat, but as the conversation went on Teite started to feel like there was more to it than that. Teite felt that Lil was acting very guilty, as if she had done something wrong. She did relay the "message" that Senadondo had given her, but she avoided looking Teite in the eye as she spoke to her. Also, when Teite asked how it was that the Haudenoshonee men might have know they were there, Lil became very flustered and broke down in tears. It was at that point that the summons had come to re-join Skoth, and she had to leave. Teite's final thoughts that she shared before they reached the harbor were that all the details didn't add up, and she warned Skoth to be wary of Lil and Duncan.

The fighting men had boarded the ships and Skoth's war leaders were standing in a circle waiting for him when they arrived at the harbor. He gave these instructions.

"We go to confront the enemies of a united Eirgalon. I appoint as my Drottin, my War Chief, Karl of Fadis Innis. Follow his commands as you would follow mine. You will be heading southwest across the bay and then up the West River to Inverbaile to confront the Haudenoshonee host. I will be taking a ship of the Heilsand men up the East River to where it joins the Mahakentuck. We will then pursue the enemy that has split off from their main host as they flee to Malsum. Go now and fight for the people of Eirgalon."

The captains of his host gave a fist to chest salute and then went to their ships. Skoth asked Karl to stay for a moment, and Duncan also lingered. Before speaking to Karl, Skoth turned to Duncan and asked, "Is there something you wish to say?"

Duncan clenched his jaw tightly, and then said, "With respect, Ard Ri, I know Karl is a childhood friend, but does he have the experience to lead this force? And why is it that you deign not to lead us?"

Skoth nodded gravely, as if carefully pondering what Duncan had shared, before responding, "I hear your concerns. I know that he will have Padrig of Heilsand, a great warrior from the East, and you, a mighty man of the West, to give him counsel and advice. But the decisions will be his. He has proven his worth in tough situations. He knows my mind. Yes, I have known him since childhood. That is one reason I trust him so completely. I know he will make good decisions. Give him good counsel, and he will follow it. As for me leading the warriors. I am leading us into this war. It is a war with Malsum. There are battles in this war beyond what you see here. I need you, Karl, and our fighting force here, but I must head another direction to another battle. Would you fail in your duty here, by questioning? You questioned me before and left in anger. Yet I brought warriors to the defense of your land. Do you still doubt me?"

Duncan hesitated for a brief moment, "No, Ard Ri. I will do as you command. May the gods protect you."

Duncan then saluted, turned, and with a determined stride proceeded to his ship.

Skoth turned to Karl and held his gaze for a moment before speaking. "Karl, or perhaps I should now call you, Drottin Karl. I need you to know more of what has transpired. Agents of Malsum have abducted Enat and Evlin. I know not the size of their forces to the west, but Duncan and his sources think it is considerable. You may find hard fighting at Inverbaile, but I think that the attack on Inverbaile and the fire plume we see is a feint. I believe that it is a diversion so that a small force may escape up the Mahakentuck to the Mohak, and then take our women to Malsum. I go that way to rescue Evlin and Enat and to search for the Loon's Necklace. However, there is a chance the women remain with the host at Inverbaile, and are being taken overland to Malsum at the Sunset Lakes. If so, pursue them, should you be able. But you will be heading into Haudenoshonee lands, so be careful. If you must, fall back to Glesga. If you are able, send a force up the river to me. You are my best friend, Karl. I am depending on you."

Karl put his arm on Skoth's shoulder, "Skoth, or I suppose I should say, Ard Ri since so many have taken to the old language form of saying high king, I will do my best. I'll handle the western route. Be the women taken west, or north, we will find them. We will defeat our foes. May the gods protect you."

Together they strode to the docks. Together they raised their swords to the sky. When the men of the ships saw this, they also raised their swords to the sky.

Skoth shouted out, "For Eirgalon!" and all responded back, echoing the call.

They went to their ships and the fleet heading to Inverbaile pulled away from the docks. Skoth's longship waited. He wanted to say a few words to his men before they left on their mission. It was a skeid of nearly one hundred feet with a shallow draft of only three feet. Powered by the oars of men on forty benches, and manned by eighty of Heilsand's finest warriors, it would quickly slice through the waters.

He climbed aboard the ship and went to stand high in the prow where all could see and hear him.

"Men of Heilsand. Warriors of Eirgalon. You know the foe we fight. You have fought them in your own city. You know their treachery. You have heard of the evil that drives them. Malsum. Today we go to confront this evil. We have a hard course before us. Malsum's men have taken as captives Evlin and Enat. While a battle rages to the west, a group of our adversaries seeks to escape with them to the north. I call on you to speed to our battle in the north."

He was going to pull his sword from it sheath to again hold it to the sky in battle cry, but he hesitated, then dropped his sword hand and held high the oak staff that Fearglas had carved for him.

Raising his voice in power, he shouted, "For Eirgalon."

This time he was greeted in response with shouts of "For Eirgalon," but also with acclamations of "For Skoth" and "For Evlin" as well as a pounding of feet on the deck of the ship.

Skoth addressed the captain of the ship, "Captain Turla, at your command take us up the East River."

Captain Turla responded with a fist salute to his chest and the words, "Yes, my Ard Ri!" and then proceeded to give the commands to get the vessel on its way.

Skoth made his way from the prow of the ship to where Erik and Teite were sitting. When he sat down, Teite patted him on the knee and said, "Well done. Don't worry. We'll catch them and free Evlin and Enat."

Skoth smiled at Teite's reassuring words until he heard Erik comment under his breath.

"Harrumph. There's plenty to worry about."

Skoth turned to him, "Okay, out with it Erik. I can tell you are dying to say something."

"Skoth, my boy, do you remember that conversation we had about cats and dogs?"

Skoth nodded, but with a quizzical expression on his face.

Erik went on. "Don't get me wrong. These were fine

words you spoke here. But at the harbor, what you did was to put the dog in charge over the cat."

Teite interrupted, "What are you talking about?"

Skoth said to her, "I'll explain later, Teite." Then he said to Erik, "So you think I should have done it differently?"

"Not at all, my boy. Tis a king's call to make. And I am no king. I'm just wondering how it will turn out. After all, tis cats and dogs to be sure."

Skoth exhaled loudly and said, "Erik, sometimes you exasperate me to no end!"

Erik grinned and said, "Aye, now that's my job."

Chapter 8 - Separated

Evlin and Enat huddled together and whispered their thoughts late into the darkness of their first night of captivity in the hands of the Haudenoshonee. They made no attempt at escape for they realized it would be futile, and perhaps deadly.

Evlin shared with Enat that in the beliefs of the Mohak there existed humans called limikkins who, when they desired, could take on the form of animals. There were few of them and usually they were more evil than good. Evlin explained that this was different from the "bear shirt" that she took on as protector of her people. Her bear form was the only shape she could assume and it was a power of good for her people. Limikkins were hard to kill when in animal form, but if one named the limikkin's true name, with a power to its face, it could be killed.

At that Enat whispered, "But we know their names: Senadondo and Gakko. Why couldn't we confront one or both of them now?"

Evlin sighed, "Because I can't touch my power now. And besides, I'm sure those aren't their real names. They are only the names they use to hide their real ones."

"So there is nothing we can do."

Finally in a whisper filled with frustration, Evlin said, "I wish there was. I wish I could change form now, but this collar won't let me. There's nothing I can do. If Leesha was here with her wand, or Skoth with his staff, they might remove this, or confront them, but I can't."

Enat whispered back, "Perhaps we can find the key to its lock."

"I'm sure it is well protected. But it might be our only hope."

From several feet away, hidden in the darkness, they heard a chortling, and then Gakko spoke, "Time for you two to stop that chattering. There is no hope for you."

There was no moon and the stars were shrouded in darkness, so that not even an animal with night vision could see what happened next. Enat lifted the Green Man medallion from around her neck. It was a gift from her mother that had led her to Fearglas, and to Evlin. She always wore it, but kept it hidden beneath her clothing. She kissed the medallion and then reaching out to find Evlin's hand she opened it, placed the medallion there and closed Evlin's hand around it. Evlin felt what it was, lifted it to her lips, and then hid it in her clothing. She would never give up hope.

Morning brought a flurry of activity to the Haudenoshonee camp. Enat asked to speak to Ayenwatha, and after several minutes he came striding across the camp to where the women were seated.

"I was told you wished to speak to me," said Ayen.

Enat stood to speak to him, and noticed how tall he was. He had seemed to dwarf Senadondo when they were together, but now, standing next to him she realized that he was taller than almost any man she knew, and well-built. The thought distracted her for a moment, but then she brought her thoughts back to what she wanted to speak to him about.

"Thank you, Chief Ayen, for coming to hear my request. I understood from your comments yesterday, that Senadondo would be taking Evlin to Malsum, but that you would be taking me to him by a different route. We are two simple women being held captive by a great host. I ask you to allow us to be sent together to Malsum. Be it with you or with Senadondo matters not. I simply ask you not to separate us. At least together we can console one another and not be as much of a burden to you."

Ayen looked thoughtful and gave a long pause before answering, "It is a logical and understandable request you make, but I must refuse it. The two of you are not simple women, by any means. I gain nothing by sending you with Evlin in Senadondo's care. And send her with him I must, for so are my orders. By keeping you with me, however, I may find some advantage in the battle to come. I am sorry, but I must say no. I promise to do my best to keep you from harm, and I will speak to Senadondo and Gakko again, reminding them to do likewise with Evlin."

Her face was a picture of dejection as she turned and faced Evlin, who stood and went to her.

Evlin said, "So be it. The future will work itself out, Enat. I will not give up hope. You must not either."

Ayen spoke again. "I can not promise a good ending for you. I know not what Malsum intends for you. But I can promise that you will not come to harm by my hand. I'll leave you two to say your good-byes before Evlin leaves with Senadondo. Enat, I will send a woman to be in charge of you when Gakko leaves. Her name is Waneek, and she is one of my aunts. She is also one of our wise women. She has not the powers that Gakko has, but she is wise. Follow her commands."

He turned away from them and walked over to where Gakko and Senadondo had assembled their small party that was to head up the Mahakentuck. There Ayen gave them additional instructions about their journey, including a strong warning that their job was to take Evlin - alive - to Malsum, and that no harm was to come to her. Ayen then left, long strides quickly taking him away to other tasks.

Enat and Evlin gave each other a last embrace before Gakko took Evlin down the trail that led to the canoes on the bank of the West River.

After watching Evlin disappear around a bend in the

path to the river, Enat turned to look in the direction Ayen had gone and saw a large woman striding purposefully toward her. She had fringes of grey streaking her hair and Enat guessed her age to be in the late forties. She projected an aura of strength and confidence, but her face belied no emotion.

She came up to Enat, looked her in the eye, and said, "I've been told that I'm to keep watch on you. I'll expect you to do what I say, and to do it when I say to do it. Do you understand?"

Enat nodded.

"Good. Then follow me," she said as she turned and started walking away. While walking, she continued to speak, "And my name is Waneek. If you need something, don't be afraid to ask. And don't try anything foolish. I wouldn't want to see you get hurt when you are my responsibility."

Enat thought the woman to be a bit blunt and tough, but then the thought crossed her mind: at least she isn't Gakko. She is far better than Gakko.

Chapter 9 – Alone

As Enat followed Waneek through the camp, she saw men dragging timbers and tree branches. They were throwing them onto a pile, as if in preparation for a huge bonfire. She wondered aloud what they might be doing, but Waneek made no effort to explain. They reached the opposite end of the camp from where they had been with Senadondo and Gakko. Crouching down beside a small campfire with a kettle of simmering stew hanging over it, Waneek motioned for Enat to come and sit next to her.

"So, Enat. What should I know about you?" asked Waneek.

Enat was quite taken by surprise. This was not what she had expected. She stuttered and stammered her reply.

"What? What do you mean?"

"Come now, child. This isn't Gakko you're talking to. You don't need to hide yourself from me, or think that you'll be giving away any war secrets to Ayenwatha. I want to know about you. I want to know about the woman I will be spending time with for the foreseeable future. Tell me about yourself."

"I don't know that there's really all that much to tell."

"Ah then, Enat. Tell me about your family and I'll tell you about mine."

So Enat shared some of her family's story, telling Waneek about her sisters, how she lost her mother, and how her father was a good man. Enat learned that Waneek was a widow, though she didn't say how she lost her husband, that she had a son and a daughter, and that Ayenwatha was the son of an elder sister. Enat began to feel at ease in Waneek's presence. The intuition that she possessed fostered a feeling that there was an innate goodness in the woman.

It suddenly struck Enat that both Waneek and Ayen fluently spoke the Eirgalon language, which was mostly Celtic with a mixture of Norse and Wabanaki terms. For that matter, Senadondo and Gakko had also demonstrated their fluency in the language. So she asked Waneek how it was that they were so fluent.

Waneek laughed for the first time in Enat's presence.

"You didn't think that your people stopped at the great river, did you?"

"I hadn't really thought about it. I guess I assumed that we had."

"Well, Enat, the truth is that your traders have been coming into our lands for generations. Some of them have even made their homes with us and married into our families. Your language is not new to us. "

"I didn't realize that. But then why do your people hate us so much and want to make war on us?"

"Enat, you have a sharp mind and you strike right to the core of the issue. I have seen the hate in the eyes and words of the men who lead us, but there is something more than hate. There is that which lies behind the hate, and the name for that is fear. There are many who fear your people, and that fear has been turned to hate. There are other motives as well, but fear lies behind them."

Enat was going to ask more, but Waneek ended that conversation, "And now, child, we must get to work and prepare a meal. The men are hungry from their tasks and they will be expecting a good meal."

As Waneek went about her work and preparations, Enat got up and helped her as she could. She reasoned that she might as well make herself useful to Waneek, and that she wasn't being disloyal to Skoth by simply helping a new friend at her tasks. As she worked, her thoughts went to Evlin. She didn't envy Evlin having to spend time with Senadondo and Gakko. She hoped that Evlin's ordeal would prove short and that her rescue would be soon.

Unfortunately, Evlin was not having a pleasant experience. When her captors reached the edge of the riverbank, they loaded themselves into two large canoes that had been prepared for them. Seven of Ayen's men got into the first canoe. The remaining five warriors, Senadondo, Gakko, and Evlin went into the second canoe.

Before getting into the canoe, Senadondo had walked up to Evlin and fingered the collar on her neck. As he did so he let his fingers trail across her throat, and Evlin felt her skin crawl in revulsion. Senadondo chuckled as he turned and she could hear his muttering taunt about a "collared, clawless, and toothless bear-witch." Gakko's laughter cackled in response.

What followed were several hours of hard paddling as the canoes pushed up the eastern eddies of the West River. Near the middle of the afternoon, the warriors beached the canoes and then they portaged the canoes nearly two miles overland and set up camp near the western bank of the Mahakentuck River. There they would wait until they could see the rising plumes of smoke created by Ayen's attack on Inverbaile. They made no campfire that might betray their presence and they posted sentries to prevent discovery. They set up the canoes for a quick dash into the river, and then they settled themselves to quietly wait out the evening and night. They didn't know how soon in the day the signal might come, but they wanted to be ready to leave at a moment's notice.

When the sun finally dropped below the horizon and the darkness began to thicken around them, Evlin watched Senadondo slip out of the camp.

Gakko noticed that Evlin had observed his leaving, "No doubt you are wondering where he has gone. He likes to slip away at this time of day to find tasty morsels to eat. He likes his meat fresh, tender, and juicy. You better hope he finds some so that he doesn't come back to nibble on you." She chortled to herself, and then continued, "I'd like to do a little exploring my self, but don't you fear, little she-bear, I'm not going to leave you alone."

As intended, that statement did nothing to ease Evlin's concerns. Evlin said nothing but her thoughts traveled to Skoth and she tried to think of ways she might escape or at least get a message to him. She was determined not to despair and lose hope, but she recognized the gravity of her situation and felt frustrated at her powerlessness.

Chapter 10 – Inverbaile

The Eirgalon ships rounded the narrow peninsula of land that lay between the waters on the western edge of Glesga and its settlement of Inverbaile to the west. Looking north up the bay the warriors could see Inverbaile on the point of land where the West River from the north and the Peecok River from the west came together and entered the bay. Karl noted to himself that it seemed an excellent defensive location for a settlement.

What became apparent as the ships drew near to Inverbaile is that while there were plumes of smoke rising from Inverbaile, the towering plume of dark smoke that they had observed in Glesga was not coming from Inverbaile. The smoke was coming from the peninsula to the east that lay between the settlement and Glesga. To the lookouts on the tower of Glesga, it had looked as if it were from Inverbaile.

Karl directed the ships to head for Inverbaile. Examination of whatever was burning across the river from it could wait. The people of the settlement were his concern.

As the Eirgalon ships made landfall at Inverbaile, they saw that the gates to the stockade were standing open and that there were several buildings ablaze. It soon became apparent that most of the men and some of the women of the settlement had died defending their homes, but that some still lived. No invaders were in sight. Karl ordered his men to form water brigades and to put out the fires they could. Then he sat down with some survivors to hear their tale.

It was mid-morning when the Haudenoshonee host had attacked the settlement. For days the inhabitants had known the "Skraelings" were gathering and they had kept their people near and inside the wooden stockade of the settlement.

It was no surprise when the attack had finally come. The lookouts on the stockade walls had spotted the flotilla of canoes coming towards them from across the river. Behind the canoes they saw a huge plume of smoke billowing from the site where the Skraelings must have been gathering. What did come as a surprise to them was that just as the canoes were coming within arrow range on the river, a large force of Skraelings had materialized on the landside of the settlement to the west. The hundreds of attackers overwhelmed the settlement. In spite of a determined defense, the stockade walls were quickly breached and the gates were thrown open.

The Skraelings had captured a number of unarmed women and children and for a while had held them under guard in an area just west of the stockade. The women were certain they were going to be taken into captivity, but instead the Skraeling leader came and talked to them. He told them that he didn't want all the "pale ones" to die. What he wanted was for them to leave this land. If they stayed, he promised he would come back, destroy all they had, and kill them. He instructed them to tell the "pale warriors" that would come from Glesga that they should take the women, children, and injured back to Glesga. Then they, and all the pale ones, should go back east to the lands beyond the sunrise. After his speech, some of the Skraelings departed into the woods west of Inverbaile and the rest of them boarded canoes and departed west by paddling up the Peecok River.

Karl and his captains listened to this, and it was decided that it was too late in the day to offer pursuit, for darkness would too soon be upon them. Karl ordered that camp be set up for the evening and any usable habitations be used. They should also do a quick inventory of any provisions and foodstuffs that might be left in the town. He also ordered Gunnar to take one of the longships and its crew across the river to scout out the cause of the fire and find any other information they could. They were to return before nightfall, and then decisions would be made as to what course of action would be taken in the morning.

Later that evening the captains of the Eirgalon ships met around a fire with Karl.

Karl started the conversation. "We came here expecting a battle, yet for reasons unknown our foes have run from us. We do know this: Inverbaile is devastated. The leader of these Haudenoshonee, a man by the name of Ayen, has ordered us to leave this land. The Haudenoshonee have fled west by land into the forest, and north by river. Gunnar, what did you find at the site of the blaze?"

Gunnar reported, "It was, indeed, the site of a camp for many of them. It appears that they piled up any camp items they would not be taking with them, as well as other wood, to make a huge fire. Otherwise, the place was picked clean. Not a clue of who was there. There were trails running to the riverbank, and obviously there had been many canoes there. There were also a couple trails running across the peninsula to the western banks of the Mahakentuck. No doubt they spied on the city of Glesga from those bluffs. But it was deserted now."

Karl took in the information and asked, "Duncan, did you have any settlers living on that strip of land?"

Duncan snorted, "Aye, there was. But when the Skraelings started prowling around and attacking one here, and one there, they packed up and fled to Glesga. I didn't have the men to send from Glesga to protect every crofter's home. So they came where they would be safe."

Gunnar added, "That's what it looked like near that bonfire campsite. We found a couple of crofter's homes and barns, but they had all been deserted for some time. It looks like the Skraelings had pretty much scavenged through them as well. There was nothing of value there."

Karl wondered aloud, "I'm still puzzled as to why they would attack like this and then turn tail and run."

"Because they are a bunch of cowardly thieves," said Duncan.

Padrig of Heilsand spoke up, "No. I wouldn't call them cowardly thieves. We have experience of their ilk in Heilsand. They are treacherous, but they are not cowardly. I think there is some treachery here."

Duncan replied, "Bah! They simply want what we have. And when they see a force of strength come at them, they flee like cowards."

Padrig shook his head. "I think not. For they fled hours before we arrived. And what are we to make of the blond woman who was seen with them?"

This brought Karl to his feet. He exclaimed, "What blonde woman?"

Padrig explained, "A couple of the women who survived and were held briefly by the Skraelings told me that they saw a pale blonde woman in one of the canoes that went up the Peecock River. It was no one they recognized from their settlement."

Karl said, "Enat."

"What?"

"That must have been Enat. High King Skoth told me that she and Evlin had been kidnapped on Glesga Isle."

Padrig turned toward Duncan, and with a puzzled look, asked, "They were sent as emissaries to you, and you let them be taken by the Skraelings?"

Duncan defended himself, saying, "That wasn't my fault. They decided to go off picking flowers in the woods. There, they were captured."

Incredulously, Padrig said, "And you just let them go off by themselves! What were you thinking?"

"But I did send a guard with them. Who, I might add, was killed defending them. And they are not powerless women, as you well know!"

"I do indeed! That just makes them more of a target for our foes!"

Karl interrupted this disagreement, "We have foes enough to fight. No need to fight with each other."

Karl was remembering his last conversation with Skoth. Skoth had thought that perhaps this fire at Inverbaile might be a feint to draw their attention away from the Mahakentuck. He wondered perhaps if Evlin was being taken that way, or if she was with the group heading west with Enat. Her presence would not have been as noticeable as the blonde Enat was. In any case, he knew he must pursue to the west, for feint or not, at least one of the women was being taken that way.

They discussed the logistics of their current situation and then Karl gave orders as to what would transpire in the morning.

Karl would be taking four of the longships up the Peecock River in pursuit of Ayen's men. This included the two ships of warriors from Fadis Innis, Padrig's ship from Heilsand, and one of Duncan's ships from Glesga. He ordered Gunnar to take the two ships of New Caledonia and proceed up the Mahakentuck to aid Skoth in his search. The settlement at Inverbaile was to be abandoned for the moment, for it would be all too easy for the Haudenoshonee to slip back in and finish what they had begun. Abandoning it might also make Ayen and Malsum think that the Eirgalonians were following their dictates to leave the land. Duncan would ferry the survivors of Inverbaile back to Glesga and then use his ships and men to patrol and defend Glesga Isle and its lands on the east bank of the Mahakentuck.

Karl's final order of the evening was that his force of men and ships heading up the Peecok were to be ready to begin pursuit with the morning light. He set his jaw in determination as he ended the meeting by saying, "Let none forget, we fight in the name of Ard Ri Skoth. We battle for the people and land of Eirgalon."

Chapter 11 - Heading North

Two groups of people were heading up the Mahakentuck River. Neither knew for certain where the other group might be, or even if the other group was there. Senadondo was fleeing north with his captive, to place her in Malsum's hand. He hoped there was no pursuit, but he sensed there might be. On the other hand, Skoth was racing northward in the hope of rescuing the captive women. He suspected that they were heading north on the river, but he was acting on a hunch. There was no hard evidence.

The other party was the fleeing kidnappers. Senadondo's trip upriver began when they saw the plume of smoke rising to the sky. It was the signal of the attack on Inverbaile and their order to commence their journey. They quickly moved their canoes into the river, loaded them, and began heading up river. They kept close to the western shore, and within minutes they were paddling with the looming palisades on their left. There were no settlements or homes built near the river's edge, so they didn't fear being seen. They did, however, take the precaution of taking Evlin's cloak from her; it was the vibrant green cloak that King Tyg of Heilsand had given her weeks ago. They replaced it with a muted brown cloak, and they covered her auburn tresses with a brown scarf, as well. To any observers from the bluff tops, they hoped to appear to be a couple of Wabanaki trading canoes headed back north.

Their travel was uneventful and they felt themselves fortunate in that the traffic on the river was near the settlements and farms that dotted the opposite shoreline. It was mid-afternoon when they reached a place where the rocky palisades diminished in size and the river's edge was becoming more open for settlements and farms. Senadondo knew that they were nearing the first pale men's settlement on the north edge of the palisades. He ordered the canoes to land. They would carefully hide the canoes from searching eyes, and quietly wait until dark to return onto the water and slip past the town. After posting a sentry to keep a lookout, he slipped away and disappeared into the brush and rocks along the base of the palisades. If someone would have been watching carefully, they would have noted that after a few minutes a red-tailed hawk took flight from the trees on the shoreline and headed out soaring over the river.

To the south, under the command of Turla, the Heilsand longship carrying Skoth raced up the East River. The lush fields and woods of Glesga Isle to their west and the Broken Lands of western Fadis Innis silently slipped past them. It was late afternoon, about the time the other ships were reaching Inverbaile, when they rounded that last tip of Glesga Isle and they shot out into the Mahakentuck. That river was almost a mile wide at this point, for in truth it was still more an estuary than a river. In some respects it was like the fjords of old Norway, plunging deep into the countryside. Turla ordered the ship to cross the river that they might run up the western shoreline. No doubt if someone was fleeing upriver, they would stay near that shoreline and away from the settlements on the eastern side.

There were no settlements for miles along this western edge of the river, because rocky palisades, some up to three hundred feet in height, rose from the shoreline. However, there were numerous places where canoes might be beached and hidden in the foliage that grew in that narrow strip of land of rocks and land at the base of the palisades, so eagle-eyed lookouts were posted. They scanned the shoreline as the longship cruised along powered by the oar strokes of the determined Eirgalonian warriors. Even with watchful eyes keenly scanning the shoreline, they didn't notice the hidden Haudenoshonee group and they passed them by.

The sun had slipped below the brow of the palisades

when Skoth's party reached the point where the river nearly doubled in width, the palisades dwindled down to small bluffs, and a small river from the west emptied into the Mahakentuck. On the north bank of that small river, there was a settlement of Celts named Dundee.

Skoth ordered the ship to tie up there for the night. He wanted to go ashore and question people concerning whether or not they had seen any suspicious traffic on the river. Skoth, Erik, and Teite made their way into the settlement while Turla gave orders to secure the ship for the night and sent out some scouting patrols along the riverbank.

The arrival of a longship full of armed warriors was not an everyday event in Dundee and they quickly acquired a sizable crowd of curious onlookers. Children had come running at the sight, and when the working men and women saw Skoth and his people coming ashore, they immediately sent word to their local chief that he might greet them.

As the people crowded around Skoth, Erik leaned toward him and whispered, "Did you notice, your royal highness, how when you arrive with one of these huge longships full of warriors, how it becomes a wee bit difficult just to walk into a local tavern and quietly find out what is going on?"

Skoth answered, just a little bit annoyed, "Thanks for the observation, Erik. I'll keep that in mind."

"Tis good, then. Oh, look, here comes Keith. He's the one in charge here."

Skoth turned and looked at Erik. "Do you know someone everywhere we go?"

"Oh no, your royal highness. Not everyone. But I'll admit I've been around the land a bit in my day. It's been a few years since I've been to Dundee, but I know ole Keith well enough."

Erik stepped forward to clear space in the crowd, as

Keith strode up to them. "Lord Keith of Dundee, I present to you, High King Skoth of Eirgalon."

Keith was a stout man in his late fifties who had an ample black beard, and an even more ample belly. He obviously was not a man for formality, as he replied, "Well, now Erik, don't you make a fine looking royal herald. And you know I don't claim lordship over any man."

"Aye, that I know. But I also know that the good folk of Dundee look to you as Chief, whether you claim a title, or not. Be that as it may, our Ard Ri of Eirgalon stands before you, and he seeks your help."

By this time, Skoth had gained a little insight into the type of man Keith was and he decided the best way to proceed was to jump into their conversation in a like manner.

"Keith! What a pleasure to meet you. It looks like you must be an old friend of my self-appointed protector and advisor."

Keith stepped forward, gave a friendly slap to Erik on his shoulder, and then extended his arm to shake with Skoth. Smiling broadly he said, "That I am. And so Ard Ri is it! We heard word of the call for an Alting at New Caledonia to name such a king, and just days ago folk returning up the river to New Alba stopped and shared the news of it. If you are a man that Erik, miscreant that he be, would give his loyalty to and fight for, then you're the right man for me."

Then Keith looked at Teite, standing next to Skoth. A puzzled look crossed his face and he asked, "And would this be your lady, Evlin? Tis not how she was described to us."

"No. This is Teite, daughter of Unaine of Fadis Innis, and she is my advisor. But it is for Evlin, that I seek your help."

"Ask what you may. We will do what we are able."

Standing there, on the street of Dundee, within hearing of all, Skoth told them of Evlin's and Enat's capture by the

---

Haudenoshonee, and of his suspicions that Evlin was being taken by a river route to Malsum. He asked if any of them had observed any activity of a suspicious nature on the river in the last couple of days, especially anyone traveling upriver.

Unfortunately, there was none who had any information to give him. Many of them had seen Duncan's two longships heading north, and that one had soon returned heading south, but no one could recall seeing any unusual Haudenoshonee or Wabanaki canoes.

The trail seemed to be at a dead end, but Skoth determined to proceed in the morning by continuing up the river. His hope was that the Glesga longship, encamped at the narrowing of the river, had seen something.

A large red-tailed hawk had circled high in the sky above Dundee as this gathering took place. Finally, it wheeled about and headed south where it descended and then disappeared into the foliage at the bottom of the last palisade.

Minutes later, Senadondo silently slipped into the hidden Haudenoshonee camp. He went over to Gakko and they quietly whispered to each other for several moments. Then he stood up and, in a voice just barely audible to the others, he said, "There are pale warriors watching and waiting for us at Dundee. After the sun sets, when darkness falls and before the moon rises, we will go back on the river again and pass them by. Until then, rest. You may need all your strength for us to escape them."

Chapter 12 - Night Flight

When darkness fell, Senadondo ordered Evlin to be gagged and to have her hands and feet bound. They slid the canoes quietly into the river and loaded her into one of them, forcing her to lay still in the bottom of it. Senadondo got into the canoe with her and five of the warriors. The other five warriors got into the other canoe. Gakko disappeared into the woods. They didn't wait for her to return but paddled far out into the river. When they heard the hooting of an owl, they turned and headed up river. They did their best to paddle quietly, for there was only a light breeze and sounds could carry a far distance over the waters. They kept their course by following the occasional hoot of an owl that sounded in front of them.

They paddled for a couple of hours before the waning half moon rose in the east and allowed them to see the shores on the sides of the river. Suddenly a large owl came swooping into the canoe and perched in the open space the Senadondo had left in front of him. Senadondo held a cloak in front of himself for a moment and then settled it on Gakko's shoulders.

He leaned forward, handed her a morsel of food from his pocket, and whispered, "Good work. Now rest, and eat. I'll be sending you out again later." Now that they could see the shores in the moonlight, he ordered his men to stay in the center of the river and to paddle with all speed. He wanted to put as much distance between him and the pursuers as possible.

Although they could still see by the moonlight, it was in the hour of the wolf before the first light of dawn, that Senadondo sent Gakko ahead to scout the river. She was gone for nearly an hour when she returned in a hurried swoop into the canoe and again transformed herself. In an almost breathless exclamation, she said, "Around the next bend in the river lies Bear Mountain. I don't know how they did it, but in the shadow of the mountain rests a longship of the pale men. They are camped on the shore, but they watch the river! We must land before we round the bend and they see us."

Quickly Senadondo directed them to make a landing on the western shore of the river. They cruised in looking for a hiding place. Finding an area with trees and low shrubs along the riverbank, they quickly pulled the canoes aground and dragged them up from the shore to be hidden in the bushes. By the time the sun broke the eastern horizon, they had settled in to hide for the day. Senadondo and Gakko left Evlin under the guard of the warriors and walked a little distance away to have a private conversation. A short time later, the red-tailed hawk again took to the sky, and Gakko returned to the campsite.

The men had taken the gag from Evlin's mouth and had even untied her so that she could relieve herself and eat some of the food they gave her.

When Gakko saw that Evlin was free of her bonds, she snarled at the warriors, "You fools! You don't know her powers! She'd rip you to shreds if she had the chance," and to Evlin she said, "I'm keeping my eye on you. One misstep and I'll slip this knife through that soft hide of yours. And don't think I won't. I don't care if Malsum wants you alive, or not. The first sense I get that you are a threat, and you'll meet the pointy end of my knife!"

Evlin had avoided speaking with Gakko, but she knew the men were watching and listening so she carefully and softly made her response. "Oh, Gakko, I think you overestimate me. I have no intentions of hurting anyone. I appreciate the small kindnesses these men have shown me. They have no need to fear me."

"Bah. Just eat your food, and shut up."

The dawning of the new day also saw the longship at Dundee swing out into the waters of the Mahakentuck River and head upstream. Lookouts were posted on each side of the ship to scan the shorelines for any indication of their prey. The crew had one new member. He was a young man of Wabanaki heritage. Keith had been astonished that the expedition had no one with them who spoke fluent Haudenoshonee with them. He insisted they take Notaku with them. Notaku's mother was a Wabanaki of the upper Mahakentuck River valley but his father was a Haudenoshonee, and Notaku had spent time living with his father's clan in the Sunset Lakes region to the west. For the last couple of years, he had been working with Keith trying to promote trade between the Mahakentuck River valley settlements, the Lenape lands to the west, and the Haudenoshonee lands to the northwest. Keith was obviously proud of the young man he was grooming to be one of his growing team of traders among the western people. His fluency in several languages, his natural charisma, and his willingness to work hard were all qualities that Keith admired in his young protégé, and he was anxious to have him be of service to the new High King of Eirgalon. Such experience would serve Notaku well in the future.

As they watched the shoreline, Skoth, Erik, and Teite discussed the events of the evening they had spent with the people of Dundee. The people had been friendly and excited to see the new High King and his associates, but friendly and casual discussions had been difficult because of the concern they had for their missing loved ones. However, even the short and casual conversations in this time of stress would have a huge positive impact on the people's loyalty to their High King in the days and years to come.

Skoth began their conversation by musing, "Are either of you beginning to wonder if we are making a mistake here?"

Teite responded, "If you mean, is it a mistake to search

for Enat and Evlin? Then no, it is not a mistake. But as to continuing up river when there is no proof they are going that way, I don't know."

Erik added, "It's not like following a trail on land. You really can't see a trail in the river. It gets right disappointing when there is no sign of them."

Skoth sighed. "It is disheartening. I thought someone at Dundee - a fisherman, a traveler, even a child playing at the river's edge - might have seen something out of the ordinary. But there was nothing unusual."

"There is that which is unusual occurring every day," said Erik, "but the question is, does it fit into what you deem as important."

Teite asked, "What are you talking about, Erik?"

"Well, it is like this. We are looking for evidence of their passing this point, but we see and hear nothing of them. So we figure there is nothing unusual. But what about that which seems to have nothing to do with those who flee from us, yet is out of the ordinary?"

Skoth gave him a puzzled look and said, "Go on. Explain what you mean."

"Aye, then. As you say, there was no sighting of them by anyone, but there were some other unusual occurrences."

"Such as?"

"Did you notice that red-tailed hawk circling over us yesterday while we were talking to Keith on the street of Dundee?"

"No. But a hawk? What's unusual about a circling hawk? Isn't that how they hunt?"

"You've seen plenty of hawks in your day, boy, but when did you ever see one hovering and hunting over a crowd of people?"

Teite was looking askance at Erik, and said, "A hawk!

That's it? That's what you think is important?"

"Ahhh. I didn't say yet that it was important. Only that it was one occurrence that was unusual."

Skoth said, "So we have a hawk that behaves unusually. Is there more?"

"Aye. Did either of your hear that owl last night?"

Teite, now nearing exasperation, said, "First a hawk, and now an owl? We hear owls all the time. Every night they are out."

"Yes, they are. But that one last night. It had a distinctive call."

"It was simply an ordinary hoot!"

"Aye. But an animal has a voice like a human, and just as you can recognize one human voice from another, you can tell one critter from another."

"So what was unusual about this owl?"

"As I said, it had a distinctive voice. Easy to recognize. But more important was where the sound came from."

Skoth spoke up, "Thanks for the nature lesson, Erik. But I recognized the call of the horned owl. I figured it was out over the river. Probably hunting. Nothing unusual about that."

"Skoth, it was headed up the river. And while some owls do, in fact, hunt over water. This owl was moving slowly. And this owl wasn't hunting."

"How do you know that?"

"The horned one hunts silently so as not to alert its prey."

"Then what was it doing out over the river for so long?"

"Exactly my point. That is unusual!"

Teite spoke as Skoth sat silently thinking about what Erik had said. "So now we have an unusual hawk and an unusual owl."

"Aye," said Erik, "Tis not much to go on, but I think Skoth is right to keep going north. We do know that, sooner or later, Evlin is to be taken to Malsum. He is to the north. By whatever route, she is being taken north. I say we go north."

Skoth nodded and said, "North it is."

They fell into their silent thoughts as they continued to watch the river and its shoreline.

They had been on the river for about an hour when Erik nudged Skoth with his elbow and pointed to the sky. From the north, high in the sky, soared a red-tailed hawk. It circled above them several times, then headed back north.

Erik looked at Skoth and said, "Unusual?" Skoth nodded in assent.

Several times during this day of travel they encountered fishing boats and traders plying the waters of the river. Each time they stopped and queried them about what they might have seen, but there was no news to encourage them.

By late afternoon, they came to the place where the river narrows in the shadow of Bear Mountain. It was there that they spotted the longship of Glesga that Duncan had sent racing up river after the abduction of the women. The Glesga men had set up camps on both sides of the river with the intention that none might travel the river without their knowledge. Skoth instructed Captain Turla to take the Heilsand longship to shore near the Glesga longship on the western side of the river.

They were greeted by the Glesgan captain, Bjorn, who had been with Duncan at the High King Alting in New Caledonia. Bjorn welcomed them into their camp. Turla had his men disembark and set up camp for the night while Skoth met with Bjorn. Bjorn was disappointed to report to Skoth that he had found no trace of the women or their captors. They were still discussing the situation when a signal horn from the far side of the river sounded. A moment later it was followed by an answering horn from Bjorn's camp.

A large canoe, paddled by six men, was coming upriver. Boats were sent out from each side of the river to intercept it.

Chapter 13 - Bear Mountain

Senadondo had returned to the hidden Haudenoshonee camp in a foul mood. He drew Gakko to the side where they spoke in animated whispers for several minutes. They obviously had some disagreement, but finally, Gakko grunted and nodded in assent. Gakko broke off their conversation, went to the center of the camp to grab her bag, and then returned with it to Senadondo.

Gakko pulled Evlin's fancy green cloak from her bag and tossed it to Senadondo, then she dug down into her bag and pulled the green man medallion from it. Evlin gasped in surprise when she saw it and quickly reached into her pocket where she had hidden it. Gone! How had that woman gotten her hands on it?

Gakko noticed her response and laughed at her. She tossed the medallion to Senadondo who grabbed it and set it on top of the cloak. They returned to the rest of the hidden group, and Senadondo laid out his plan to the warriors.

"The six of you," he point to six of the ten men, "will take one canoe on to the river and head north. As the river narrows, you will encounter a couple of those longships of the pale men. Act as though you are attempting to flee from them, but allow yourselves to be captured. Tell them Ayen ordered you to take the bear-witch to Malsum but that she attacked you, so you subdued her, tied rocks to her and drowned her in the river. Let them find the cloak and medallion, as proof that you had her. Later, try to escape and make your way to Malsum."

The men did as they were ordered, and when they left in their canoe, the others packed up and left by walking westward with the intention of meeting up with Ayen south of the Blue Mountains. They walked single file, with Gakko directly behind Evlin. They left her hands unbound so she could help carry their gear, but Gakko let Evlin know that she had her knife ready. Mohak land was still far to the north. It was going to be a long journey as they avoided the local inhabitants.

The warriors in the canoe heard the horns of the Eirgalon Celts and saw the intercepting canoes coming at them from both sides of the river. It soon became apparent that flight was not an option. They quickly surrendered and allowed themselves to be taken to the western shore where High King Skoth and his men awaited them. They beached their canoe on the river's edge; and were quickly taken from the canoe and made to sit on the beach. Their weapons and possessions were taken from them and placed in a pile before them.

When questioned as to what they were doing and where they were going, they told the story that Senadondo had instructed them to share. They only spoke in Haudenoshonee and acted as if they couldn't understand anything else, but with Notaku there to interpret they told their tale. They pointed to their pile of possessions that contained the cloak and the medallion as proof that they had captured Evlin, but that they had disposed of her. They made no mention of Enat and acted confused when Skoth had Notaku question them about her.

Then Teite stepped out of a tent and headed across the clearing toward them. Her intention was to join in the questioning, but she didn't anticipate the reaction her appearance caused. As sisters, Teite and Enat bore a striking resemblance to each other. The third sister, Leesha, had a shade of soft brown hair, but both Enat and Teite had the same shade of honey blonde hair. From a distance, to these men who did not know the sisters, it appeared to be Enat, whom they had captured with Evlin, that was walking toward them.

Their reactions startled Skoth's men and caught them by surprise. Three of the men threw themselves prostrate and motionless on the ground. The other three jumped to their feet and tried to grab weapons to attack. The guards responded quickly and efficiently. Two of the men were stabbed to death by the guard's swords, but the other was knocked unconscious to the ground.

Captain Bjorn immediately ordered his men to securely bind the four remaining Haudenoshonee With their hands and feet bound and the men sitting on the ground, the questioning began again. Tiete stood to the side while Notaku asked in their language why they had fallen to the ground. The men kept casting furtive glances at her, but held their tongues. The man who had been knocked unconscious started to moan and his eyes flickered opened. When he saw Teite standing before him, he moaned louder and closed his eyes tightly.

Skoth stepped directly before them and with his staff he pointed at Teite. He said, "Here stands before you the daughter of Unaine of Fadis Innis." Then he moved his staff to hold it above the cringing men. "What have you to say? Speak now!"

One of the men, the one the others looked to as their leader, replied, "Please, sir, we were just following orders. Don't let the witch destroy us." Again he looked to Teite.

Teite stepped to Skoth's side. "Why do you call me a witch?"

The man's eyes widened. "We didn't know your power when we seized you. How did you escape Ayen? Do not curse us for what we have done. We have only done what we have been told to do. Senadondo made us do it."

Teite gently put her hand on Skoth's arm and softly said to him, "Come with me."

They walked away from the men to a distance where

they could not be overheard.

There Teite said to Skoth, "I think that these men believe I am Enat. You know how similar we are in looks. If that is the case, then they think I have escaped. Let me question them. I know a few of their words, but let me see if any of them speak Celtic. If not, Notaku can translate for me."

Skoth nodded and said, "You may be right. Give it a try."

They returned to the prisoners and Teite began the questioning. "I know you are men of the Haudenoshonee, but you are to speak the language of Eirgalon; that all who are here might understand."

The leader nodded and said, "I know it. I will do as you command."

At this moment, Teite realized how careful she must be. She wanted to find out information, yet if she revealed too much about what she didn't know then the men would know she wasn't Enat and her power over them would be lost.

She pointed to the pile of possessions and asked, "Where were you taking the cloak and medallion?"

"Senadondo ordered us to take them north."

"Tell me all. Or I will have these warriors spill your blood and I will curse your journey through the sky as you leave this life."

The men obviously understood what she meant, and they gestured at their leader to speak.

"Please, please, no. Let me tell you. It was Senadondo. He sent us to be captured. He knew the pale ones with the longships would capture us here and would recognize the cloak and medallion of the bear-witch. He wanted us to convince the pale warriors that she was dead."

"Go on. Why?"

"Because then they would give up the search for her, and would go back down river."

"What are his plans?"

"To take the bear-witch by land and meet with Ayen south of the Blue Mountains, and then back to the Mahakentuck River. But does Ayen live? How did you escape?"

"How did Senadondo know we were waiting for you?"

"He didn't know you were here, Enat. Or if he did, he didn't tell us. But you know some of his powers." He turned his head to the side and spat, "He and that sneaky Gakko. Curse all limikkins! You can't trust them. Please, Enat, forgive us."

Teite again reached out her arm to Skoth and asked him to step away with her for a moment.

When they were out of earshot, Teite said, "I think I should tell him who I am. I think that if I am honest with him that he will come to trust me. There is good in him. I feel it."

Skoth hesitated and responded, "Teite, I don't know. You had a feeling that you could trust Neal, and the darkness that controlled him almost killed you. How sure can you be? How can we take such a chance?"

"I'm not asking you to give him a knife and to stand before me. I'm only asking that you trust me enough to tell him the truth about who I am. Then we can take it from there."

With a sigh of resignation, Skoth said, "Aye, then. Try it your way."

They walked back to the prisoners and, holding the gaze of the leader, Teite said to them, "I fear you have misunderstood who I am. I am indeed a daughter of Unaine of Fadis Innis, but my name is Teite, not Enat. We are

75

sisters."

The leader's eyes hardened as he looked at her. "You have deceived us."

"No. Your thoughts and fears have deceived you. I would have you know who I am and yet speak freely with me. Will you?"

The man hesitated and looked at his fellow prisoners. The two sitting next to him nodded, but the man who had been knocked unconscious and was still moaning tried to shake his head.

Cautiously the leader asked, "Do you have the power to curse our afterlife journey through the sky?"

Teite gave a light chuckle and said, "Well, I can certainly curse you, but I'm not sure that it would have much effect. There are others here with power, perhaps they could. But I think it is your actions that would curse you more than anything I could say. I believe honesty is best, and that if we do what is right and good, then such will be returned to us." She smiled at him.

It was a rather disarming smile and made him cock his head to the side as if in deep thought. Then he took a deep breath and exhaled as if he had made a decision.

"So be it. Mistress Teite, what more would you know from me?"

"Do Enat and Evlin still live."

"I believe so. Both lived when I saw them last."

"Were you one of the men who actually captured them?"

"Yes, I was. Senadondo was in command. He arranged it. I just followed his orders."

"I have a hard time believing that you could capture them unaware and take them captive."

"That was Senadondo's doing. He is a limikkin - a

shapeshifter. He appeared to them as a little girl and then he stabbed them with a sleeping dart."

"But when she awoke? Surely when Evlin awoke, she would have escaped."

The man shook his head. "I don't understand all that he did, but Senadondo kept her drugged and asleep until he put a chain collar around her neck. He told us it was a special collar from Malsum and that the magic in it would keep her from touching her power."

"And you say they are with this Senadondo now, and that he is taking them by land to meet up with Ayen?"

"No, and yes. Only Evlin is with Senadondo. Ten of us left by river with Senadondo and Gakko to take Evlin to Malsum. Enat stayed with Ayen. Of their fate, I know naught. Only that they were planning to cross the land south of the Blue Mountains and then follow the Wissawkin River as it flows to the north to where it joins the Mahakentuck."

Skoth was impressed by the openness with which the leader was answering Teite. He asked him, "Do you know who I am?"

The leader looked at him carefully and answered, "I know not your name. But everyone here gives deference to you. By whatever name you use, you are the one in command here."

"I am Skoth. The one named as High King of the people and land of Eirgalon. Do you know of me?"

"I know that one named Skoth has been declared the king of all the pale ones. If you be that one, Malsum teaches us that you seek to destroy us and our way of life, and that we must drive you and your people from the land."

Skoth sighed. "That is not what I seek. We will talk. I promise that I will share with you the vision of peace I have for this land. But first I must meet with my men, and make plans. I thank you for what you have shared, and I hope you will come to see that this world is not the way that you have been taught it is."

He turned and went away leading Teite and his captains to the main tent in the encampment. It was getting late, too late in the day to proceed with action, but not too late to make plans. Skoth didn't want to make a costly error by acting too quickly, but he also felt that timely action was of the essence.

Erik followed Skoth and the rest of them toward the tent, but before he entered he turned and looked back at the four prisoners on the beach. The one who had been knocked unconscious was now fully alert and was looking at him with a glare of pure hatred. Erik muttered to himself, "Too bad that one didn't fall by the sword like the other two. Mark my words, there'll be trouble from that one."

Chapter 14 – Retreat

To the south and west of where Skoth was on the Mahakentuck River, Ayen was retreating with his force of warriors up the valley of the small Peecock River. In determined pursuit were four Eirgalon longships. Drottin Karl, the head warchief of Skoth's forces and his lifelong friend, was continually frustrated by the pursuit.

Every couple of hours as he tried to push his longships upriver they were met by a small force of Ayen's warriors lying in wait to ambush them. The river was narrowing too much to afford the longships much maneuverability. Canoes would rush out from the riverbanks, firing arrows and engaging them in battle. After a brief battle, often with but few casualties on either side, Ayen's warriors would simply abandon any canoes they had used in the attack, and then melt away into the woods. This had the effect of turning a spirited rush up the river into a slow, arduous process. It left Karl wondering how far ahead of them were the main portions of Ayen's forces, as well as the prisoner, Enat.

The direction up the river had been northward, but then the river turned to the west. Then it turned even more and was heading to the southwest. After proceeding in that direction for two more miles and being drawn into a couple of more skirmishes, the longships came to an unsurpassable area of falls and rapids. The Haudenoshonee warriors put up strong resistance at this place, harassing them by shooting arrows at them from the riverbanks. When the Celtic warriors went ashore, the Haudenoshonee men would momentarily engage them in heavy fighting, but would then disengage, only to reappear a few minutes later and re-engage in combat. Finally, as night fell, the Haudenoshonee attackers disappeared entirely.

Many miles to the north, Ayen had his people set up their camp for the night. The rear-guard delaying strategy he had deployed had enabled him to put a safe distance between him and the warriors of the pale ones. He had split his main force away from his forces that were retreating up the river at its northern bend, but the small skirmishes had kept drawing the Eirgalon forces upstream, and away from him. Even if those pale ones returned to the northernmost bend of the river and pursued on foot, they would have a hard time catching up to his retreating woods-wise force.

The travel had been arduous for Enat, who had thought herself to be in good physical condition. When the time came to make camp for the night, she welcomed the chance to rest. Waneek, her appointed guardian, astounded her. The Haudenoshonee woman never tired! She was old enough to be Enat's mother, yet she carried as much in her pack as any man. Even though Enat had carried only half what Waneek did, she had struggled to keep pace with her. When they stopped for the night, Waneek immediately went to work to prepare the food and to feed the men. Even though these men were her enemies, Enat felt a sense of obligation to help Waneek as she went about her chores. So, side-by-side, they worked.

Ayen allowed them to make cooking fires for the night. Earlier in the day, he had sent several men forward to hunt for game, so in short order there were several spits of venison and game fowl roasting for their evening meal.

After all had eaten and they were settling in for the night, the cooking fires had burnt low and small groups gathered around the smoldering fires. There were more women with the group than Enat had noticed previously and she asked Waneek about this.

Waneek kept her face devoid of emotion and replied, "One doesn't always immediately see all there is to see. Ayen did bring some women with this war party, for we are distant from our homeland. Perhaps he is wise enough to know that men can not always take care of themselves."

That comment made Enat raise her eyes from the glowing embers of the fire to search Waneek's face. Enat wondered if Waneek was completely serious, or if she might be joking. Waneek cast a glance her way and Enat saw a twinkle in those deep brown eyes. It might have just been a reflection of the fire, but Enat thought it was more.

Enat, mimicking the straight face of Waneek, said, "I know what you mean. Some men think they know it all, but behind every great man there are some wise women."

The conversation might have gone further; but throughout the camp, conversations went soft and then silenced completely as the sound of a flute wafted softly through the air.

Enat was used to hearing the lively and cheerful piping of the Celtic flute, but this had a tone that was gentle and seemed to speak of the earth to her. The melody was sad and mournful. It made her mind recall the bagpipe funeral dirges she knew from back home. There were sections that emoted strength and life, but they intermingled and were overpowered by the sadness until it ended with notes that felt light and airy.

Enat softly whispered to Waneek, "What is the meaning of this melody?"

"It is called the Weeping Willow. It is a song of mourning for our dead. Some of our warriors have given their lives in this war and now they go to their journey in the sky. We weep for them because we miss them. The willow bends its branches as if weeping, but it does not break. We are like the willow. We grieve, but we do not break."

Several more songs were played. Lighter in tone, they lightened the mood of the host. The final song of the evening imitated the wailing and laughing calls of the loon. A chill tingled up Enat's spine as she heard the final notes trail off into the night shadows.

Enat hesitated, not wanting to break the spell of the moment, but as others started moving away from the fires, she whispered to Waneek, "Does that last tune have a name?"

Waneek looked her in the eye, and then with just a smidge of a smile on her face, she said, "It is called the Loon's Necklace. It was well played, don't you think?"

Enat's eyes went wide in surprise as she heard the name, and then her eyes went even wider in amazement when she saw the flute player stand at a distant fire and turn toward them as he put his instrument away. He had sat with his back to them, but now she could see him clearly. She recognized the imposing figure of Ayen.

Softly Waneek said, "You seem surprised. Was it because of the song, or because you recognize the player?"

Enat stammered, "I am surprised. By both. The song was beautiful. And I didn't know it was Ayen playing."

"Ah, so. My nephew is a man of many talents. He has the mind of a warrior, yet he has the heart of a poet."

Enat thought for a moment, and then decided to risk asking a question. "Forgive me if I ask what shouldn't be asked, but why does Ayen follow Malsum?"

"That's not something I can answer, my child. I don't fully understand it myself. I know that Ayen has a good heart. Also, that he is fiercely loyal. But what Malsum has done to earn such loyalty, I know not. He has never told me. Now, time to rest it is. We have long days of hard travel before us."

Chapter 15 – Wausacom

Far to the east, Leesha and Tkaden had left New Caledonia in good spirits. The events of the High Alting were fresh in their minds and they were filled with hope for the future of their land. But when Skoth had proposed the plan sending her and Tkaden north to his hometown and raising a force of warriors to head west, Leesha was unsure if it was the right action to take. Skoth may now be High King of Eirgalon, but he was also the best friend of her childhood and she knew him in ways no one else did. She could tell that he was unsure of what the best course of action was, but that he was loath to let others know of his uncertainty. She also knew that if she confronted, or questioned him too deeply in front of others, he might well dig in his heels and refuse to listen to her at all.

She understood that he wanted the northern Wabanaki people to feel that they were a strong part of the High Kingdom of Eirgalon, but she wondered if asking them to take up arms against the Haudenoshonee of the western lands was wise. Wouldn't they just feel as if they were being used as pawns? Weren't there better ways to continue the integration of their cultures?

When she voiced her concerns with her intended husband, Tkaden of the Wabanaki, he reassured her that he had considered that; however, he thought that asking them to join in the defense of their homeland and of the society that had already been created with the Celts was precisely the sort of calling that would join them fast together. He used the illustration of making a laminated bow with different woods glued together to make a stronger and yet more flexible bow.

They traveled north with Tkomik, Tkaden's father, and the rest of the Wabanaki delegations. Many conversations were shared on the days of travel as the people traveled back to Wausacom and neighboring communities. Leesha noticed that the old Wabanaki shaman, who had originally placed Tkaden forward as one to be the fulfillment of what was being called the "High King Prophecy," now avoided any contact with him. Dakatomi was suspected by Skoth's circle of supporters of plotting against him and even attempting to kill him. She had been warned by her sisters to keep her distance from him, but she couldn't resist the temptation to spy on him.

So as they traveled, she decided to try to use the power of her wand to search out what he was doing. Tkaden's grandmother, a powerful wise woman in her day, had coached her on how to use the fine rowan wand that Leesha's mother had left for her.

One evening, as they were camped along the banks of a small river, she retired early for the night while most of the other travelers were still gathered around their campfires. Before entering the tent, she very gently cupped a large moth in her hand that had landed on the tent. She went into the tent she shared with Tkaden and settled herself on their sleeping rolls. Pulling her wand from its leather pouch, she stilled her mind and softly whispered an incantation. She waved her wand over the moth and with a gentle puff of air from her mouth she blew the moth out of her hand. It lifted off of her hand and then went fluttering into the twilight in search of Dakatomi. Then, still holding her wand in her hand, she settled back into a crossed-leg sitting position and closed her eyes to listen.

As the moth fluttered through the camp, she heard the conversations of people as though she was walking wherever the moth went. The moth fluttered about the camp, moving from campfire to campfire, tent to tent, but never did she hear Dakatomi's voice. Finally, when she was about to give up and release the spell, the moth landed on a high tree branch several paces into the woods. Below she could make out whispering voices. One of them was that of the old shaman. The other was unknown to her.

Dakatomi whispered, "His power is strong. And he has those meddling women around him. There is nothing more I can do."

The other voice, in a hiss more than a whisper said, "Stop whining old man. You have your own powers."

"But they outfox me every time."

"Stay with young Tkaden and his Leesha. If you can't defeat them, then slow them, as you are able. That is what Malsum desires."

"I will try."

Success will bring you reward. Fail, and you will be punished. I suggest you succeed."

Suddenly, Leesha noticed the high-frequency clicking sound of a bat and then the sound she had been hearing from the moth was gone. The spell was broken.

She sat there for several moments contemplating what to do. She could confront Dakatomi, but even if he admitted conspiring against Skoth, it would accomplish nothing. He could never be trusted. She could tell Tkaden about what she had heard. But she wondered what good would come of that. There was little to nothing he could or would do about it. He had his own suspicions of the shaman, but he still cared about him. So, at least for the present, she decided to do nothing with the information. She determined she would keep an eye (or perhaps two eyes!) on the tricky shaman.

Chapter 16 - Let Them Come To Us

The discussion became heated in Bjorn's tent on the banks of the Mahakentuck River where Skoth and his advisors had gone to discuss the information from their captives and to plan a course of action. Teite insisted that the words of the captive leader could be trusted, but the others weren't so sure.

Turla, captain of the Heilsand ship, voiced his concern, "What if it is just part of an elaborate ruse this Senadondo character has concocted to throw us off his scent? If we can be persuaded to think that Evlin is dead, or when a prisoner changes his story, to think that she is being taken by land - then we might well give up our watch on the river, and he will slip past us and be gone."

"What if what he says is true?" asked Erik. "Then we are wasting time gabbing about it here, and the trail is getting colder as we speak. We should get moving now."

"Would you have us abandon our ships, and go on a merry chase tramping through the woods?" queried Bjorn.

Teite chimed in, "I don't know what we should do. But I do know I believe the man. Evlin is alive and they are escaping by land. What if they don't come back to the river?"

This was the tone of the conversation as they verbally sparred back and forth for several minutes.

Finally, Skoth voiced his thoughts. "I, too, think that the man speaks true, but I don't think we can catch them by land. Senadondo is too wiley. And they have too much of a lead."

"Listen here!" Erik raised his voice. "You know we can track them. You saw me track down the Skraelings when they grabbed Enat and Leesha. You've walked the lands with Fearglas. If there are any who could stay on the trail and catch up to them - we could! Let's get going!"

Skoth shook his head slowly, "No, Erik. Not this time. This time we'll let them come to us. We'll go north to where the Wissawkin River enters the Mahakentuck and wait for them there. This time, let them come to us."

Both Turla and Bjorn were silently nodding their heads in assent to this. Tiete looked thoughtful and did not disagree, but Erik objected.

"I think you are wrong not to chase them. What if you set a trap up north, and they simply go around it? You might not even know they have gotten around it until it is too late! Hot pursuit is best! And what if Senadondo lied to the men we have here? Maybe they intend to go all the way by land!"

"Erik, I respect what you are saying. But I think that, given the forces we have at hand, setting the trap up the river is best."

Erik sighed in resignation. He knew how hard it was to argue with Skoth when Skoth's mind was made up. So he tried a different tack.

"Then set your trap, but let me take a couple of my men and give chase."

Skoth slowly tilted his head and thoughtfully said, "You know that they'll know they are being pursued. Our prisoner called their leader a limikkin. They have some powers."

"Aye, that they do," agreed Erik.

"They'll try to set traps for you to stumble into."

"I'm sure they will, but don't you see - if they feel the pursuit behind them…"

Skoth smiled and finished Erik's sentence, "Then they might not see the trap set before them."

"Aye. And who knows. Maybe I'll even get lucky and catch them before you do."

"Go then. Take the men you want and leave in the morning."

"Begging your pardon, but if you permit, we'll leave now. All I want to take with me are Jake and Rolf. Send a small boat to take us, and that leader with the loose tongue, to show us where their last campsite was. Then we can pick up the trail at first light."

"But the evening shadows are already deep upon us."

"All the more reason to hasten our departure."

"You want the prisoner to go with you on the chase?"

"No, no. Let him show us the campsite where we can pick up the trail then he can return with the boat and you can do with him what you want."

Skoth gave a long sigh filled with determination. "Go then, and may the gods direct you."

Erik smiled and responded, "If the gods want to help a wee bit, I won't be turning away any favors, but it is my skills I'm counting on. And you, High King Skoth, may the gods favor you. Oh, and one more matter. Watch out for that prisoner who rose in action against us and yet still lives. He has the evil eye for you, that's for sure!"

Preparations were quickly made. The small group clambered into a boat oared by four of Bjorn's men and shoved off into the river current. Hugging the western riverbank, they disappeared into the gloaming light of the evening.

Teite turned to Skoth and asked, "Do you really think he can catch them? And only the three of them? From what the prisoners said, this Senadondo character has at least four other men with him."

"If anyone can catch them, Erik can. Those three are

formidable. They can take care of themselves. And perhaps their pursuit will serve a purpose, even if they can't catch them as Erik hopes. It may run them into our waiting arms."

Bjorn walked over to the two of them and asked, "What would you like us to do with the prisoners?"

Skoth glanced their direction and said, "Post a guard - a double guard - over them for the night. We'll get more information from them tomorrow. And tell your guards to keep a special watch on that one who attacked."

After Bjorn left to attend to the prisoners, Teite pulled the Green Man medallion from her pocket. Turning it over in her hand, she said to Skoth, "This medallion raises questions for me. Why did Evlin have it, and not Enat? How, or why, would it have taken it from either of them? And, maybe more importantly, is it time to summon the help of the Green Man?"

"Good questions. All of them. And I have not the answers for them. I, too, wonder about summoning Fearglas, but I sense it is not yet the time or place. Evlin's need is great, but now her captors are not only fleeing us, they are coming to us. We go up the river and we wait for them."

Chapter 17 - Overland Chase

As soon as Senadondo saw the warriors depart in the canoe, he led his reduced troop into the woods and uphill to the ridge on the western side of the river valley. Single file they walked, with Senadondo in the lead and with Evlin in the middle. And always, just one pace behind Evlin walked Gakko. Senadondo pushed his group hard. In the remaining daylight hours, he wanted to put several miles between them and the river. Surely the pale ones would not find the location of the camp. The Haudenoshonee warriors, even when questioned, would not reveal it. He may not have told them all of his plans, but they knew enough to fool the pale ones. But just in case something went wrong, he wanted to be far from the river.

Through woods, over and around hills, they trekked. Senadondo did an excellent job of avoiding any contact with the few local inhabitants of the area. Finally, as darkness was falling they came to the shore of a small lake, and there Senadondo ordered them to camp for the night.

Suddenly there was a swarm of dragonflies surrounding them. Evlin held out her hands together before her and raised them to her face. A large dragonfly landed on her open hands. Evlin whispered something then softly exhaled upon the dragonfly. It lifted from her hands and hovered before her.

At that moment, Gakko screeched something incomprehensible. She disappeared as her clothes fell to the ground and a kestrel appeared and took flight. The dragonfly zipped toward the water of the small lake and plunged beneath its surface just inches before the streaking kestrel would have seized it. The kestrel hovered over the water for a few moments then went screeching off into the woods.

Senadondo grabbed her pile of clothes and walked several paces into the woods where he tossed them on the ground and then he returned to the shoreline where the men and Evlin were watching him. A few moments later Gakko reappeared, walking into camp as she was adjusting her clothing. She was obviously flustered.

"That was a cursed water sprite! We must get away from here. She'll warn the pale ones of where we are."

Senadondo chuckled, "Oh, really? You think those idiots are following us? By now they're either searching the river bottom for their dear, departed bear-witch, or else drinking themselves into a stupor in their mourning for her. Don't worry, Gakko. The sprite may have escaped you, but it has no one to tell."

"Foolish old man, you know nothing! For all you know, they could be on the trail right behind us as we speak."

"Old woman, quit your whining. You get our bear-witch settled for the night and keep watch with these men. I'll go check on the pale men's river camp. I don't know how long I'll be gone, but be ready to leave with the first light of dawn."

With that comment, he turned and strode off into the woods and was gone. Gakko glared at Evlin and spat. Then with malice in her voice, she said, "I'll be watching you. And if any more of those nasty little sprites turn up," she clacked her teeth together and continued, "they'll be snapped up just like that!"

The men who were with them glanced back and forth at each other, and at Gakko and Evlin, but said nothing.

Gakko noticed their glances and threatened, "And you sluggards, what are you standing around looking at. Make us a small fire and get us something to eat!" And pointing at Evlin she continued, " And keep your eyes on that one. If she gets away, or if she speaks with another one of those sprites, you'll pay with your lives! Now get moving!"

They scrambled to do as she commanded.

Back on the river, the boat of pursuers guided by the Haudenoshonee captive was just touching the shore near where the last rest stop of the abductors had been.

Erik, Jake, and Rolf quickly jumped out of the boat. A brief torchlight perusal of the area allowed them to find recent breakage of foliage and then the hidden canoe. Satisfied that they were in the right location, they shoved their transport boat back into the river and sent the captive and his guards back upstream to the main camp.

Erik gave his instructions to Rolf and Jake, "We'll take turns standing watch. I'll go first. We'll search the area and pick up the trail at first light and be off. So get as much rest as you can."

None of them noticed the small set of eyes peering at them in the darkness of the night, nor the rapid departure of those eyes.

Senadondo came trotting back into the camp by the lake during the hour of the wolf, that hour of deepest darkness before the first light of day brightens the skies. He immediately woke them all and told them to get prepared; they would be moving with the first light.

Gakko questioned him, "Well, old man, what did you see? What has got you all riled up? You were so calm last night.'

"It is those cursed pale ones. The ones at the river camp are doing nothing, but they have sent a small group to follow us. We must get moving. I'll set a trap for them down the path, but for now we must move."

Within minutes they had picked up all their gear and were ready to leave. As Senadondo led them away from the lake, Evlin gave one last wistful look at the calm morning waters and said a silent prayer that the sprite might somehow get her message to Skoth.

It was several hours later when Erik and his men warily stepped from the woods into the clearing on the lakeshore. All three of the men were expert trackers and could easily pick out signs that someone had camped as recently as last night at this site. In places the grass was bruised and crushed where bodies had lain down for the night. Jake pointed out one spot where seven small sticks and been placed next to each other and one of those had the bark scraped off of it.

Erik held those sticks in his hand and stood for a moment, looking over the lake as the dragonflies darted back and forth across the waters. Suddenly, what he thought was a huge dragonfly was hovering above him. When he glanced up at it, it zipped toward his huge hand that was holding the sticks. He felt a sharp burning pain as it touched him and darted off. Looking back at his hand, he could see a small image of a bear seared into his hand.

He muttered aloud, more to himself than to anyone else, "I reckon that was no dragonfly. A water sprite it was. And this mark of the bear is proof enough that Evlin, our little bear-witch was here." Speaking louder to his men he added, "Aye. For sure it is that we are on the right trail. It is hot before us. But they may know we are following. We must hurry, but we must take care. We'll take a brief moment to eat and drink and then be off again. Have either of you found their trail from this place?"

Rolf replied, "Here it is. It looks like someone is scuffing the ground and that they aren't taking the time to try and cover their tracks. It looks to me like they are trying to move quickly."

Erik nodded, exhaled with determination, and said, "Then they know we are after them. Let's get moving."

Chapter 18 - Mixed Emotions

Ayen led his force of Haudenoshonee warriors to the northwest. It was his intention to guide them through the area of woods, lakes, hills, and ridges to the headwaters of the Wissawkin River and then to follow the valley as the river flowed northward to where it joined the mighty Mahakentuck. The lowlands in the valley were settled and farmed by historic rivals of his Mohak people, the Lenape, and by a scattering of the Celtic immigrants, but he didn't anticipate they would hinder a force of his size as they were simply passing quickly through the territory. He had no plans to engage with them and even planned to avoid contact with them as much as possible.

They moved with a steady efficiency through the ridgelands and it wasn't long before they had worked their way through these lands and come to the upper valley of the Wissawkin. Ayen did not think the Celtic warriors of Eirgalon would catch up to his people: however, he did keep a strong rearguard in case the unexpected happened.

Although Enat was alone as the sole captive of Ayen, she did not feel entirely alone. She felt a growing kinship with Waneek and knew that even though she was a prisoner, she was safe under the watchful eye of her appointed guardian. She also felt a growing admiration and fascination with Ayen. When they would gather around the evening campfires, he would visit each fire briefly but would always end up at her fire and spend the rest of the evening there. At first she supposed that it was because Waneek was his aunt and that he was showing deference to his family, but then as he always engaged her in conversation, she began to wonder if it was because of her.

Ayen appeared to be a deep thinker, and often paused

to organize his thoughts before speaking. One evening he seemed especially quiet and deep in thought when he suddenly turned to her and startled her by asking, "Waneek has told me that you have a sister that is promised in marriage to a man of the Wabanaki. Are you promised to someone as well?"

Enat stammered her response, "Yes, well, no, not really. I mean there is this man, but we haven't made any promises. I always thought we would get married, but I don't know. He hasn't exactly asked."

"And if he asked?"

"Well, then I would think about it."

"What does your father say?"

"Oh, Da likes him. Sure enough he does, but he is not about to order me to do anything. The choice is mine."

"You are a headstrong young woman. He must be a strong man."

"That he is. But since you asked me, how about you? Is there some maiden that you, or your family, has in mind for you?"

On the other side of the fire, Waneek gave a little grunt and a slight smile crossed her face; she liked the spark in this young woman.

Now it was Ayen's turn to sputter a bit. "No, there is none for me. Or, at least none that I want. Family, maybe Auntie here, may have some ideas for me, but there is none I want."

Waneek couldn't let that comment pass by without saying something. "Ayen, here, is a good man. He has a strong heart and would make a good husband and father, but he rejects any we place before him. He likes to say he hasn't the time for raising a family, but sooner or later the time will come."

Ayen insisted, "I really have no time for a family. I have Malsum's War I must fight. Even now, as you well know, we have been away from our homes for several months. It would not be right for me to take a wife."

"Bah! Malsum's War you say. Just why is it that we must fight this war to chase these people out? Look at this young woman before you. She is one of them. Is she such a terrible beast we must make war on her people?"

Ayen said nothing but stared at Waneek for several moments. Then he glanced at Enat and looked back at Waneek. He clenched his jaw tight but said nothing. Then he slowly stood and walked away from the campfire and disappeared into the darkness of the woods.

Enat looked at Waneek. When Waneek took her eyes from watching the place that Ayen had entered the woods, she met Enat's gaze and saw Enat raise an eyebrow in question.

"Don't worry about him, Enat. This is the way he is. I wanted him to think through what he was doing and so I said what I did. Now he needs time to be off by himself and to think. For some people, a time of solitude is needed for them to understand their thoughts and feelings."

"Will he be gone long?"

"There's no telling, Enat. But you are here, and I want to talk with you. Tell me about that young man of yours of whom you said you weren't sure."

Enat smiled as she thought of Karl. "He is much like Ayen. He is strong, smart, and is a good man with a good heart. He is loyal and determined. I think you'd like him."

"You speak well of him, yet you are unsure whether you would be his wife?"

"Aye. Truth be told, we've known each other since we were children. And we've always liked each other, but sometimes I fear we don't have a strong passion between us.

I fear we are more friends than true lovers."

"Come now girl, it isn't a bad decision to marry a good friend."

"I know. We do like each. But I want more."

Waneek nodded knowingly. "I understand. I had a man that meant the world to me. Oh, the sparks we made." She chuckled a moment at the memories, and then went on, "Ah, well, that time is past. And we are in the middle of this crazy war. Don't give up. You may yet find your true love when all this is over. But now it is time to get some rest. I'm sure Ayen will be pushing us hard again tomorrow."

So Enat covered herself with her cloak and tried to sleep, but her thoughts moved to Karl, and then to Ayen.

Miles away, on the other side of the ridgelands, Karl was encamped with his men. He had retreated with his forces to the northernmost bend of the Peecock River. There he made the decision to pick a hundred of his fittest warriors to pursue the Haudenoshonee overland. The remaining men and the four longships he sent, under the command of Padrig, back down the river. They were to return to Glesga and then head up the Mahakentuck to join Skoth's forces.

Karl pushed his men hard in the pursuit of his foe, but Ayen's forces were moving quickly and were maintaining their day lead on them. He had some doubts about what he was doing, though he didn't share those concerns with his men. It was apparent that the Haudenoshonee were not trying to hide their trail, but were trying to travel quickly. The lure up the river to the falls while the main enemy force had veered off to travel north overland had secured for his opponents breathing room from the hot pursuit of the Celtic warriors. It felt to Karl as though he was being lured to follow them. But was it a trap? Perhaps his force was now too small to fight a major battle against a foe of undetermined size. By the number of firepits that they had seen in the deserted Haudenoshonee campsites, Karl

---

estimated the opposing force to be larger than his own. But maybe Skoth was right, and this was just a lure to open up the escape route up the Mahakentuck River. If so, giving nominal pursuit and then sending the longships back to Skoth on the river was the right course of action to have taken.

As he slept a fitful sleep that night, images of his deceased friend, Neal, flashed through his mind. He had always thought of Neal as the smart one. A real bookworm and scholar he had been. He would have been a master druid. But he had been killed by the effects of the poisoned knife intended for Skoth. Karl had gone to sleep thinking that if Neal were with him, he would be able to help him think through the strategy of this chase. He would know what to do. So when Karl roused from sleep early in the morning, he wasn't surprised he had dreamt of Neal. He only remembered bits and pieces of his dreams, but in those fragments he got the sense that Neal had been speaking to him and that Neal was telling him to keep going.

Karl actually grinned to himself as he thought of Neal and thought to himself, "Imagine that, Neal telling me to go on. Dead friends don't really speak in dreams. But, in any case, I think he's right. On I go!"

Chapter 19 - Setting the River Trap

After Erik and his men left Skoth to pursue Evlin's captors, Skoth directed his forces up the Mahakentuck River to the small Celtic settlement called Euanglen, at the mouth of the Wissawkin River on the western shore of the Mahakentuck River. The small village was on the south side of the Wissawkin River, so Skoth ordered his main war camp to be set up on the north side of the Wissawkin River. He had decided to leave Bjorn and his ship of men posted as a checkpoint and communication link on the river at Bear Mountain.

Within days Skoth had seven longships and their men at his command, for the fleets commanded by Gunnar and Padrig arrived in short order. Rather than keep all his men in one large camp, he directed them to establish a string of smaller camps that ran from his base camp on the banks of the Mahakentuck westward for several miles to the eaves of the Blue Mountains. Only with great difficulty and great luck would any party be able to sneak past them.

Soon, many of the local Lenape and Celtic inhabitants of the river valley established a little village next to Skoth's camp as they came to trade and sell provisions to Skoth's army of warriors. Skoth groaned inwardly when he heard the people were referring to the settlement as Kingstown as he imagined the teasing Erik would be giving him about that. Well, he thought, at least it was better than being called Skothville or some such name that Erik would have come up with!

Skoth knew that Teite had become an accomplished reader of the runes, but until this point he had been hesitant to ask her for a reading. However, one evening he asked her if she would come to his tent and be willing to do a private reading for him.

When she entered his tent that evening, Teite noticed that Skoth already made arrangements for the reading. A small lantern was hanging from the center pole of the tent and a table large enough for her to spread out the throwing cloth for the runes was set up. There were also two chairs placed next to the table. No doubt the locals had provided the table and chairs, since they looked more substantial than anything the warriors would have carried on the longships.

It was a warm summer evening, but Skoth instructed the guards posted outside the tent that he didn't want to be disturbed and then he closed the flaps of the tent door.

Teite tried to joke with him. "So secretive. Are you trying to keep prying eyes from seeing us together, or are you just trying to keep the mosquitoes out?"

Skoth, however, was not in a joking mood and replied somberly, "No. It is just that I don't want to be interrupted. Somebody always wants to talk to me about something. I want us to be alone."

Teite left her joviality disperse and said, "I understand. So let's sit down and get to it."

They sat down and Teite spread the throwing cloth over the table and set the bag of runes upon it. Then she said, "Before you draw and throw the runes, I think we should talk for a while about what it is that you want the runes to speak to."

Skoth sighed, and began to speak, "It has been days now. Evlin is still in the hands of her captors. Who knows what they have done to her. To be collared like that has to be hurting her. I worry that I have made the wrong decision in trying to set a trap here. What if they try to trek through the Blue Mountains? And what of Enat? Now that Karl has sent so many men here - will he be able to rescue her? And what of the search for the loon's necklace? I am doing nothing about that! Or the fight with Malsum? Should I be raising a large army to march on him? Should I be summoning Fearglas? My mind is a jumble of thoughts and worries!"

"Skoth, I wish I could reassure you about all these concerns. But I can't. You can only try to do your best. You are making wise and thoughtful decisions, but who knows what the outcome will be?"

Again Skoth sighed. For a moment he hung his head, but then (as though with resolve to carry on) he lifted his head and looked at her to ask a question.

"Have you been questioning our prisoners and the local people about the loon's necklace? Have you found any information that can help us?"

Teite replied, "As you suggested, I have been talking to our prisoners and to some of the local people. I try to be discreet, so as to not tell them what we are looking for, but I haven't found anything of great value yet. The Lenape people don't seem to have the legends that are tied to the story of the loon's necklace, but I think there may be with the Mohak of the Haudenoshonee folk. The prisoners do talk to me, except that one surly fellow, but they are wary. I'm not about to give up trying!"

"That's good. Keep it up. I'm sure you'll uncover something of help. Now, what about this reading? How do we proceed?"

"First we have to clarify that jumble of thoughts. You have to be more specific about what you desire to understand. You spewed out numerous thoughts and questions. Before you touch the runes, we must have a clear question from you. And the type of question will determine the number of runes you cast. If it is a simple yes or no question, then it may only be one rune. If it is more complex, then there will be more runes. So, what do you desire to focus on? What is your question?"

"For right now, I want to focus on Evlin. I guess the best way to say it is to ask what I can do to rescue her. I don't suppose it really helps to ask if I have made the right decisions, since what's done is done, but perhaps if I had some indication of a course of action to pursue. Does that sound focused enough?"

"Yes. That will work. Your intentions are clear. For now, I will have you reach into the bag four times to draw out the runes. Then, without looking at them, cast them on the throwing cloth. Please reach into the bag and select the first rune."

Skoth reached into the bag, drew a rune and tossed it onto the cloth. It landed upright and was the rune Ansur.

Teite told him, "This is a good omen. It indicates that you are looking for guidance and are open to counsel. This suggests that the outcome will be good for you. Had you tossed it face down, the opposite would be true. Now, reach in and draw three runes, and cast them on the cloth."

Again he reached in, and this time he pulled forth the three runes and tossed them in the center of the cloth. They were Geofu, Is, and Th. All three were faced upward.

Teite exhaled loudly and said, "These are powerful runes for you. They can be called Gift, Ice, and Thorn. I sense that you have before you a great gift. I wonder if, since you mentioned him earlier, that it might be Fearglas. The choice is yours, but you need not fear to summon him."

Skoth nodded thoughtfully and queried, "And the others?"

"Ice indicates waiting. That fits your situation. You have set a trap. Now you must wait for your prey to enter the trap."

"You're right. That makes sense. The hunter must have patience and wait. What about the thorn."

"Ah, that one bothers me, for it indicates the suffering of some pain. It is like a thorn in the flesh. It may mean physical pain, or it may mean some sort of mental test.

Whichever it is, it will cause you pain."

Skoth sighed with resignation and made a motion as if to rise.

Teite held out her hand, "Wait!"

"What? You said four runes. I have cast four."

"Skoth, you weren't listening carefully. I said to reach into the bag four times. On the second time you drew three stones. You still have two more times to draw."

She held out the bag to him and he drew another and threw it on the cloth. It was Beorc.

"This is sometimes called Birch. It is a symbol of new life. In the upright position you threw it, it is a very positive indication of a female's relationship with you. Now draw one more rune that will show you the likely outcome of the actions you are undertaking. Open it and look at it in your hand before you place it on the cloth."

Skoth reached into the bag and drew forth Ing. He held it in his gaze for a long time as he held it in his hand, and then he placed it gently in the center of the cloth.

Teite gave a soft whistle before she began, "Whew, this is open to many interpretations. It certainly has to do with Evlin, since that is what your focus question was about. It symbolizes that the difficulty concerning her that you have been undergoing is drawing to a close. It could also mean that both of you will have peace soon. That is good. But there is also a strong aspect of fertility here. It may be an indication of new life."

"Just what do you mean by that? New Life?"

"It could be figurative, or it could be literal. It could mean that you will soon have her here to enjoy your new life together, or it could mean she is with child."

"What? How?"

Teite chuckled, "I didn't think I'd have to explain to

you how babies are made!"

He stammered, "Well. No. Of course not."

"Teite went on, "I'm not saying that she is pregnant, mind you. I'm simply saying that the way the runes were cast are open to such an interpretation."

Skoth's jaw hardened in determination as he said, "Now, more than ever. We must get her back."

Teite nodded as he continued, "I know you've been holding the Green Man medallion of Enat's. If you would allow, I would borrow it as I summon Fearglas. I don't need it for him to hear my call, but it can't hurt."

Teite reached under her tunic and handed it to Skoth.

As she gathered up the runes and throwing cloth, he grabbed his staff, carved by the Green Man himself, opened the tent flap and walked out into the semi-darkness of the flickering campfires. From the door of the tent, she saw him disappear into the woods.

Chapter 20 - Night Visitor

After Skoth left, Tiete simply wanted to be alone for a while. The discussion of the possibility of Evlin being pregnant had prompted her to think of the man she had loved, Neal. She walked down to the river's edge, sat on a boulder, and gazed out over the dark waters of the river. She could see the lights of Euanglen to the south across the small Wissawkin River; and to the east, across the wide Mahakentuck, she could make out the flickering lights of small settlements and homesteads. Looking up the river, she could see that the northern skies of this balmy summer night were shimmering with the lights Teite's folk called the "merry dancers."

The daytime winds had softened into slight wafting breezes that carried the sounds of the night echoing across the gently flowing waters. She listened closely to the sounds of nature as she sat and thought of Neal, but the human sounds of camp life often overlaid them. Voices, sometimes soft, but sometimes filled with the laughter and boasting of fighting men disrupted her thoughts.

She heard a voice say, "I'm sorry. So sorry." It stopped her thoughts dead in their tracks. It sounded so much like she remembered Neal's voice. She strained to hear, and then she heard the voice again. This time it was closer, and louder. She sensed someone behind her and to the left. Slowly she turned slightly to her left where she could see the "merry dancers" fill the sky. In front of those pulsating lights stood a shadow. Startled, she jumped to her feet.

A voice, Neal's voice, said, "Stay. Come no closer."

"Neal? Is that you?"

"Teite. I am sorry. So sorry. I never meant to hurt you."

"How? What? Who?"

"Please, no questions. Just listen to me. And please forgive me."

"I'm listening."

"I never meant to hurt you. The power that possessed me forced me to try to kill you before you could share your information with anyone. I didn't want to do it. I couldn't stop it. I was too weak."

"But why? I loved you."

"I'm sorry. I loved you too. But I was too weak."

"Even though you attacked me, I know the true Neal wouldn't willingly have hurt me. There really is nothing to forgive."

"Thank you. I can still help you. Gluskabi has given me a gift. I can make amends for what I have done. As I make my way across the sky bridge," the shadow seemed to wave a hand across the flowing northern lights, "I may speak to you and give you a message from him."

"A message?"

"Yes. He says to tell you that you should look to the north and that he who makes rivers holds the key to the quest."

"He who makes rivers? Who, or what is that?"

"That is the message. That is all I can say. I must go. Never forget that I loved you, but you must go on."

And then the shadow seemed to dissolve before her eyes, melting into the dancing shapes of the green and golden lights in the northern skies. Her heart ached as she felt again her love for him and knew that he was gone from her forever.

At that moment, a man approached her from the camp. The flickering flames of the campfires silhouetted him. When he spoke, she recognized him. It was Gunnar.

He said to her, "My lady, Teite. One of my sentries told me you had come down here to the water's edge. Forgive me if I intrude, but I thought I heard you speaking to someone."

She glanced toward where the shadow of Neal had been.

"No. I'm all alone. But come, sit with me. Talk to me."

They sat side by side on the banks of the river for a long time. They talked about their activities of the last few weeks, for she had been with Skoth and he had been with Karl. Then, to her surprise, she found herself sharing stories of her life on Fadis Innis. She even spoke of Neal, though she told him naught of the shadow she had just spoken to. They were in the process of rising and returning to the camp when Skoth stumbled out of the woods.

"It is done!" he announced. "I have called on Fearglas to give us aid."

"What will he do?"

"I honestly don't know. The Green Man has a will and way of his own. I can't predict him. But I know he is good to his core. So whatever he does, it will be done for good."

Teite hesitated and then said, "Gunnar, would you mind if we say good night? I have news of great importance I need to share with Skoth."

Gunnar, ever the polite warrior, said, "Not at all. I have enjoyed our moments together. May you sleep peacefully, my lady."

With a smile on his face, for he was indeed content with what had passed between them, he turned and made his way back to his own lodging.

Skoth watched the interplay between them and raised an eyebrow.

"You two look good together," he said. Then he gave

an exhausted sigh and continued, "Is this really necessary, Teite? I can scarcely stand after the work of the day and the summoning of Fearglas. Truth be told, it took more out of me than I thought it would."

"Yes. It won't take long, but this is not something I want to keep to myself. I must share it with you now."

"Aye, then. Let's go into my tent. We can sit while you share this news that you think is of such great importance."

When they were seated in the tent, Teite began the telling of her encounter with Neal's shadow. Skoth sat silently and listened intently as she described what had happened. When she was done, he closed his eyes in thought.

Finally, he said, "I'm glad you insisted on sharing this. I'm not positive about the exact meaning of that phrase: he who makes rivers has the key to the quest. But I am sure it is a strong message that we must head up the river. I think that perhaps it means that we must go to the headwaters of the Mahakentuck, or perhaps the Mohak, for the source of the river is where the rivers are made. What think you?"

"That makes sense to me. We see loons throughout the land. But the northern lakes are where they make their nests and raise their young. The rivers begin in those lakes. When do you think we should go?"

"I'll think about it and decide after I have rested. In any case, the decision can probably wait a few days. For now, we must wait. Wait and see what falls into our trap."

When the new day dawned, Skoth felt renewed energy. He still wondered why the summoning of Fearglas to their aide had expended so much of his energy, but he knew well that he didn't know all there was to know in this world. He did come to another decision that morning. He decided to send a small scout team up the Wissawkin River.

He called for Notaku, the multi-talented protégé of Keith, and gave him instructions to take a crew and head up the Wissawkin River under the guise of conducting a trade mission. His real purpose would be as a scout to listen for any word of Haudenoshonee men on the move and to communicate that information back to Skoth at Kingstown. Skoth gave him the authority to arrange for any canoes, trade goods, and hire men he may need to make the mission authentic. He also instructed him to include a couple of the Fadis Innis men-at-arms, specifically Rudi and Magnus. He knew from his days as a youngster at Dunsheelin that these men were often at the side of Erik, and that Erik trusted them. If Erik trusted them, he had no doubt that they had some skills to blend into this reconnaissance mission.

As Notaku walked away from him, eager to be entrusted with such a mission for his High King, Skoth smiled to himself. He would wait. But there was no need to wait idly.

Chapter 21 - Chase in the Ridgelands

The days were becoming harder for Evlin. She first began to notice her growing weakness the morning they left the lake of the dragonflies. She was progressively feeling weaker and nauseous as the days went on.

Two days of travel later she stumbled and fell to a heap on the ground when they stopped to rest for the night. Senadondo looked at her with a strange leer and asked her what was wrong. When she told him how tired she was and how sick she felt, he grinned and then laughed. The four Haudenoshonee warriors looked on at them with varying degrees of curiosity and disgust, for what honor is there in taunting a captive.

When he had finished laughing, he said, "Malsum said this might happen after we put the collar on you. He said that once you were cut off from your spiritual power your physical strength would weaken too. He thought it would take longer to have an effect on you. It looks like you're not as strong and powerful as everyone thinks you are."

Senadondo broke out into laughter again, and this time Gakko joined in with that hideous cackle of hers. Evlin made no reply, but lay still on the ground in exhaustion.

Senadondo turned to the four warriors and said, "You must lay an ambush for our pursuers. We are at the edge of the ridgelands and are about to descend into the lowlands of the Wissawkin River. Those last gullies and ridges we passed through should give you ample places to ambush them. In the first light of morning, you are to backtrack along our path until you find a good spot. Arrange yourselves so that none of them will escape you. Gakko and I will take the bear-witch on from here. We must go as fast as we can now for I don't know how much longer she will last and I want to get her to Malsum. We can't wait for Ayen to arrive from the south. We will steal a canoe and speed down river to the Mahakentuck. After you kill the pale ones, wait and watch for Ayen. Join up with him and tell him what we have done."

The leader of the warriors replied, "We will do as you command. But those are skilled and accomplished warriors who follow us. You say there are only three, but what if there are more?"

"Fool! I told you there were only three. Do you doubt me?"

"No. But it may be hard to surprise them."

"Then use all the skill you famed Haudenoshonee fighting men claim to have. But perhaps I can help. Each of you give me one of your arrows right now. I will return them to you before you leave in the morning. Be careful not to touch the arrowheads, and use them for the first shot in your ambush. They will be deadly!"

Senadondo turned to Gakko, "And you, get some food inside that creature," he pointed to Evlin. "She may be losing strength, but I can't risk taking the collar off of her, and I can't risk giving her any more of the sleeping drug I gave her the first day. If we take the collar off, she may kill us, and if I give her the drug it may kill her. Feed her so she can make it to where we can steal a canoe."

When light started filtering through the trees, the four warriors collected their arrows from Senadondo. Meanwhile, Gakko woke Evlin and dragged her to her feet. The men started to backtrack down the deer path they had been following at the end of the day and the other three went the opposite direction.

The Haudenoshonee warriors carefully selected the place for the ambush. The previous day they had followed the deer path down a ravine that had some brush and trees growing in it. There was a place where this ravine had relatively steep sides; and from the top ridge of the ravine there were occasional open spots between the foliage where they should be able to get some clear shots if the pale ones were grouped closely together.

As the mid-day sun moved slowly to high overhead, they lay spaced out on both sides of the ravine and waited patiently. They saw a doe and her fawn ambling up the path in the ravine, and then minutes later they came trotting back. It was an indication that something, or someone, was coming their way.

One of the pale ones came into view. The Haudenoshonee leader cursed under his breath for he could see that the pale ones had spaced themselves far enough apart so that it was unlikely they would all be open enough for clear shots at the same time. He waited until the first man passed him and should be in view of his men furthest down the path. He shot at the second man, and hit his mark in the left leg. The man yelled in pain. Then, he could see another arrow come from the opposite ridge and strike the pale one in the shoulder.

When the lead man, Rolf, heard the sound behind him he immediately threw himself to the left side of the path into the brush. Arrows pierced the space where he had been.

Erik was bringing up the rear of the pursuing men when he saw Jake stumble to the side of the path and heard his shout. He immediately looked to the ridges of the ravine, but he saw no one. Glancing to the sides he saw that he could climb to the ridge on his right, so he carefully made his way to the top. With stealth, he made his way along the ridge. Peering around a tree, he saw a Haudenoshonee warrior, with bow drawn, warily kneeling and trying to see into the ravine.

Erik drew his bow and let fly. With a thunk, the arrow plunged into the torso of the man. The warrior's arrow flew errant into the sky and he tumbled to the ground. Quickly Erik moved forward and finished him off with his knife. Immediately he looked further down the ridge to see if there were more men lying in ambush. He didn't see anyone at first, and he gradually worked his way along the ridge. Carefully sneaking a look over the trunk of a large fallen tree, he spotted a second man. The warrior kept peering into the ravine and then he moved slowly up the ridge toward Erik. Erik could hear the warrior making his way toward him. He set his bow to the side and quietly drew his sword. When he sensed that the Haudenoshonee warrior was on the other side of the fallen tree, he leapt up and threw himself over the tree to attack the man. The warrior had no time to drop his bow and pull his long knife before Erik had slashed him in the neck and dropped him to the ground.

Erik knew that this was enough noise to alert any other attackers. And he knew there must be more. As they had been following the trail the last few days, they had figured out that they were following six or seven people, and they knew that one of them was Evlin. Even if he had disposed of two of them, Erik knew there was a possibility of four or five others that he needed to be wary of. He started to work his way back along the ridge of the ravine the way he had come, so he might descend into the ravine and cross to the other ridge.

While Erik was dealing with the men on the right ridge, Rolf was cautiously working his way up the left side of the ravine. He knew there were likely to be archers on both sides of the ravine -it is what he would have done if he had set a trap at this place - so he kept looking up his side of the ravine, as well as glancing across to the far side. It was during one of these glances that he caught the motion of Erik leaping over the tree to attack the warrior. He didn't know what had happened to Jake, but it gave him satisfaction to know that Erik was at work.

Rolf spotted the man with the bow a moment before the warrior released his arrow. It was just enough time to slip behind a large pine tree growing on the bank of the ravine.

As he worked his way along the ravine ridge, Erik kept

an eye open for action on the opposite ridge and saw the motion when the warrior released his arrow at Rolf and drew another arrow. Erik carefully notched another arrow and sent it flying across the ridge. Again there was a satisfying thunk as it met its mark and sent the warrior falling forward into the ravine.

Rolf stepped forward to finish him off as he tumbled down to him.

The leader of the four warriors saw his partner falling into the ravine and sensed that the tables had turned on him. He determined it would be better to make his way to Ayen and get him the news of what had happened rather than to risk dying at the hands of these pale ones. Quietly and quickly, he melted away into the woods and disappeared from the scene of the ambush.

Erik and Rolf spent the next several minutes searching the environs of the ravine and ridges but finding no further attackers. Erik did find the spot where the fourth man had lain in wait, but he lost his trail in the woods and rocky ground. When they returned to the deer path in the center of the ravine, they found Jake, but there was nothing they could do for him. Neither of those initial arrows had pierced a vital organ or severed any artery, but the poison-laced arrowheads had done their work and his heart had stopped.

They briefly considered what to do. While they cared not about the men who had ambushed them and they felt that they should quickly get back on the trail of Evlin and her remaining captors, they also felt they needed to take care of Jake. They couldn't just leave him for scavengers. So they took a few moments to scrape out a shallow trough and they covered him with rocks as best they could. Before leaving, they promised to return some day and give him a proper farewell.

The attack had set them back a couple of hours and they rued the hours it had cost them as well as grieving the death of their friend. But they went on and by the time darkness came upon them they had reached the place where their prey had spent the previous night. It was too dark to proceed, but they could read the tracks leading into the lowlands. Now there were only three they pursued.

They took turns keeping watch during the night and with first light they picked up the trail and were on their way. It wasn't long before both of them noticed that the pursued were no longer trying to hide their trail.

Erik said, "Do you notice that one of them is leaving a lot of scuff marks on the trail?'

Rolf replied, "Aye. It looks like one of them is injured and the others are dragging 'em along."

Erik's eyes narrowed as he spoke. "It looks to me like that one is Evlin. I don't know what they have done to her, but we must pick up our pace. Let's move it!"

Following the track was much easier now and they were determined to make up time and close the gap between them. They redoubled their efforts as they noticed the terrain had shifted from the ridges and ravines of the ridgelands to a land of gentler hills with woods and valleys. They had come to the lowlands of the Wissawkin River.

Erik turned to Rolf and said, "I fear we must move even faster now. I think our prey will look for a water route. I'd wager they'll be looking to steal a canoe and to use the water to escape us. Once they get on the water, they'll be hard to catch unless we can get our own canoe."

They were starting to pass through some small fields that skirted Lenape villages and the occasional Celtic crofter's homestead. The terrain was more open and obviously more inhabited than the ridgelands and the trail they were following carefully avoided the activity of the local people.

It was close to noon when Erik and Rolf came to the place where the trail ended at the banks of a stream. To them it was obvious that a canoe that had been on land had been shoved into the water and was gone. They knew their prey was now moving faster than they by paddling with the flow of the stream.

Rolf said, "Well that does it. It looks like they are getting ahead of us. And that was the only canoe here. What do we do now, boss?"

Erik thought for a moment and said, "Did you notice that finely tilled field of that crofter a few minutes ago?

"Aye. Tis a hard-working man that lives there, no doubt."

"By the looks of that field, I suspect that crofter has a horse or two."

"And you're thinking we might just borrow them to try a get ahead. Right?"

"Aye. Though I'll not steal the man's livelihood. I'll explain our need and get the horses from him by buying them or by borrowing them. In any case, I'm betting the man can tell us the fastest way to the Wassawkin River without having to follow all the curves and bends of that stream."

With haste they made their way to the crofter's home. There they found a middle-aged Celtic man, his Lenape wife, and their children. Erik briefly explained their situation and need, but unfortunately the crofter's horses consisted of one sturdy mare and a yearling foal. He couldn't see parting with them, and in any case it was doubtful they could carry the two large warriors. The crofter suggested that he could take them to some friends a few miles away, who also had more and sturdier horses, and who might be willing to sell them.

Erik shook his head. "We don't have the time to waste. I know how horse dickering goes. We have to get moving."

Then the crofter glanced at his oldest boy. He was a teenage boy with flaming red hair, just growing into the strength of his manhood.

He suggested, "Why don't I have my boy here, I named him Red, after Erik the Red, don't ya know. Why don't I have him lead you on the fastest paths down to the Wassawkin. That stream you mentioned the canoe is on, why it curves and bends and bends some more. If you've got a load you want to get to market, it's nice enough to let the waters do your work for you and carry you downstream, but sure enough, you can get to the river faster by walking. I'd even let you load your gear, little as it is since you have obviously to travel in haste, on the old mare here and the boy can lead it for you."

Erik quickly agreed to the offer and gave him a few coins in appreciation for the help. At first the crofter declined it, because he wanted to help, for that was the right thing to do. But Erik insisted, after all the use of the mare and the time of the youth were worth something to a hard-working farm family. Within minutes, they were ready to depart. The crofter and his wife gave them some food for the trip and, being parents, a few words of instructions for their boy.

They headed off down the path at a good pace with a renewed sense of optimism that they would catch up to Evlin and her captors.

Without having to search for a trail, the men moved with what seemed to them breakneck speed. By nightfall, they had come to the sizeable Lenape village that was built at the confluence of the stream and the Wissawkin River. No one in the village had seen a canoe of travellers descend the stream into the settlement, so Eric and Rolf were sure they had jumped in front of their prey.

When young Red told some of the local leaders about Erik's mission, for he fluently spoke both the Celtic language and the Lenape tongue, the leaders offered them lodging for the night. Erik thanked them, but told them that he and Rolf intended to take turns sleeping and keeping watch at the stream to make sure that the canoe wouldn't slip past them during the night. And so, they waited.

Chapter 22 - On the Wissawkin

Just southeast of the Lenape village, shortly before sunset, Senadondo beached the canoe and they dragged it out of the water, hiding it in a small grove of trees. Then they worked their way into a thicket of brush where they could hide for the night.

Evlin was obviously exhausted. Even though she had lain in the bottom of the canoe for the last several hours, she felt as though she could barely walk. She didn't like the looks of the traveling food that Gakko shoved into her hands, but she knew she must eat to gain some strength. The nuts and dried berries made her feel nauseous, but she nibbled on them in spite of the foul taste and swallowed them. Soon she fell into a tortuous slumber.

After darkness had fallen and only stars lit the sky, for it was clear and in the time of the new moon, Senadondo sent Gakko to scout out the settlement. Perhaps the deep darkness of night would be the time to get back into the canoe and slip through the settlement and head down the river. Certainly once they were on the river, the sight of a native couple traveling down river would not seem unusual to anyone they encountered. Evlin would be unnoticed. She could lie in the bottom of the canoe as she had done this past day.

After an hour, Gakko crawled back into the thicket.

She hissed at Senadondo, "Those sneaky pale warriors are there! I think it must be two of them who were following us! They are waiting on the bank of the stream. One sleeps, but the other watches. Somehow they got in front of us!"

Senadondo muttered a curse and said, "Then we move by land. We'll go around the village and straight to the river. There we will find another canoe, steal it and get away from them. Get the bear-witch up and let's get moving. Now!"

The river was only a short mile from where they had lain hidden in the thicket, for as the river flowed downstream to the north it curved toward the east. However, because of Evlin's weakened condition and their desire to remain silent and undetected, the journey took a couple of hours. This first light of a new day was just beginning to give light to the eastern skies when they came to the river. Senadondo told Gakko to stay with Evlin while he went to find a canoe.

Later, but before the sun rose, he returned paddling a canoe down the river.

"I had to go back toward the village to find something we could take. Get her in and let's get moving."

Evlin could hear Senadondo and Gakko softly chortling to themselves about how they had out-foxed the pale ones again. But as Gakko was pushing her towards the canoe, her nauseous feeling overcame her. She knelt on the riverbank and vomited into the waters. "Senadondo leapt out of the canoe and roughly pushed Evlin into the canoe while cursing at Gakko.

"You fool! Never let her touch the waters! Did you forget the watersprite? Who knows what might happen!

Gakko muttered her curses back at him as she climbed into the canoe. She roughly covered Evlin by throwing a cloak over her, so to the casual observer she would look like a pile of baggage as she lay in the canoe, and then they shoved off and began the trip down the river to where it would join the Mahakentuck at the Celtic settlement of Euanglen.

About an hour after dawn, Erik and Rolf were standing near the bank of the stream getting ready to send Red back to his parents and talking with some of the village elders, when a canoe floated into sight. It was paddled by a young boy. As he approached, they could see the excitement on his face. He beached the canoe, jumped out and ran up to the strangers and elders.

"Look what I found!" he exclaimed, "It was hidden behind some trees upstream. I know it wasn't there before. I go out fishing near there almost every day, and it wasn't there yesterday. Maybe the people you are looking for used it and left it there."

Although Erik could understand a little of the Lenape tongue he couldn't speak it well, so he had Red translate for him. Erik had Red ask him if he had seen any people near the canoe.

"No one," was the answer, "but I did look, and I yelled. No one answered so I jumped in it and brought it here."

While they were talking, Rolf had stepped over to the canoe and looked it over. He came back to Erik and whispered to him that he could see Evlin's name rune scratched on the bottom of the canoe.

Erik spoke to the gathering crowd, pausing periodically so that Red could repeat his words in Lenape.

"I'm sure this is the canoe that they stole upstream. No doubt they wanted to avoid being seen, so they decided not to bring the canoe past the village. Do any of you recognize this canoe?"

One of the elders said it looked like one that belonged to his brother that lived upstream and it had his mark upon it..

Erik nodded thoughtfully and then said, "My friend and I need this canoe to chase those thieves. The theft of this canoe is but the last in their long line of misdeeds. We have been traveling light and don't have much to trade, but on behalf of your brother, what would you take in trade for this canoe?"

The elder responded, "It is an old canoe, but my brother still uses it. However you have great need, and your cause is just." He pointed to Erik's knife, which was a treasured knife that King Unaine had given him as a present many years before. "Give me the knife, and we'll call it a trade."

Erik didn't hesitate. He knew that the knife had a value far beyond an old canoe. It had been forged by one of the finest craftsmen in the world, and it was useful to boot. It had a balance and heft that felt perfect in his hand. He doubted he'd ever find another like it in all the land. But he knew what was of true value. If it cost him this precious gift to enable him to rescue Evlin, there was no question.

He handed the knife to the elder who took it and carefully turned it over in his hand. The old man looked at the knife and then looked up into Erik's eyes and handed it back to him while shaking his head.

Erik had Red ask him why he wouldn't take the knife.

Red and the elder conversed back and forth for several exchanges and then Red turned to Erik and explained.

"He wants you to have the canoe. When you gave him the knife, he saw how much you valued the life of your friend over any possession - even a possession of great value. He says that he will pay his brother for the canoe. It is his gift to you. He wishes to honor you."

Erik, seldom at a loss for words, didn't really know what to say.

Finally he stammered out, "Tell him thank you. And that I believe that he is a man of honor."

Again, Red and the elder spoke back and forth and then Red told Erik that there was one more request that he had of him.

Erik raised an eyebrow and asked, "And that is …?"

"He wants you to return in the future and tell him how this ends."

Erik smiled and said, "I'll do my best."

Within minutes they had said their farewells. They got

in the canoe and with determination paddled off downstream in search of their prey.

Chapter 23 – Fearglas

By Senadondo's reckoning, they should have at least a couple of hours head start on any pursuit by the pale ones who were guarding the stream at the village. He didn't doubt that they would eventually pursue them; but since they were waiting at the village for them, it was unlikely that they would leave immediately. In the event that the abandoned canoe would soon be discovered, it was still likely that it would be several hours before the pales ones would pick up the pursuit.

Nonetheless, Senadondo and Gakko used their hidden strength, for limikkins may look frail but have unseen strength in their very nature, to speed the canoe along with the natural flow of the river. Senadondo had determined that, given Evlin's failing health and the uncanny pursuit by those pale warriors, it would be best to push hard to the north and not to wait for Ayen's forces as they were coming from the south.

There was considerable traffic on the river. They frequently passed groups of Lenape who were fishing with spears and who had at some locations set up weirs to catch large numbers of fish. They also saw the occasion Celtic settler, for the Celts had entered this valley generations ago. Though out-numbered by the native Lenape, they lived among them in a relatively peaceful co-existence.

Senadondo carefully steered his canoe so that others only greeted them from a distance and he never stopped to make conversation with any of them. Because they were trying to travel quickly, they occasionally passed other people also traveling downstream, who did sometimes look at them with curiosity. Senadondo and Gakko just waved at them as they went by. As the sun started to settle toward the western horizon, Senadondo deemed it wise to look for a place to settle in for the night. Perhaps they could rest for a few hours and then under the starlight proceed further and avoid any watching eyes.

They came upon a sizable island in the stream that rose out of the riverbed and divided the flow of the current evenly around its sides. There were some large trees and areas of brush on the island but it looked as though there was no one occupying the island. Senadondo decided it was a good place to rest. They beached the canoe and tried to pull it far enough into the dense summer foliage so that no other travellers or local folks could observe it. Dragging Evlin out of the canoe they propped her up under an old oak tree near the center of the island. While Gakko tried to force her to eat some food, Senadondo went to make a quick survey of the island.

He returned after only a few minutes and said, "It looks clear. Only a few squirrels and small varmints here. We'll rest for a few hours; and then if the skies stay clear, we can proceed under the starlight. If it clouds over, I think we'll have to wait for the daylight."

Gakko gave a slight nod and muttered a "mmph", and then turned her back to him.

He said, "I'm going to go scout back up river for a few minutes. Watch her carefully while I'm gone."

Gakko sneered back at him, "Don't tell me how to do my job. Look at her. She's so weak she can barely lift a stick."

Senadondo just returned the attitude with a snort of derision at her and then stepped behind some brush near the shore as he transformed himself into an ordinary screech owl and took flight up river.

Meanwhile, Erik and Rolf had bent their backs to the task and had put all their energy into speeding their canoe down the river. However, they often slowed to hail other folk on the river and ask them if they had seen other travellers hurrying down the river. While not everyone responded to them, or perhaps didn't fully understand them, there were enough who told them of the man and woman in the canoe for them to know they were gaining on them. But Erik knew they would have to pull to the side of the river soon and rest for the night, or risk missing the others in the darkness of the night. The sun had set and night was descending upon them when they rounded a bend in the river and saw the island in the river before them.

The small screech owl heading up the river saw them the moment they saw the island, and that was the very moment that they heard a scream from the island only a hundred yards ahead. The men redoubled their efforts at the paddles and went shooting forward to the island, while the screech owl also turned and darted back in that direction.

The owl arrived first and landed on a branch high in the old oak tree. As it looked downward, it saw a wizened old man, dressed in green with wild brown hair, holding Gakko by the throat. Her screaming faded away as the man tightened his grasp.

Gakko was flailing about and Senadondo wondered why she didn't shift her shape to escape the man.

Then the man in green spoke, "You'll not be able to use your limikkin power to escape my grasp. As you have blocked my daughter from touching her power, my hands prevent you from touching yours. Now, where is that key to unlock the collar?"

Fearglas loosened his grip on her, ever so slightly that she might respond.

"I don't have it!" she spat! "Senadondo carries the key!"

High above her the little owl gave a screech and flew away. Gakko glanced upward and saw him fly away. The green man's eyes followed hers.

She gurgled a laugh and squeezed out the words, "And now he's gone and so is the key. Now she dies. As do you!"

As Fearglas' eyes looked upward Gakko had slipped her hand inside her tunic reaching for the dagger she always carried.

Erik burst through the brush in time to hear those words and to see her hand slip a knife from her tunic. In one fluid motion, he lifted the knife from his belt and threw it at her. It plunged into her back and she screamed as she dropped the knife to the ground.

Limikkins are difficult to kill, for when hurt they can transform themselves. In effect, they can heal themselves from what might be mortal wounds. But since Fearglas' hold prevented her from using her shapeshifting powers, she felt the pain. She bled and the life ebbed out of her. She could not escape. Fearglas lowered her to the ground; but before he released her, he spoke the words of release for her.

"I know your true name. You are 'the one born in the viper's nest' and now you are named. Now you are released from life."

Gakko's eyes went wide in death and the last breath went out of her. She lay motionless on the ground. Fearglas released her and went to kneel at the side of his daughter.

Rolf kept a watchful eye as Erik bent over Gakko to retrieve his knife, but there was nothing to fear. She had indeed passed from this life. Erik pulled his knife from the body and carefully wiped it clean thinking, "I do like this knife." He kept hold of the knife as he looked to Fearglas and Evlin.

Evlin was still seated leaning on the tree and her eyes fluttered in disbelief as she tried to focus on Fearglas.

She sighed in relief, "Father" and fainted.

Chapter 24 – Sacrifice

Fearglas moved from a kneeling to a sitting position next to her and pulled her into his arms. He felt her forehead and wrist, and then a look of surprise crossed his face and he placed his hand upon her abdomen. His eyes went wide and the concern was obvious on his face.

"Child, you feel so cold. Even on this warm summer evening." He looked up at the men and said, "Quickly, gather some wood to start a fire. Use as many of these dry oak branches that have fallen, as you can."

Within minutes, the men had pulled together a pile of several oak branches and smaller twigs for kindling the fire. Then Fearglas asked them to retrieve his oaken walking staff that lay several paces away. He had laid it aside when he had seized Gakko. Taking the staff, he touched it to the pile of wood and with a spark, a fire sprang to life. Moments later the space beneath the old oak was illuminated and warmed by a blazing bonfire.

In the light of the fire, Fearglas touched and examined the collar and lock that was fastened around Evlin's neck. He asked Erik if he carried any water that Evlin might drink, and Erik handed him his waterskin. Fearglas lifted it to her lips and dribbled a small amount into her mouth. She licked her lips and swallowed a mouthful as consciousness returned to her.

She looked up into his eyes and then laid her head upon his chest as she said softly, "Father. It is you. Now I am safe."

Because she had her head nestled into his chest, she couldn't see him sadly shake his head.

"Sleep, my daughter. Sleep. We will see what the morning brings."

He gently held her in his arms for several hours, as the men kept the fire burning, then he softly laid her down and covered her with his cloak.

The men had been keeping a watchful eye for Senadondo and had posted themselves on opposite sides of the couple. Fearglas stepped to the side of the fire opposite Evlin and motioned for the men to join him.

"You need not worry about the other limikkin tonight," Fearglas said, "for by now he is far away as he goes to his master, Malsum. But come sit by me. There are instructions I must give you."

Erik gave a last glance upward into the old oak where the screech owl had been, gave a brief look to the northern skies, and then joined Fearglas and Rolf seated by the fire.

"How is she?" asked Erik.

Fearglas slowly shook his head and took a deep breath before he responded.

"She is failing. That cursed collared has kept her from spirit power and is siphoning away her physical strength. Unless it is removed, and soon, she will die. The other limikkin took the key to the collar's lock with him. We can't unlock it and remove it."

Erik said, "Well, then let's break it off. Even if we put a scratch or bruise on her neck. We need to get it off."

"Would that we could, good Erik. But this is a collar wrought with the magic of a god. Without the key for it, there is only one way I can remove it."

Erik cocked his head in query, "And that would be, how?"

"I can use my strength to destroy it."

"But you haven't done that yet. So there must be a

price to pay."

"Aye, a huge price. But it is a price I will pay. Her mother gave her life for her. Now I must do the same."

"I'm not sure I like the sound of this."

"Nor I. But it is the only way. And it must be done soon or she will die, and the hope for your people that she carries within her will perish with her."

Erik objected, "No, no, no. It can't be. If some life needs to be traded for hers, let it be mine."

"A generous offer, my huge-hearted friend. But it can not be so. The ageless strength and power of the Green Man are what is needed to dissolve the metal of the collar into dust. But we must do it soon. Go, and pull from this river a waterskin filled with its moving water and bring it to me."

Erik sighed in resignation, but nodded to Rolf to go and do as had been requested.

Fearglas continued his instructions.

"When all breath has left my body, I leave her in your charge. Get her safely down the river to her husband. It was his summons that brought me to her. Make sure you let him know that without his action, she would have died."

"Aye, I promise."

"And I would ask a favor of you. Take my body to the grove of ancient oaks that lies on the slope of the north side of this river. I passed through it on my way here. You will see an oak, old and gnarly, struck by lightning and fallen to the earth. Place my body beneath that tree. Leave no marking, just leave me."

"But Evlin will want . . ."

"She will understand. There is the cycle of life. Yes, there is death, but life begins anew. You may think this is the end of my life, but it is only a beginning."

Rolf had returned with the water skin, so Fearglas

made the preparations. He smoothed the grassy soil several feet away from the fire. He carefully removed all the sticks and stones on it. Then he lifted Evlin and carried her there, gently laying her directly on the grass and soil. He told them to let the fire die down. The skies were already brightening, but were cloudy and had the feel of rain.

Taking a swig of water from the waterskin, he swished it about in his mouth and then cupping his hands he filled them with it. He opened those hands over her face and wiped her cheek and brow with the waters. Her eyes opened slightly, as she focused her sight upon him and a smile crept across her lips. He touched his wet fingers to her lips as if to still them from saying anything. Then he leaned forward and kissed her upon the forehead.

Taking another deep draught from the waterskin, he filled his mouth, swished it around, and then released it into his cupped hands. He then opened his hands over her neck and washed her neck and the collar with the water.

Then holding her hand, he lay down on his back next to her. He looked into the green foliage of the old oak tree and his eyes began to glaze over.

To Erik's eyes it looked as though the collar around Evlin's throat began to rust, and then it dissolved completely and tumbled as particles of dust into the grass and soil beneath her.

Evlin inhaled a deep breath and her eyes opened wide. She squeezed her father's hand tightly and felt a feeble squeeze in return. She rolled to her side to look at him, and then quickly sat up and leaned over him.

"Father. What have you done?"

His eyes remained unfocused, but he said with a whisper, "I did what needed to be done." And then with his last gasp he added, "Chase the hate away, Evi. Embrace life." And then so softly she could hardly hear him, he added, "And take care of my granddaughter." And he breathed his last.

She laid her head upon his chest and wept.

Chapter 25 - Moving On

Erik and Rolf stood nearby for several moments, and then as unobtrusively as possible moved several yards further away to serve as silent sentinels in this moment of grieving. They allowed her the time and space she needed.

When her tears had subsided, she lifted her head to them and motioned for them to come closer.

"How did you, and he," she motioned to her father, "come to be here?"

"Why, Rolf here, and poor Jake, and I, we tracked you, my lady. Although, I'll admit we had some help along the way. Like a water sprite," and he held out his hand for her to see the mark of the bear, "and some good Lenape folk. But as for your father, why he came because Skoth summoned him. Before he took that collar off you, he told us to tell you that it was the only way to save you, and that if Skoth hadn't asked him for his help, why, you'd be dead."

She let his words sink into her thoughts, and then she said, "I'll want you to tell me more later. I still feel very weak, but I feel like myself again now that the cursed collar is gone. I'll need your help to give my father a farewell that befits the Green Man."

"Aye, my lady, he told us what to do." He recounted the instructions Fearglas had given them and then he pointed at Gakko's body that they had covered and carried to near the shore, "But what about that? What should we do with her?"

Rolf, normally not one for many words, spoke up, "I say we leave her here to rot. Let the carrion have her."

Evlin shook her head, "No, although given the way she treated me, that is tempting. But we'll not let her evil infect the land. We'll have to burn her. If we turn this limikkin's body to ash, the evil that possessed it will fall to ash with it and be gone forever. Build a pyre on the edge of the river touching the waters. We will burn her to ash and then when the waters rise with the next rain, they will wash the ashes away."

They assembled the wood for the pyre as instructed, and then placing Gakko upon the pyre they prepared to light it with coals that remained from the fire that Fearglas had ignited last night. Then Erik turned to Evlin and spoke.

"Begging your pardon, my lady, but I think we should take Fearglas to his resting place first. This kind of fire and smoke plume will certainly draw folk's attention. And there are lots of folks on, and near, this river. Fearglas said to leave his resting place unmarked and unknown. I'd like to make sure those wishes are followed. How about if I take him across the river and tend to him first? Rolf can stay here and make sure nothing happens and then, when I signal him from the other shore, he can torch the pyre."

A faint smile crept across her face. It was the first in a long time.

"A touching gesture, Erik. And so good of you, but you'll not do it alone. I will accompany you and say my final farewells to him at his resting place beneath the oak."

Rolf said, "I'll gladly stay and light the flame under this one. Go take the Green Man in one canoe and do what you must. I'll keep watch here. When you are done, give me the signal from the shore and take off in your canoe. I'll get the fire blazing here and then jump in the other canoe and catch up to you."

They did as they had planned and soon the body of the Green Man was nestled into the soil beneath the trunk of a mighty oak tree and covered with a fine blanket of oak leaves. Erik walked a distance away so that Evlin might say her farewells to her father in private. His eyes teared up as he saw her final gesture to be the placing of the sturdy walking staff upon his grave.

She turned and walked toward Erik and he tried to discreetly wipe his eyes so she wouldn't notice. But she did.

She reached out and took his hand, the one that had the mark from the watersprite emblazoned into it. She lifted his rough and calloused hand, dirty as it was, to her lips and kissed it on the bear's mark.

Looking up into his eyes, she said, " Good and faithful Erik. Thank you. Thank you for your loyalty and your caring heart. Thank you for doing this for him," she nodded her head toward the mighty oak, "and thank you for staying on my trail."

Erik, uncomfortable, for he was not one given to sentimental words, stammered and said, "Awwhhh, lassie. It's what anyone would do."

"No, Erik. It isn't. And you and I both know that's true. But now you know how I feel," she paused and then added, with a little bit of the old lilt and life in her voice, "and now I reckon I've embarrassed you enough."

Letting go of his hand she turned and started walking back to the canoe. He stood motionless for a moment. She kept walking but turned her head back to him and beckoned, "C'mon, let's go see what we can do about making this a better world."

He took a couple quick steps to catch up with her and said, "Yes, my lady."

When they returned to the river, Erik saw Rolf standing on the island near the pyre watching and waiting for the signal. Erik gave him a huge wave and then got in the canoe with Evlin and shoved off.

Rolf took the coals and kindled the brush beneath the pyre into a fire. It soon became a blazing beacon with smoke drifting to the heavens. The sky was cloudy and threatened a summer shower, but the rain held off and the blaze grew fierce. When Rolf was certain that the fire would finish its job unabated, he jumped in his canoe and paddled downstream to join his friends.

A couple of hours later the rains did come, and the river did rise slightly, and the ashes began to be washed from where they had fallen to be carried into the river and dispersed.

Chapter 26 – Esepus

Once Erik pushed the canoe into the steady waters of the river, he simply allowed the current of the river to carry them forward. They drifted downstream without speaking. Erik allowed her the privacy of her thoughts. Truth be told, he didn't really know what he could say that might help. Rolf caught up with them after a couple of hours, just when it was beginning to rain, and they pulled to the shore to sit out the shower under the spreading branches of a large chestnut tree.

A couple of Lenape men who had been spear fishing from their canoes on the river stood on the shore of the far bank where they had taken cover from the rain. They watched the three travelers intently and when the rain started to subside, they jumped into their canoe and hurriedly took off down the river.

"That doesn't look good!" said Rolf.

"I wouldn't bet on it either way," calmly replied Erik, "but we better be ready for anything."

Evlin looked from one to the other before speaking.

"You two are just looking for trouble."

Erik looked at her and said, "Well, it seems to me that you've gone through a mountain of trouble already. You don't need any more. I aim to see that you get back to Skoth without another scratch on you!"

Rolf added, "Aye. That goes for me too!"

Evlin rolled her eyes. Even with the trauma of the last several days still fresh in her mind, she couldn't help but think, "Men! Always thinking they have to protect their women! As if we can't do anything for ourselves."

What she said to them was, "What do you propose? We've come to a part of this valley with lots of fertile fields, good hunting grounds, and a good many people. And, as we can see, they know we are here. Do you think we can avoid them all?"

Erik answered, "Right enough you are. But I'd rather not meet a bunch of them on water. It's decidedly hard to swing a sword while seated in a canoe. I'd say we start walking, and pick a path away from the river."

"No, Erik. They obviously saw that we are here. And it looked to me as I watched their gestures that they were curious about us. If we take off on foot, leaving those canoes here, they will be even more suspicious of us."

"Well, then, my lady. What do you suggest we do?"

She looked around, "This looks like a good spot to sit and to have a bite to eat. I feel famished all of a sudden. Let's see what kind of traveling fare you have in those packs of yours."

Erik and Rolf stared at her, and then at each other for several moments. No doubt they were wondering how she could be thinking of food at a time like this.

She went on, "I know it is a little bit damp here, but the rain is letting up. I expect they'll soon be back with some of their friends. You two will look a lot less intimidating if you are sitting down and eating with me. Besides, truly, I am really hungry!"

They acceded to her wishes and were soon sitting on a couple of fallen logs high on the bank above the river's edge, munching on some of their dried jerky from their packs and of what remained from the food given to them by the crofter's wife what seemed so long ago, when a small flotilla of canoes rounded the nearest bend in river. The men in the lead canoe pointed to the travelers on the riverbank and headed in their direction. The other canoes followed. They didn't hesitate, but came right up to the shore and found a place to beach their canoes next to the two already there. None of them had weapons drawn, but they obviously did carry bows and arrows, along with the knives and fishing spears. A middle-aged man got out off his canoe and led the procession scrambling up the bank of the river.

Standing before them, he spoke greetings in Lenape, which both Erik and Rolf could understand since a dialect of Lenape was used on the western end of the isle of Fadis Innis.

"I am Talli, sachem of the village of Esepus. What do you know?"

Evlin responded, "This and that."

The sachem squinted his eyes and looked at her closely for she responded to his traditional words of greeting with the correct traditional words of response.

Evlin continued, "I haven't seen you in a long time."

Talli lifted his hands toward her as he said, "It is you! Evlin! It has been a long time. Is your father with you?"

Evlin had been smiling at him, but a look of sadness crossed her face momentarily before she lifted again her smile and responded as she shook her head, "No, and I grieve for him."

"What? You grieve? Is the Green Man of the Woods departed from us?"

"I fear I must tell you he has. I travel today with my friends," she said as she motioned to Erik and Rolf. They stood there with mouths agape as they listened to this conversation. They had anticipated having to defend Evlin, yet now they stood here listening to her converse with a Lenape sachem as if the two of them were old friends.

"That is sad news, my child. Will you tell me the tale of his passing?"

"It is still so fresh in my heart," Evlin began and then

took a deep breath, swallowed, and continued, "but you were friends. He would want you to know. Perhaps around the fire tonight."

"Around the fire. So it will be," replied Talli. "Come. Let us not stand here on the bank of the river while my people would greet you. Come."

As they made their way down the bank and settled into their canoes, one could hear Erik mutter quietly to Rolf, "Thor's hammer! That girl never ceases to amaze me."

It was only minutes, and they had only rounded a couple of bends in the river, before they came to the Lenape village of Esepus on the banks of the Wissawkin River. It was a stockaded village, for in this area the Lenape villages had been periodically attacked for generations by the Mohak peoples to the north and west. There was a large stockaded log fence around the entire village with passageway entries at each end. Inside the stockade were rows of longhouses for extended family units and clans. The enclosure was set back from the river by several dozen yards and surrounded with numerous tilled fields that were filled with corn, squash, and beans. It appeared to be home to several hundred men, women, and children.

As they followed the sachem walking from the river to the village, Erik leaned over to Evlin and said, "You might have told us that you were friends with the folks hereabouts."

She gave a little laugh, "I wasn't exactly sure where we were. I haven't exactly been myself the last few days."

Erik knew she was still full of grief, but nonetheless it was good to see her trying to make a joke of what had happened to her. It was a sign that she would heal.

The people of the village welcomed them with open arms and the children especially were entranced by the large Celtic warriors who looked fierce one moment, but who then had faces, which crinkled in laughter at the activities around them. They were well-fed and attended to. When the sun settled low to the horizon, the villagers assembled the logs to make a large bonfire.

The sachem called them forth to join him and they were seated on blankets in a place of honor. He then made of speech of welcome and made a request that Evlin might tell the gathering what had happened to the Green Man of the Woods.

Erik watched her as she rose and all eyes fell upon her. He knew not whereof she drew the strength to do such, on this the night after suffering such a loss, but yet she did it. Sometimes telling the story brings a balm of healing to those who grieve.

With words like magic and the movements of a dancer, she made her way around the fire. First, she drew them in as she told them of the Green Man, and then she entranced them as she shared the "Romance of the Green Man and His Sheela." Some listeners wiped tears from their eyes, and sighs mingled with sniffles spread amongst the crowd. Then she went on to tell the tale of the years after her mother's death and of the coming of Skoth and their romance, and of how he became the High King of Eirgalon.

Erik noticed a slight quaver in her voice as she began to tell them the most recent of events, but on she went, driven by the spirit energy of those enmeshed in the listening of the tale. She tried to modestly protest that the telling of the story wasn't polished, that the words needed a poet's touch, but they cared not, for as she spoke it was as if she were re-living the events and they were living them with her. There were several hisses when she told them of the limikkins, and murmurings of disgust when she told of how they had treated her. When she told them of the rescue on the island and of her father's sacrifice for her, they felt their hearts breaking for her. They were spellbound by her.

And when she softly whispered her father's final words, both women and men let loose their tears. She ended with the words that graced her parent's story "So dream with me and dance with me, and chase the hate away, live life in full embrace, in honor of the Green Man and his Sheela."

Silence descended upon the village. Even the children were silent. The only noise was the crackling of the bonfire in their midst.

As Evlin went to sit down between Talli and Erik, Talli rose and spoke to his people, "This is the first telling of this story. We have been greatly honored. For our old friend, the Green Man of the Woods, and for his daughter, The Bear-Witch of the East, we do honor now by dancing the Bear Dance of our people."

He lifted the drum that he held in his hand and began the rhythmic drumming. The people, men and women, young and old, came to their feet and started the counterclockwise motion around the fire.

This was a dance for all the people; so when women of the village reached out to pull Erik to his feet, he rose and joined them in the dance. Evlin grinned, for she remembered once that when Skoth had been speaking to her about his old mentor and protector, he had said that Erik had never been one to turn down the invitation of a woman.

The night became a celebration of the life of the Green Man of the Woods as they recalled the times he had visited with them. Long into the night they danced and the sounds of people of Esepus echoed up and down the valley.

Chapter 27 - Notaku Arrives at Esepus

Erik intended to get the three of them back on the river and headed to Skoth early the next morning, but it didn't work out that way. After the dancing and celebration of the previous night, the village came to life with the slow laziness of a sultry summer day. When Evlin insisted that she wanted to stay among the villagers another day, Erik acquiesced. It was obvious that the people of Esepus adored her, and as this was a fortified village, there was little danger to her. Erik reckoned her to be as safe here as she would be almost anywhere.

It was mid-morning when there was a flurry of activity as a number of children came running into the stockade shouting about traders on the river. The trade expedition, headed by Notaku, had arrived.

Erik and Rolf slipped on their gear and walked out of the stockade entrance. Across the field, they could see a crowd had gathered at the bank of the river. They couldn't see the traders or their canoes since the bank was too high and they were too far back from the bank. Finally, they saw a young man who looked confident and sure of himself step over the top of the riverbank. He was followed by a couple of more men and then, to Erik's surprise, he recognized the next men. They were his old comrades-in-arms, Rudi and Magnus.

Talli, who had come to stand beside Erik outside the stockade, noticed Erik's smile when he saw the others, and asked, "Do you know these men?"

"Aye, some of them. Good men and friends, they are."

"Then they are welcome here. Let's go meet them."

Talli led them down the path to the river where the traders awaited them.

Talli welcomed them with traditional words of greeting and Notaku responded in kind. Erik and Rolf waited patiently behind him, but when Talli motioned to them they stepped forward.

Talli said, "These friends say that they have friends among you."

Notaku looked at Erik and Rolf and recalled meeting them on the trip from Dundee to Bear Mountain. Though he had met them but briefly, he knew they were loyal to High King Skoth.

"These men are known to me." Notaku replied, "I would call them friends."

"Then you are welcome among us."

Erik sighed, for he was not one given to formalities. He turned to Talli, and pointing to Rudi and Magnus, he said, "Those two are my men. We have been together for years. And you should know up front that our loyalties are to High King Skoth and his queen, Evlin. You'll not find two better fighting men."

And with that said, both he and Rolf stepped forward to welcome their comrades with slaps on the back and hearty bear hugs. Talli looked on smiling, for though his people often used formal word and greetings, he appreciated the honest emotions and actions of good and decent people. Formal words spoken in greeting show politeness and respect, but honest words of friendship have value beyond compare.

Notaku was a little surprised at Erik's openness, for he had hoped that Skoth's warriors would be seen simply as a couple of his trading men as they traveled up the river. That plan, at least at Esepus, would have to be abandoned.

When Erik and Rolf had finished greeting their friends,

Notaku turned to Erik and said, "Well met, good Erik. I see that there are only two of you. Your friend, Jake, I believe his name was. Is he not with you?"

Erik shook his head, "Sadly, no. He fell under the arrows of the Haudenoshonee."

"And your chase? Did you ..?" he hesitated, for he wasn't sure what to say in front of Talli and the others.

Erik grinned, "Ah, yes. The chase. Aye, it was quite a chase."

He glanced back toward the entrance to the stockade. Evlin and a number of the women had stepped outside the stockade and were watching them.

He continued, "We may not have chased them all the way to Skoth's trap, but, as you can see, we have met with success. On the morrow, we plan to complete our journey down the river." He hesitated, laughed at himself, and went on, "I was going to say that we were going to return Evlin to her husband, but I think 'escort' might be a better word. She has a mind of her own and goes where she wants."

Talli invited the traders into the village and they spent much of the day talking trade and commerce. Talli and the people of Esepus already had been trading up and down the river with the Celtic traders and settlers and knew well the town of Euanglen. Some of the men had even visited there several times. They had also heard of the force of Celtic warriors that had come up the Mahakentuck and were camped across the river from Euanglen in the place that was now being called Kingstown.

Talli questioned the purpose of the large war part; and as Erik listened, he thought Notaku did a good job of giving a diplomatic response. Notaku tried to reassure him that the warriors were in response to the threat from the Haudenoshonee war party that was to the south of them and that was thought to be headed this way. High King Skoth had no desire to make war with the Lenape. In fact, Notaku offered the friendship and cooperation of the High King in defending the Lenape of Esepus and the Wissawkin Valley against the Mohaks who had raided them over the years.

The men of Esepus listen carefully to all the words of the trader and emissary Notaku, and in the end, they decided to make several trade deals with the young man. They also decided to send a delegation with Evlin when she left, that they might meet with Skoth and discuss the suggested alliance.

Erik was content enough to spend another evening within the friendly confines of Esepus and enjoy the company of the people there. Before he joined the others at the village fire, he spent some time sitting with his old friends and making plans. He admired how Skoth had chosen Rudi and Magnus to accompany the trade mission. A small part of him was tempted to go back up the river with them that he might track down the man that had shot Jake, but he knew his job was to watch over Skoth and Evlin. At the end of their discussion, it was decided that Rolf would join the expedition up the river. While Senadondo and the others may have been taken care of, there was still the likelihood that Ayen and his force of men, with Enat as their captive, was heading their way.

While the men of Esepus and the traders of Kingstown parlayed and planned, Evlin visited with the Wise Women of the village. The Celtic communities had groups of women they referred to as the "Women's Circle" and these women had a similar function. The men may make the military, political, and trade decisions of the village, but it was often the women who let them know what would be the right decisions to make.

As Evlin spent time with the women walking about the village, she noticed the women's sweathouse built into the side of a nearby hill (the men had their sweat house on a hill on the other side of the village). She felt the urge to have a thorough cleansing of her body and spirit after the travails of the travel with Gakko, and because she knew it would be improper as a visitor to ask if she could use it, she simply complimented how wonderful it looked and how fortunate they were to have it.

Immediately the eldest wise woman, Gela, said, "How rude of us, child. After all you have gone through! You need a session in our sweat-house!"

Quickly Gela gave instructions to some of the young girls that were adoringly following wherever Evlin went. Moments later they went running off to prepare the sweathouse.

It wasn't long before the Evlin and Gela were in the sweathouse beginning to enjoy the heat. Gela wanted to be alone with Evlin and guide her through this cleansing for the sweathouse was not only a physical cleansing, but a spiritual one as well. By allowing Evlin to speak in the privacy of the sweathouse, she could cleanse her spirit of the evil that had tried to harm her.

Evlin was telling Gela about her father's final words and she confided to her that she had not shared all of them with the people around the bonfire.

Gela understood that sometimes words between a father and daughter are not to be shared, but she knew that sharing them was what Evlin wanted and needed to do at this time.

She asked, "What was it that you failed to say?"

Evlin shook her head as she spoke, "They are words I didn't really understand. I mean, I heard them, barely, for his voice was faint, but they made no sense to me."

"What were they, my child?"

"He said to take care of his granddaughter. That's what I don't understand. I didn't know he had any other children, and I certainly didn't know he had grandchildren. Why wouldn't he have told me before?"

Gela looked at her incredulously. Then she leaned forward and placing her hands on the sides of Evlin's head she touched her forehead to Evlin's. Keeping their heads touching, she slowly moved her hands down Evlin's body, over her shoulders and arms down to her abdomen, where she let them rest for a long moment. Then pulling her head back and taking Evlin's hands to move them to Evlin's abdomen, she looked at Evlin and asked a question.

"How have you been feeling lately?"

"What do you mean?" Evlin responded, and then the realization of what Gela was asking hit her and she continued, "I can't be. I mean how?"

Gela chuckled, "Oh, I believe you are. As for the how of it, you're old enough to know how that happens. How many moons have you missed?"

"Two. But I thought it was because of the stress and the collar. Are you sure that I am with child."

"Your father's words are proof enough to me. But trust me, I have a few powers of my own. Now, let's get you out of this heat. The sweat-house is no place for a pregnant woman."

Calling out to the young girls who were attending to them, they opened the door flaps of the sweathouse. As they made their way back to Gela's longhouse in the village, the words of Fearglas kept echoing through Evlin's thoughts, "Take care of my granddaughter." Life was beautiful, but it was also getting more complicated.

147

Chapter 28 – Reunion

Another beautiful summer day broke upon them and by midmorning the visitors to Esepus were back on the waters of the river. Notaku's traders were heading upriver and Evlin and her entourage were making their way to Skoth at Kingstown.

Evlin said nothing about her condition to any of her fellow travellers, but there were a couple of times she caught Erik looking at her with a quizzical look on his face. She felt a little guilty about not sharing it with him, but she wanted Skoth to be the first to know.

Sentries posted along the river observed them long before they reached Kingstown, and Skoth was waiting at the river's edge when they arrived. A few paces behind him stood Teite and several of his officers. Stretching out behind them was a sizable camp, which was turning into a town. Skoth's men had not sat idly by. While many of them were scattered along the line of outposts he had strung to the eaves of the Blue Mountains, there were many who remained stationed in Kingstown. It did, indeed, give every indication of becoming a town, for the men had kept busy felling trees and had constructed several log cabins.

He walked out into the water as her canoe edged up to shore; and even before it was beached, he lifted her from it. Swinging her in his arms he carried her to the shore. Long he held her in his embrace before he let her feet touch the ground, and even when he did so he continued to hold her tightly in his arms. Though there were greetings and activity all around them, it was as though they were in a world by themselves.

Finally, Erik broke the mood. He had beached his

canoe, climbed out of it, and politely stood to the side. But now he spoke,

"Well, now, should I also be expecting such a greeting?"

Skoth looked at Erik, and released Evlin from his hug, whereupon she quickly turned and embraced Teite.

Skoth stepped toward Erik, and in a most unkingly fashion threw his arms around the elder warrior in a huge bear hug and gave him hearty slaps upon his back.

Erik was surprised, but quickly recovered and returned the embrace of warrior brothers.

When Skoth released him, Erik grinned at Skoth, "I reckon I should be reporting back to my Ard Ri. It looks like you've kept the men busy here. No doubt you'll have something in mind for me as well."

Skoth laughed, for his spirits were high with the return of his beloved.

"I'm sure I can find something for you do to. But in all seriousness, I want to hear about all what you encountered and what happened. As soon as we can, this evening, we'll sit together and you will tell me everything."

"So be it. You spend some time with Evlin. My report can wait til then. But the one word I would tell you now, before you go on to anything else, is that you made the right choice. Fearglas, himself, told me that it was your summoning of him that saved Evlin's life. I can explain more later, but he wanted you to know that!"

Skoth nodded thoughtfully and responded, "Thank you for telling me, and I will most definitely want to hear more later."

After making formal greetings with the Esepus delegation and providing them with a promise to sit and discuss in depth with them trade and relations on the morrow, he turned and took again his wife in his arms and carried her into the largest of the newly built cabins, jokingly referred to by the men as the King's Castle, where they might have some privacy.

While Skoth had every intention of carrying her to the bedroom of his cabin, she would have none of it. When the door of the cabin had been pulled shut, she insisted he set her down. Even though she wanted to remain in his embrace, she pulled herself away. She stood before him and took his hands in hers and looked into his eyes.

"You know how I feel about my father."

"Aye, never has a daughter been as loving as you, and he calls you the apple of his eye."

She smiled a sort of mischievous smile, "Exactly. And don't you think every man should have a daughter to be the apple of his eye, as you say?"

"Aye, but none could ever match you."

She smiled again, "Yours would."

Now he laughed, "When that time comes, maybe so, for she will undoubtedly be like you."

She pulled his hands forward to place them on her abdomen and said, "That time comes now. Are you ready for a daughter that will be the apple of your eye?"

His eyes went wide as the realization of what she was saying struck him.

"You mean? You really are? How?"

She laughed, "How?! That is what I said when the Wise Woman, Gela, announced it to me. And she said that by this point in my life I should know the 'how' of how such wonders happen." She laughed again and went on with a serious question as she searched his eyes, "Are you happy with this?"

He pulled her into his arms and kissed her gently on the lips.

———

"Of course. I thought I had lost you, and now I not only have you back I have a daughter." Then he cocked his head to the side in wonder, and asked, "How do you know it is a daughter. Maybe we'll have a son."

"It's a girl. I know because Father's last words to me were to take care of his granddaughter."

Skoth smiled and said, "Then I'm sure it is so." Then he abruptly stopped and a look of dismay crossed his face. "Wait . . . his last words? You mean . . ." and he could say no more.

She put her finger to his lips and said as she led him to the bedroom, "Shhh. Say no more. There is much I must tell you. Come, let us lay together and I will tell all."

They made their way to the bed, and within the privacy of their room she lay curled up in his arms. There she told him all that had happened to her since they had parted.

Chapter 29 - The Flight North

Ayen kept his group of Haudenoshonee warriors moving northeast following the flow of the Wissawkin River toward the Mahakentuck. His standing orders were to avoid contact with the locals when possible and to travel as quickly as possible. He sent able-bodied men out to hunt and forage, so that his people could travel long hours and yet eat fresh provisions. If sometimes that resulted in some poaching of the local's livestock and fields, then so be it. The Lenape of the valley were traditional foes of the Mohaks and they were no friends of the new Haudenoshonee Union.

Large groups of people moved slower than smaller groups, and Ayen was concerned that those who followed him might be moving faster than his people, so he always kept a strong enough rear guard trailing his main force. That rear guard could both slow any pursuers and warn him of their approach.

They hadn't been long in the valley, before one of his advance foragers brought the lone remaining warrior of Senadondo's group to him. Upon hearing his report Ayen knew that even if, and that was a big if, Senadondo made it through the valley and through the forces of the pale ones on the Mahakentuck, there was no way Ayen and his men could catch up to them to help them.

After digesting the information, Ayen changed his strategy. Each day he broke off about a third of his people and sent them heading northwest, out of the Wissawkin valley, to skirt the Blue Mountains on their western side. They would traverse the hills and valleys to the south of the Haudenoshonee homeland and return to the land of the sunset lakes in a couple of weeks.

Enat noticed that each night the camp seemed smaller than the previous night, but no one explained to her what was happening. On the third day, Ayen led a small group of a dozen people, including Waneek and Enat, and he also left the main group to head northward into the hills.

Each day when Karl's men found the previous night's Haudenoshonee campsite, they reported that it was smaller than the previous one. Within days it was obvious that Karl's men now outnumbered what remained of the fleeing host. And then the day came when they lost the trail of the main host in its entirety, for what remained had split into several small groups and scattered. He had no doubt that Enat was with one of the small groups that the Haudenoshonee had split into, but which one? Was it one from two days ago, or yesterday, or today? His trackers told him that most of the groups had turned northwest out of the valley, but what good would it do to follow them now? He would be leading his men through terrain they didn't know, in pursuit of scattered people who were heading into their homeland and who would have the support of their people. It was as if he had been tracking a covey of quail that had now scattered to the four winds. Perhaps they would group together again. Perhaps he would find the one he was looking for. But the odds were not in his favor, and he knew he had a decidedly small force to invade the Haudenoshonee homelands.

They set up their camp that night near the village where Erik and Rolf had waited by the creek overnight in hopes of capturing their prey. As fortune would have it, that was also the village that Notaku on his trading expedition reached that very day.

Rolf had just introduced Notaku to the village elders when a couple of young boys came running into the village shouting about the Celtic warriors who were setting up a camp to the southwest. Rolf assured the elders they had nothing to fear from these men and then took leave from them that he might go and speak with the new arrivals.

153

Minutes later he was striding, with the young boys at his side, up to one of the sentries of the camp and asking to see Drottin Karl. The surprised sentry took him to Karl who looked at Rolf with as much surprise as the sentry had.

"Rolf! What are you doing here?"

"Why, I've been trying to track down some of the same folks you have. These young men," he pointed to the Lenape boys, "saw you setting up camp and came to warn their village. I'm there with a group of our traders that Skoth sent upriver. Why don't you send some of your men to the village? Notaku is the name of our trader; he'll help them get some fresh provisions."

Karl ordered a group of his men to follow the young boys to the town as Rolf had suggested, and then Karl invited Rolf to sit and tell him what had transpired.

Rolf gave him the short summary of the pursuit, Jake's death, Evlin's rescue, and the demise of Fearglas. He reaffirmed to Karl that they believed that Enat was with the group of Haudenoshonee that Karl had been trailing.

When Karl asked Rolf for his advice, he responded, "Mind you, I'm not the one to be making the decisions here, but I'd suggest you leave a few men here in the upper part of the valley to work with the Celtic settlers and Lenape folk. It wouldn't hurt to give them a little protection just in case any of those Haudenoshonee have stuck around. Give them some reassurance. Then I'd take the rest and head on back to Skoth. I haven't the foggiest idea of what he'll do now that his trap is empty, but I reckon he'll have something in mind."

Karl mulled the suggestions over for a bit before responding, "I think you have a good plan there, Rolf. It would be wise to have some men stationed here. It wouldn't have to be a large troop, but enough to make a positive presence here. And I know just the man to be in charge of it."

Rolf protested for a bit, but eventually Karl persuaded him to accept the task. They talked of which men to include in Rolf's troop and agreed that they should be volunteers, and should include some of the Fadis Innis men. However, any who stayed should be unmarried, since they might be away from home for several more months and possibly through the coming winter. It would also be helpful if they spoke, or at least understood Lenape. That meant it was more likely the men would be from Glesga and Fadis Innis since Lenape was spoken more in those areas than in eastern Eirgalon.

By the end of their discussion Karl's men were returning with provisions from the village that Notaku had helped them get by bargaining and trading.

The next morning Karl moved out with his men, heading toward Kingstown. Notaku stayed in the village for another day working with Rolf and his men to establish good relations with the village elders. Then he moved on up the river, to spread more good will and promote more trade between the Lenape and the people of Eirgalon.

The presence of their traditional foes, the Mohak and the other Haudenoshonee warriors, in their valley had unsettled the Lenape, as well as the few Celts who lived in the area. They welcomed the presence of a few of the warriors of Eirgalon who would live and work in their midst. Rolf and Karl made sure to select men who he knew to be level-headed and respectful of others. When Karl and Notaku departed, going their separate ways, they felt comfortable knowing that the future of the area of the Wissawkin valley, was in good hands.

Chapter 30 - Celebration at Kingstown

Skoth and Evlin spent the afternoon together in the cabin, as she told him of her ordeal, and as he shared what had happened during his quest to rescue her. But when evening came, they were ready to celebrate with their people by sharing their news. Skoth was anxious to hear Erik's report and to get his advice, but in the light of Evlin's news, that could wait til morning.

It was one of those wonderful days of midsummer when the heat of the day has peaked and people gather in the pleasant charm of a sultry evening. Skoth had left for a few minutes to meet with his men just as Teite was bringing them some food. Skoth said he had to check on a few matters and that he would eat with the men, and left Teite to enjoy the food and to spend some time alone with Evlin.

Teite warned Evlin that some of the warriors who had escorted her on the flight with Senadondo were being held at the camp. She mentioned that three of them seemed to be questioning their previous loyalty to Malsum, but that one of them was still openly hostile.

Then Teite told her about the visit of Neal.

Evlin listened carefully, and at the end of Teite's narrative, she asked, "What makes you so sure it was Neal? Could it have been some unseen power playing a trick on you?"

"I've thought about that. In stories from the ancients, there are times the gods have played tricks upon unwitting humans. But, with this, I don't think so. I felt no malevolence there. Neal was in shadow form as he stood in front of the Merry Dancers in the Sky, but it was his voice. Those were his mannerisms. I just know it was him."

"And you say that the message from Gluskabi was that 'He who makes rivers' holds the key to Skoth's quest? And you say Skoth is planning on searching the headwaters of the Mahakentuck and Mohak Rivers to find the loon's necklace?"

"That's right. I think it is the logical course of action to take. Don't you?"

"Maybe. But I have another idea. You mentioned the warriors that were with me; do you know which of the Haudenoshonee nations they hail from?"

Teite gave a thoughtful look, and then answered, "Why, I'm not sure. I think the man who speaks most is Mohak, but I'm not really sure. Does it matter?"

"It might. I've got an idea. Take me to them."

They quickly finished cleaning up from the meal and left the cabin heading in the direction of the prisoners.

Erik had been waiting at a discreet distance outside the cabin, hoping to talk with Skoth for a few minutes when Skoth would return from his errands. When the two women came out of the cabin with those determined looks on their faces, he decided it might be wise to follow them. He thought to himself, "When a woman has a look like that on her face something is about to happen."

With his long strides he caught up with them and said, "Well, there, my lassies. Seems like you two are on a mission. I hope you don't mind if I just tag along with you. Just to satisfy my curiosity mind you."

Evlin smiled and replied, "Ah, dear, Erik. My gallant protector. I think we'll be safe enough. But you are certainly welcome to accompany us. We're going to pay a visit to our prisoners."

"Then I certainly do want to come along. I'm not so sure they'll be too pleased to see you, seeing how their mission was to take you away from us."

Surprisingly, she gave a little laugh as she spoke, "I don't believe they are bad men. They weren't the ones who were so cruel to me. They were only following the orders of the limikkin."

"Be that as it may, they have yet to prove that they can be trusted. And keep an eye out for the squinty-eyed fellow. He'd like as not to gut the either of you if he had the chance."

The four men saw the women and Erik approaching them, but they showed no surprise. The activity of the camp and the conversations among their guards had announced Evlin's rescue and arrival in Kingstown to them indirectly, even if they had not been directly informed of it.

The men stood to face Evlin as she approached them. Three of them, including the one who spoke for them, kept their eyes downcast before her. The fourth one, referred to by Erik as the squinty-eyed one, looked straight at her with a glare of hostility. Their hands had been bound again as a precaution when Evlin arrived in the camp, but their feet were unfettered. There were two warriors of Eirgalon standing guard and watching them. They also rose to attention when the trio approached.

Evlin addressed the men with a form of formal Mohak speech, "Warriors of the Haudenoshonee people. Lift your eyes to me. You see me stand before you: without a collar, free and strong. I would speak with you."

The men raised their eyes and looked at her. The one who had been their spokesman since arriving declared, "We hear you, Bear-witch of the East, and we see your power. Forgive us for any harm we have done you. We are at your mercy."

"You may yet prove what you say. It sounds to my ear, that you are a man of the Mohak nation. Are the others with you, the same?"

"Yes, and no. I mean yes, I am Mohak. These two," he pointed first at the two who stood closest to him, "are of the

Oneida, and he is of the Seneca."

The two with him nodded and the squinty-eyed third one spat upon the ground. The Eirgalon guard closest to him took a step closer.

"It is you I wish to speak with. I have a question for you."

The squinty-eyed warrior, blurted out, "Don't answer her. Say nothing to her. She will bewitch you!"

The guard closest to him said, "That will be enough out of you."

He grabbed him by an elbow to silence him and pull him away from the rest of them. The man stumbled as if he was falling and pulled the guard off-balance. He then grabbed the guard's knife from its sheath at his waist. Though his hands were still tied, he held the knife in them and plunged toward Evlin.

He never made it near her. Erik had sensed the possibility of danger and had been standing with his hand resting on the pommel of his sword. The drawing of his sword and his stroke were swift and sure. The man tumbled to the ground. Dead.

The action had happened so quickly that the other prisoners stood in stunned silence.

Erik spoke up, "Ladies, let's step over to the cabin while this mess gets cleaned up. You two, " he motioned to the two Oneida men, "carry this man's body to where the guards tell you and do what you must for him." Then he motioned to the Mohak man, "You come with us, and do whatever the lady tells you to do."

When Erik gave orders like that, no one questioned him. Seeing him in action, Teite was reminded of all the years she saw him in action as her father's chief bodyguard. No one ever gave King Unaine a hard time when Erik was around.

———

The two women, Erik, and the Mohak man walked to the King's Castle. There they met up with Skoth, who was returning from the errands he had being running. They went into the main room of the log structure, which had a large stone hearth, still under construction, at one end. Near the hearth was a large, heavy rough-hewn table with benches around it.

Erik was still in charge and gave directions, even to Skoth, about where to sit. Erik had the two women seated at one end of the table, the Mohak man on the other end, and he and Skoth on the longer sides. this man had made no move to threaten Evlin, and Erik would make sure that the opportunity didn't arise.

Evlin started the conversation by telling Skoth that she was glad he had come back so he could hear this discussion for himself. Then she thanked the Mohak warrior for the small kindnesses he had shown her while they were traveling and that she realized he had not approved of the way Senadondo and Gakko had treated her. Then she came to the question she had wanted to ask him.

"How well do you know He Who Makes Rivers?"

He looked a little startled by the question, but said nothing as if he was trying to think the answer through.

She spoke again, this time in his native tongue, "You know I have met him, but I want to know how well you know him."

"I know him well. We are of the same village, though he is several years older than I."

"Please tell me more. Are you of the same clan?"

"No. I am of the Wolf clan of the Mohak. His mother is of the Bear clan. His father was an Onondaga."

"Do you follow He Who Makes Rivers, or do you follow Malsum?"

The man took a deep gulp and slightly shook his head.

160

"I have no love for Malsum, but where my chief leads, I will follow. I follow Ayenwatha."

Skoth interrupted, "Wait! Are you saying that He Who Makes Rivers is Ayenwatha?"

Evlin smiled as the man answered, "Yes. In the tongue of our people his name means He Who Makes Rivers."

Skoth looked to Teite and held her gaze for a moment, and then said, "I think this means some changes to our course of action."

Chapter 31 - Two Wolves

Once Ayen was no longer with the combined group of warriors from all the Haudenoshonee nations, and with only his small band of Mohak men surrounding him Enat saw his demeanor change slightly. He still projected an aura of power and strength, but she saw a new facet of his character emerge as he sometimes joked with the men who had been his friends since childhood.

Ayen kept them moving at a steady pace through the woodland hills and valleys on the western edge of the Blue Mountains. There was no straight path to follow, and the men needed to hunt for game as they traveled, so the days of travel turned into weeks. Ayen no longer feared he was being followed.

One evening as they were sitting around the evening campfire, and in a roundabout way, Waneek asked him where they were headed. She said she missed their home village and that she sure hoped they would return to it sooner rather than later.

Ayen reassured her that she would see it soon because that was where he was headed.

The sun had set, and no moon had yet risen so they could only see each other by the light of the flickering fire, and Waneek sensed that Ayen was in a relaxed and talkative mood. Enat just stayed quiet and listened. She had picked up much of the Mohak language over the last couple of weeks and could now carry on a better than rudimentary conversation in it. But she remained silent and watched how Waneek led the conversation.

"It will be good to see the home lodges again, don't you agree, Ayen?"

"That it will. It has been long months since Malsum sent our war party to the south."

"But now you return to our village, and not to him."

"I will go to him. But first I intend to return you to our home."

"And what of my friend, Enat? Will she go with you?"

"No. I think not. She will stay at Tionnontoguen with you."

"Does not Malsum want her?"

Ayen paused in thought before replying, "Perhaps he does. But it was the Bear-Witch that he sought. Enat was not his intended prey." He paused again, and then went on, "She will be safe enough with you."

"Safe from him, you mean."

"Perhaps," he said, and then went on, "and now it is time for a little music."

Ayen pulled out his flute and began to play. He played for a long time and the music of the flute around the fire melded into the music of the night surrounding them as the woods came alive with the sounds of the nocturnal creatures beginning to stir. His last song of the evening was one that Enat recognized. It was the one she had heard him play so many nights ago, the Loon's Necklace. In the wonder and beauty of that night, as the constellations sprang to life in the sky above them, Enat wondered about that song and about Ayen. The song was haunting and beautiful, and obviously full of meaning to Ayen. She went to sleep that night wondering what that might be.

The days marched onward into the dog days of late summer and the party of travelers entered more populated Mohak territory. Their hearts were lightened by the prospect of returning home. On the evening of the day before they would finish their journey and arrive in Tionnontoguen, they stayed in a small village where Ayen and his men were treated as heroes. Many eyes looked upon Enat with great curiosity and with some suspicion.

As the sun began to reach for the western horizon, Ayen asked Enat to walk with him. He took her to a high hill where they could see the Mohak valley spreading out before them. They sat in the light of the setting sun in silence for a brief time. She waited and said nothing. She had learned from observing him in his interactions with Waneek that he was one to speak when he was ready. Finally he spoke to her.

"Enat, I wish to speak with you before we come to the home of my people."

"I'm listening."

I want you to know that you will be safe there. I must depart immediately and go to Malsum at Onondaga, but I will be leaving you in Waneek's care. No harm will come to you."

"Thank you. May I ask why you aren't going to deliver me to Malsum? I thought that was the plan."

"There is no need for him to have you. If, as warchief of the Haudenoshonee, I must deal with High King Skoth, or your father, then it is best that you were with me."

Enat thought about this and decided that since he was talking she would venture another question.

"Is there no other reason?"

The barest visage of a smile crossed his face as he said, "I would have you learn of my people. Live with them. Live as one of them. Learn our ways and our hearts. See what this world looks like from our eyes."

Enat nodded. Then to his surprise, she reached out and took his hand. He had been looking out over the valley as he spoke, but when she did this he did not pull his hand away, but turned and looked into her eyes. For a long moment they simply looked deep into each other's eyes, as if to understand the depth of the other's thoughts and soul.

Then Ayen stood, and pulled her up before releasing her hand.

He said, "We'd better go back. We have a busy day ahead of us tomorrow."

True to his word, within a few hours of arriving in Tionnontoguen, Ayen had departed again to make his way to Malsum's capital at Onondaga. His greetings and farewells with his extended family and clan were warm and sincere. But as neither father nor mother yet lived, and he had no siblings or children, his closest relatives were his aunts. Waneek held him briefly in her arms, promised to watch out for Enat, and in no uncertain terms told him to be wary of Malsum.

Waneek's final words to Ayen before he left were, "Son of my sister, be careful which wolf you feed."

Enat could see that Ayen heard the words, but noted that he gave no response to them. She wondered what they meant. In the privacy of their longhouse that evening, she asked Waneek what those words meant.

Waneek smiled and said, "You have noticed that Ayen is a man of many facets. You have seen him be a harsh and cunning warchief, you have heard his soul in the music of the flute, and you have also seen him be a gentle and caring friend. I was reminding him to consider which parts of his nature to feed. For feeding the wolf is a phrase we use to teach our young. It is as if each person has within themselves two wolves, one of a good nature and one of an evil nature. They war with each other. But which side will win? The wolf you serve and feed will become strong, and the other wolf will weaken. So which wolf will win? It will be the wolf you feed. These are words we tell our young people, but even when we grow and become old, perhaps even grow to lead the people, we must remember which side we feed. Ayen is a man of war and a man of peace. I asked him to remember which wolf he would feed."

Enat smiled in agreement. There was much wisdom in the way the women of the Mohak dealt with their male counterparts. She was struck by the sudden realization that she was looking forward to spending the winter with them. She was not to be disappointed, for in the time between Ayen's departure and when he would return, and then throughout the long winter, Enat would learn to appreciate much of the wisdom and way of life of these people.

Chapter 32 – Skaktafl

The realization that He Who Makes Rivers could possibly, and most likely did, refer to Ayenwatha, caused Skoth to spend some time considering what action to undertake. While his people spent several days reveling in the return of Evlin, and the news of her pregnancy, Skoth continued his efforts to reinforce and build a strong positive relationship between the Lenape people of the Wissawkin Valley and his people of Eirgalon. In his meetings with the delegation from Esepus, he reassured them of his peaceful and cooperative intentions. He also sent men to various Celtic, Lenape, and Wabanaki settlements throughout the Mahakentuck valley to let them know of his intention to develop a strong confederation of commerce and protection throughout the valley and of the growing center of administration that was being built at Kingstown.

The decisions concerning future actions were his to make, and he agonized over what to do. He had several important factors to consider: first, he must continue the quest for the loon's necklace; second, he could not fail to take action for Enat; third, he had a wife with child to care for; fourth, how long dare he hold the longships of men from southern and eastern Eirgalon away from home; fifth, what was he to make of the lack of news from Tkaden and Leesha amongst the Wabanaki; sixth, did the episode with the limikkin and the death of Fearglas bespeak a power wielded by Malsum that he could not match; seventh, while he spent his time in the western reaches of Eirgalon would the eastern lands remain loyal; eighth, Duncan of Glesga still seemed a wild card, what should he make of him; and ninth, he was sure there was a ninth, a tenth, and many more, but certainly this was enough for now.

Skoth was developing a growing appreciation for the levelheaded and even-handed way that he had witnessed Unaine rule in Fadis Innis as Skoth was growing up. There were times he wished he could hand it all over to Chief Unaine just the way Unaine had handed it to him when he had placed the king rune into Skoth's hand so many months ago.

It was in the middle of August when a messenger from Tkaden and Leesha arrived. He informed Skoth that it was taking longer than expected to persuade the settlements in the interior of northern Eirgalon to come together and assemble a force to head west and help in action against the Haudenoshonee. They would not be joining Skoth in the Mahakentuck Valley this year. Whatever force they could muster would assemble after the winter and join them in the spring of next year.

That knowledge helped Skoth make some decisions. There would be no major offensive military action by the High King's men for the next several months. Fall and winter would be a time to consolidate, defend, and plan for next spring. And he knew that they must be ready to defend, for Malsum had already shown that he would send men out over the winter months to conduct raiding forays. The Heilsand incident was proof enough of that, for those Haudenoshonee men must have traveled in the late winter months to make such an attack.

Skoth was surprised one day when Erik came to him and insisted that they sit down and play a game of chess, as many were starting to call the traditional game of Skaktafl. Erik beat him soundly and quickly the first game, and then taunted him into playing a second game. This time Skoth focused more of his attention on the game, but Erik still beat him. Erik taunted him a bit more. He always had known how to raise Skoth's ire. Frustrated, Skoth insisted on a third game. He put all his concentration into it, but again Erik was victorious.

After Skoth conceded again, Erik asked him, "Now, what did you learn from this?"

Skoth thought a moment and said jokingly, "Not to play chess with you," and then with more seriousness, "and, I reckon, a little humility. I didn't think you were much of a chess player, and I thought I was better than you. I wasn't."

"Aye, humility tis a good lesson to learn, and it never pays to underestimate your opponent."

"Is that what you think I am doing with Malsum and Ayen?"

Erik shook his head. "I'm not saying that. While I'm not privy to all your thoughts, I'm quite certain you worry about what surprises they may spring on you. What I want you to do is to think about how and why I won those games. Of course the first couple of games could be credited to your underestimating me, but not the third. You were putting your full concentration and effort into that one."

"I don't know, Erik. I kept trying to attack you, but you always had too strong of a defensive position."

"Yes. And how did I get that position?"

"You didn't attack me right away. You spent your first several moves setting up your position."

Erik smiled, "Aye, now you have it. Sometimes, in order to win, you have to take the time to set the board in a way that will help you later on." He paused for effect and then went on. "And how do you feel about what you are doing about this campaign as you sit here in Kingstown?"

"I'm frustrated that I'm not doing anything."

"Oh, but you are, my boy. You're setting the board. Now, mind you, I'm not telling you that you're doing a good, or a poor, job of it, but setting the board you are."

Skoth nodded in understanding, "I think you're right. It doesn't look like there will be any major fighting in the near future, but there are pieces I can be setting into place. Perhaps I shouldn't worry so much about not accomplishing so much right now, and I should be satisfied with arranging the pieces on the board to accomplish more down the road."

Erik smiled again and said, "Looks to me like you won those three games of chess after all."

Skoth chuckled and said, "Maybe I did, at that," then a quizzical look crossed his face and he added, "and by the way, Erik, just how did you get so good at chess?"

Erik laughed and replied, "What did you think Unaine, Theofinn, and I would do all those times while we were just sitting around waiting to find out about the next adventure or trouble you and your friends had gotten yourselves into?"

Then Erik turned and walked away, while Skoth sat there shaking his head in wonder at the elder warrior who was much more than just another man with a sword.

Chapter 33 - Setting the Board

During the next several weeks and months Skoth went about setting the board, as Erik had called it, in his developing duel with Malsum. He sent most of the longships back to their home ports, although he allowed men, who volunteered to stay in service to their High King, to remain with him in Kingstown. With each of the leaders of those ships, he sent messages to the various kings and chiefs around the land of Eirgalon. In those messages he informed them of events that had occurred and requested that on the spring equinox of the coming year they would send longships of warriors up the Mahakentuck to him. Malsum had brought this war to them, and Skoth proposed taking it back to him.

Skoth returned the messenger from Tkaden and Leesha letting them know he would be looking for their support as they had promised.

Under the command of his chief war captain and friend of his childhood, Drottin Karl, he sent a group of warriors to winter in the area of New Alba (northern and westernmost of any Celtic settlement) at the confluence of the Mohak and Mahakentuck Rivers. In effect, they were to be Skoth's advance guard. Their orders were to protect the far-flung Celtic trading outpost from any Haudenoshonee attack and, if possible, to foster positive relations with their nearest Mohak neighbors west of them in the Mohak valley.

When Gunnar left to return to New Caledonia, there was a tearful farewell with Teite. The two of them had obviously grown very fond of each other. Gunnar had even asked Teite to accompany him, but she refused to leave saying that, for the moment, her place was with Evlin and Skoth. Gunnar accepted this, but was adamant that he would be returning in the spring with his warriors and that she had better be waiting for him.

One day, as Skoth was helping some of his men in the building of a large hall connected to the King's Castle cabin where he and Evlin had been living, he heard the men referring to it as "Tara." When he asked about it, the men responded that Erik had reminded them that on the emerald isle across the sea, the name of the seat of the High King's power was called Tara, so they decided that's what they should call the High King's home in Eirgalon. People might still call the town around it Kingstown, but Tara, lying in the center of fertile Mahakentuck valley was the High King's home.

Skoth's mind had been troubled over the issue of finances. As High King there were expenses that he incurred. How was he to pay them? As a young man he had never given much thought as to how a king was able to afford running the king's hall, but now the reality of it dawned full upon him. Fortunately for him, he had Teite, Unaine's daughter and admittedly a smart woman, to give him advice as to how her father had operated as king of Fadis Innis. Erik was also there to give his advice and to help him cement ties of loyalty and fealty within the fertile Mahakentuck valley. As High King, Skoth would not be totally dependent upon the goodwill and loyalty of the lesser kings of Eirgalon, because the lands around Tara would provide a strong base for him. He would not be at the mercy of others "gifts," although he would receive them; and when called upon for additional troops the other kingdoms would provide them.

Teite also explained to High King Skoth the concept of an economic league that she had read about while at the Academy in Dunsheelin. She told him of how there was an economic trading association of cities across the ocean in Europe that was called the League of Hanse. She suggested that he promote such a trading league in Eirgalon because trade could tie a people closer together than military force of arms could. Skoth liked that idea and when Notaku returned from his trade mission up the Wissawkin River, he had him sit down with Teite and make plans as to how to encourage such an endeavor in Eirgalon.

One development that amazed Skoth was that the three men of the Haudenoshonee who had guarded Evlin during her abduction at the hands of Senadondo now pledged their personal loyalty to her. The two Oneida men, Kenda and Tekaya, never spoke much, but they learned quickly and they did whatever they were told. The Mohak man, Anoka, who came from the same village as Ayen, was the spokesman for the three. He would spend time with Evlin, and the others, telling them of the ways of the Mohak, and he was so fierce in his loyalty to Evlin, that not even Skoth feared to leave him alone with her.

Skoth had sent a message requesting King Duncan of Glesga to come up the river and visit him in the fall before the river might ice over. And so it was that on a fine fall day, with the leaves of the valley turning into a multi-hued celebration of color, two longships of Glesga came cruising up the river and docked at the newly constructed wharf at Kingstown. One was Duncan's ship, and the other was the familiar longship of Captain Bjorn.

Evlin had also sent a message to Lil, requesting that she accompany her husband. Evlin and Skoth stood, with Teite and Erik at their sides, as they waited in the open square before the wharf. They could see King Duncan give his hand to help his lady step off the ship and then make their way forward across the wharf to greet the High King.

Skoth lifted his voice as they approached and spoke first in greeting, "Welcome, King Duncan of Glesga, to Kingstown, Tara of the land of Eirgalon."

Duncan crossed his right arm across his chest and responded, "Hail, High King Skoth."

It wasn't heavy with formality, and to Erik's wizened eyes it was obvious that Duncan wasn't exactly bending the knee with great show of fealty to his suzerain. The words may have acknowledged it, but the actions belied the true feelings. If anything, it was apparent that Duncan saw them more as equals. Lil, standing at Duncan's side, bowed deeply and kept her eyes averted as she spoke with a weak voice, "My Lord and my Lady."

Skoth invited them to come to the newly constructed great hall of Tara, knowing that it was certainly rough-hewn and simply functional rather than richly decorated, but that it was a physical reminder of the new political structure in Eirgalon. It was a mid-afternoon of a sunny autumn day, but there was a chill wind in the air, so to enter into the Great Hall and have a hearthfire burning was a welcome treat.

When they arrived and were walking into the hall, Duncan said, "Well, well. It looks like you're making quite a little home for yourself here. I'm not sure why our High King would want to make his hall so far up north and away from the sea, but it is quaint enough."

Before Skoth had a chance to answer, Evlin piped in, "Why thank you, King Duncan. I rather like the idea of it being quaint. That is so nice of you to say so." Then she shifted her comments to Lil, "Please, Lil, would you come and join Teite and me, as I show you around our new home? We'll leave the men to talk about all that man stuff that they like to talk about."

Lil's eyes widened in fright at the invitation to be alone with Evlin and Teite, for she was unsure what Evlin knew about her role in Evlin's abduction near Glesga. She gulped a swallow and meekly followed them out of the great hall into the original cabin that had become the private quarters of Evlin and Skoth.

The men stayed in the great hall and settled themselves around the largest of the tables in the room. The tables and chairs were nothing fancy, but they were solid and served well for the hard-working men and women who had come to serve the High King. Erik and Teite had formed a discrete duo that examined and assembled the women and men who ran the king's household. They had a wealth of people to choose from, for there were many who had been drawn to this new settlement. Kingstown had become quite a conglomeration of cultures where all were welcome. A quick walkabout of the burgeoning young city revealed people of Celtic, Wabanaki, and Lenape cultures. There were even a few Mohak people in the mix. Erik and Teite had chosen members of each cultural group to be a part of the king's household. Culture didn't matter. What mattered was loyalty to Skoth and Evlin.

When they were settled around the table and some of the kitchen workers had brought out some beverages for them, the freshly pressed apple juice was a delight. Then Skoth started the more serious conversation.

"I was hoping you'd feel safe enough to make this little trip up river before the river froze. I take it that you no longer feel threatened by a large force of Haudenoshonee warriors at your doorstep."

Duncan replied, "Why no. They seem to have run back to their homes up north. We chased them away this time. But they might be back. They are a sneaky lot. I notice that you have quite a few of them hanging around here. Do you think that is wise?"

At that moment, Erik, who sitting at the far end of the table with Bjorn, slapped his leg and whistled. He looked about the room as if searching, and when his gaze passed Skoth he winked and said, "Where is that dog of mine when I want him?"

The outburst by Erik startled Skoth, until Skoth picked up on Erik's wink and remembered the dog and cat conversation he had with Erik many months ago about King Duncan.

Skoth said, with fake chagrin, "Aw, Erik, he's probably just sniffing around. We were, however, talking about more serious matters. Why don't you explain to Duncan why you think it is wise to have a varied group working in our hall."

Erik made a point of clearing his throat before he began his explanation.

"Aye. It works like this King Duncan. You, yourself know that in this part of the country many Celtic men took Wabanaki or Lenape wives. Why I even understand your wife is the daughter of such a union."

"Yes, yes. She is the daughter of MacGregor of New Alba in the far north and his Wabanaki wife. But that's different. MacGregor raised her in our Celtic culture. Lil is as much a Celt as any of us."

"Aye, ye make my point for me. When people of every group in Eirgalon live and work together, we become one people."

"That's not really what I mean, but look at it, you folks are so far north here and close to the Skraeling territories, that living with them makes you less like us and more like them."

Erik gave a little shrug with his shoulders and then said, "Ah, well, it seems to be working for us. There's much to respect in the Lenape, the Wabanaki, and even the Mohak folk. I'd venture to say that the loyalty of the folks around our High King and his lady is quite strong."

Duncan gave a little snort of derision and said, "We'll see about that when Skraeling hordes start attacking. I'll be taking no chances like that."

Erik made an obvious gesture of glancing about the room. When he spotted a young boy, the child of one of the kitchen workers, standing by the door he spoke in a louder voice directed at the boy.

"You, boy, go see if you can find that dog of mine!"

Skoth grinned on the inside, though he did not let this expression show on his face. He thought that maybe Erik was putting on too much of an act, but Duncan's smugness was no act.

Skoth decided that it was time to move on to something else so he interjected, "King Duncan, I wanted you to hear from me, that both Chief Keith of Dundee and Chief MacGregor of New Alba have renounced any claim of kingship over their territories. They declare they are vassals, and that their lands are territories, of the Kingdom of Tara."

Duncan said nothing, but looked at Skoth with a strange look on his face.

Skoth continued, "To be clear, the domain of Tara runs from the northern edge of your lands to the headwaters of the Mahakentuck."

"All the settlements of Euanglen and the central Mahakentuck valley acquiesce to this?"

"All have done so."

Duncan smirked as he said, "That's an ambitious endeavor on your part, uniting that large of territory into one kingdom. At least now Malsum and his men will go after you before they come after me."

It wasn't exactly the response Skoth was anticipating, and it did nothing to raise Duncan's stature in Skoth's eyes, but Glesga was one of the lands of Eirgalon and Skoth was its High King. He would serve it as he served all of Eirgalon.

Skoth smiled and said, "I'm glad you understand. Now there's one more item I have to explain to you."

Skoth spent the next couple of hours explaining the workings of the new economic trading arrangement that was going to be established in Eirgalon. Although Duncan was dismissive of the idea at first because it came from the Old World of Europe, Skoth brought him around to understand how such a league, operating under the protection and peace of the High Kingdom of Eirgalon, would bring prosperity for its members. When Duncan realized that much of the trade to and from the growing kingdom of Tara would be passing through Glesga, his demeanor suddenly became very agreeable.

At that moment, Skoth saw Erik smile. Later that night Erik shared with Skoth what he had been thinking, which was that Duncan looked like the cat that has pounced on the sparrow. But just wait, this cat may find that what he thought was a sparrow is more likely to be an eagle.

Chapter 34 – Redemption

Lil was very unsure of herself as she went into the private quarters of the king with Evlin and Teite. She remembered well how Teite had probed her in that brief conversation following the abduction. What she didn't know is that Anoka was one of the men that was with Senadondo on that raid and that he had already spoken to Evlin about Lil's duplicity in that action.

Evlin and Teite acted pleasant and welcomed her warmly, but they were very much alert and prepared for any suspicious activity.

They made themselves comfortable in what was now the sitting room of the private quarters. The matron of the kitchen had brought them some spiced cranberry tea. It was a perfect tea to flavor this autumn season, and as they sipped on it, Teite mentioned how it was one of her sister Enat's favorites.

Lil swallowed her tea, and then swallowed again. Her face went pale with dread.

Evlin asked, "Are you alright, Lil?"

Lil just nodded, but didn't say anything.

Teite said, "Oh, I'm sorry, dear. Did my mention of Enat disturb you? I know that must have been an awful moment when they kidnapped her. What a terrible sight it must have been to see your guard cut down in front of your eyes."

Evlin decided now was the moment to test Lil's truthfulness. "It really must have been terrible. The poison made me pass out immediately, but you must have seen it all. Did you see the limikkin? Why did it allow you to go free?

Surely it must have known that you were the wife of Duncan, lord and master of Glesga? One of my captors told me later what happened, but it must have been terrible for you."

Lil set her cup down and leaned forward, putting her head in her hands.

Lil started to cry, "I didn't want to do it. It made me. I'm sorry."

Interspersed through several minutes of tearful sobbing, Lil told how she had been lured into the plan to take Evlin and Enat captive. Senadondo had appeared to her the previous evening on the roof of the castle solarium in Glesga where she had been enjoying the warm summer night. He had promised her that Malsum would fulfill her greatest wish. She had been barren and had no children with Duncan, and it was her heart's desire to get pregnant and have a child for Duncan.

Evlin asked her, "And are you with child? Has Malsum fulfilled your wish?"

With a mixture of anguish, disgust, and embarrassment she said softly, "No. I was deceived and used. There is no excuse. I tried to trade an evil deed for that which I thought was good."

Evlin compassionately said, "You can not change what you have done. But what you can do is to make amends. What is there that you would do?"

Lil thought for a few moments, "First, I must say I am sorry to you. I wish I could also tell Enat I am sorry, but she still suffers from my action and is far away. I would help her if I could, but I know not how."

Teite spoke, "I know my sister would accept your sincere apology, but as you say she is not here, and who knows what hardship she is dealing with. Perhaps the time will come when you can make amends to her. But what of Evlin, is there anything you can do for her?"

Lil looked to Evlin with questioning eyes, beseeching her to offer some possibility. Any possibility. A discussion followed of ways in which Lil might be of assistance in the future relationships between Glesga and the High King. After all, she was the wife of King Duncan and the daughter of Chief MacGregor of New Alba. Above all Lil promised that if Malsum or Senadondo contacted her by any means, she would communicate that to Evlin.

Duncan and Lil only stayed a couple of days with their hosts at Tara before returning downriver to their home in Glesga. Bjorn and his ship of men would stay for another week to give assistance in the construction of a stockade wall around the Great Hall and courtyard. When Bjorn's ship departed the following week, he allowed several of his men to stay. It seemed as if whenever groups of people from any culture (Celtic, Lenape, or Wabanaki), be they warriors, traders, or settlers, visited the new capital of Tara some of them stayed. There was a positive atmosphere around the growing settlement and people wanted to be a part of that.

Chapter 35 – Birth

Winter descended in a soft fashion upon Eirgalon in that first year of High King Skoth's rule. The temperature dropped as was to be expected, but no extremely bitter cold snaps distressed them. Snows fell, but they were of a relatively gentle nature and without the driving blizzards that some years afflicted the land. The Wissawkin River froze over in late December, and by the middle of January the ice on the Mahakentuck River extended south beyond Kingstown. Some years the region enjoyed a "January thaw" but this year the temperature remained moderate. In many ways it was the most average of winters.

On some of the days men assembled ice boats, basically a couple of skis and a sail, and went skimming across the frozen expanse of the Mahakentuck River. Winter could be harsh, and there were always tasks to be done such as chopping firewood, taking care of livestock, hunting, fishing, and hauling fresh water. And even in the cold winter, men continued to work at adding permanent structures to the growing city that more and more of them were calling Tara, as they dropped the former moniker of Kingstown. However, they did find time to enjoy life as well, and the thrill of the ice sailing appealed to the risk-taking nature of the young men. While there were a few accidents, at least none of them resulted in a fatality.

It was on one of these sunny sailing days of mid-January that two groups of visitors arrived. One from the west and one from the east. From the west came a group of Lenape from the settlement of Esepus. In that group came Gela, one of the wise women of the village. When asked why she had made the journey in the dead of winter, Gela had laughingly replied, "I thought it would be good to have at least one Wise Woman present at the birth of this child."

From far to the east, having trekked for weeks over many a hill and through many a dale, came a party from Wausacom. Fortunately, it had not been a harsh winter and they had stopped at every village and settlement along the way. But it was still winter travel and it had been arduous. The men who had been ice sailing across the wide expanse of the Mahakentuck were the first to notice the travelers. From the eastern shore the travelers led their pack horses carefully onto the ice and headed directly toward Tara. The ice sailors did not want to spook the horses so they remained a considerable distance from them, though they acknowledged them with arms held high in welcoming waves. A couple of the ice sailors skimmed back to Tara to give advance warning of their winter visitors.

Evlin and Skoth were in the Great Hall of Tara exchanging their greetings and sharing news with Gela and the visitors from Esepus when a young boy came running into the hall shouting about visitors from the east crossing the Mahakentuck.

Evlin, who earlier had been outside with Skoth watching the sailing, expressed that they should go back outside to watch and greet the folk from the east. Almost before anyone could respond, Anoka brought her outer winter garments to her. They rebundled themselves and went out and to the river's edge to watch the procession approach.

Slowly and carefully the people of the east led their horses across the ice. Skoth noted to Erik, who was standing nearby that even from a distance the horses looked to be of the sturdy Icelandic stock. They made some of the best and most dependable of pack horses.

It wasn't until the travellers reached the shore that they recognized any of them. One of them reached up and pulled back her hood. Then they saw and recognized Leesha. At Leesha's side was another woman. Leesha introduced her as the wife of Chief Tkomik. It was Tkaden's mother, Maeve.

183

Greetings and welcomes were shared all around. Skoth ordered the pack animals to be cared for, and the visitors were ushered into the warmth of the Great Hall.

Once inside and shed of their winter outer garments, Maeve embraced Evlin. Holding her tight she said, "Niece of my husband, I have longed to meet you ever since my son and his wife," she smiled at Leesha, "brought word of you."

Evlin responded, "How wonderful it is to meet you. I too have looked forward to meeting you. Tkaden and Tkomik, and Leesha too, have said wonderful stories about you. But why would you travel in the depth of winter?"

With a smile Maeve answered, "When word from Skoth came to us in the fall about his plans for next spring, the messenger also shared word of your being with child. I have no doubt that Wise Women of this area," she glanced a knowing smile at Gela and when on, "can give you any assistance you may need, but I felt I must be here as well. We are family and it never hurts to have one of the Women's Circle with you when you are giving birth."

Leesha, not one to be left out of any conversation, chimed in, "And, for a certainty, Skoth is like a brother to me. You don't think I'd be missing this!"

And so it was that a couple of weeks later, on the first day of February, when Evlin felt her water burst and felt the first contractions of labor, she was surrounded by many strong women. Maeve and Gela had witnessed the birth of many a child and their presence gave reassurance to Evlin that all would be well. The sisters, Teite and Leesha, sat with her and gave her their strength through their presence as well.

Where was Skoth? He was indeed present, but he was willing to stay in the background. He let Evlin know he was there, perhaps that was reassuring, but it was the strength of the women surrounding her that carried her through the labor and delivery. Maeve performed the primary midwifery duties and Gela assisted her as needed.

As Maeve swaddled the newborn in her hands she reached one hand to a small cupful of water that she had ready for this moment. She anointed the child with one drop at a time as she said words of an ancient birthing ritual of her Celtic people.

"A wee drop of the sky on your forehead, my love. Shield thee from despair.

A wee drop of the land on your forehead, my love. Protect thee from the evil one.

A wee drop of the sea on your forehead, my love. Guard thee from danger."

Maeve then asked Skoth to bring a burning candle forward. He placed it on a chair between them. Then three times she passed the child across the flame to him, and three times he passed her back while Gela, Teite, and Leesha softly murmured prayers of protection.

Then, taking in hand the oak staff that Fearglas had fashioned for him. Skoth circled Maeve as she held the child. Five times he made the circle as he called for her protection: in battle, during travel, against spiritual foes, from magical danger, and from physical danger.

The final action of blessing involved the mother, Evlin, taking the child and touching the child's forehead to the ground while quietly invoking her mother's blessing upon the child. So there, in the bedroom, before the hearthfire that warmed the room, in a small circle that had been left exposed to the soil of the earth, Evlin blessed her child.

Maeve motioned to the basin of warm water that Gela had prepared for what might be called the baptismal washing of the child. It was to be her first washing in the waters of this world, and it was here that she would be given her birth name. Maeve looked to Evlin and then to Skoth as she carried the child to Gela for the washing.

She asked, "What is the child's name?"

185

Evlin looked at Skoth. He nodded and Evlin said, "She is born the day of Imbolc, her name is Brigit. She heralds the springtime of our people."

As Gela washed the child in the warm waters she called her by name, "Brigit."

And all in the room responded, "So mote it be."

When they had returned the washed and newly christened Brigit to her mother's arms, Skoth stepped forward to give Evlin a hug and kiss. He followed that by giving Brigit a kiss on the forehead and then he left the room to the women. With a smile on his face, he made his way into the Great Hall to announce to the people of Eirgalon the arrival of Brigit.

Chapter 36 - Longhouse Conversation

Far to the north and west, on the opposite side of the Blue Mountains, Enat was spending the winter with Ayen's people in the town of Tionnontoguen. After Ayen had delivered Waneek and Enat to his home village, he had immediately departed to head west up the Mohak River and meet with Malsum at Onondaga, the capital of the Haudenoshonee nation. It was two months later and far into autumn when he had returned.

Ayen said little about what had transpired with Malsum during his visit with the mysterious leader. He only said that in the spring Malsum would be sending an army of warriors from the western groups of Seneca, Cayuga, Onondaga, and Oneida to assemble at the eastern edge of the traditional Mohak lands. From there they would be moving on the Wabanaki, Celt, and Lenape settlements down the Mahakentuck Valley.

Participating in the village life of the Mohak people enabled Enat to learn their language and become fluent in it. She also found that the day-to-day life and relationships of the people was not much different from what she had experienced in her life on Fadis Innis and her visit to the Wabanaki folk of Eirgalon. There were certain cultural traditions which deviated from what she had known, but she found there was much more similarity than what she had expected.

One tradition that struck her was that while the Wise Women of the Mohak resembled the Wise Women of the Wabanaki and the Women's Circle of the Celts, there was one area where they had even more influence. Enat had grown up observing, and even been a participant in, how the women worked behind the scenes to influence the male leadership of the communities. In Mohak society, the Wise Women actually got together and chose the men that would be their chiefs and leaders.

One winter evening, around the time of the longest night of the year, Enat ventured to start a discussion. Tradition held that during these long winter months, the families and clans would gather in their longhouses. In the evening they would tell stories and thus the histories and legends of the people would be passed on. In this manner, the young people would learn the values and teachings of their people. This led to close family units where loyalty and respect were strong. So it was on this evening, the stories had been told and the younger ones had been settled in for the night. The elder ones remained gathered around the center fire of the longhouse, including Enat, Waneek, and Ayen.

Enat ventured to say, "I see how the Wise Women of the community gather together and choose which men are to be the leaders of the community, and I can see how they would have chosen Ayen to lead for he is wise, compassionate, and cares for the people," she blushed a little at complimenting him, but she went on, "but there is something I don't understand. I'm not sure if I should ask."

Waneek looked her over carefully and said, "You are here among us. You have become as family to us. Ask. We shall do our best to answer you."

Enat took a deep breath and then went on, "As I have said, I can see the wisdom in choosing Ayen to lead you. But," she paused again and then blurted out, "what of Malsum? Of what I have heard of him, there is power and knowledge, but where is the care and compassion? Why would the Wise Women choose him? How did he come to be the one to lead your people?"

A few heads turned toward Ayen, but most of them turned toward Waneek, and when Ayen looked at her as well, she nodded and began to speak.

"You have asked some difficult questions. I don't know that there are good answers for them. What I can tell you is that our Mohak women did not choose him. I will tell you the story as I know it. But it is a new tale, with parts unclear. I know not all the details. If someone has more to add when I am done," she looked to Ayen but then went on, "then they may add it."

Waneek took a moment to organize her thoughts, then took a deep breath, and began to tell the story.

"Not so many years ago, on the shores of the beautiful lake we call Ontario, there lived a Huron wise woman. She had a vision that her daughter would have a boy who would stop the warring that was taking place among the people of the land. For Huron, Mohak, Seneca, and all the rest were constantly at war with each other, fighting each other for control of hunting grounds and fine fields. In her vision she saw this boy become a man who united the nations in peace. He would persuade the warring nations to put aside their weapons and to live together in peace. With respect, negotiation, and cooperation, they would unite and prosper.

And then her daughter brought forth a child, and that child received his own vision when he went on his vision quest. Deganawida, which means "he who brings two rivers together" for so he had been named at birth, had a vision that he would unite the people of the land. They would become one people, the Haudenoshonee.

But the old woman was bothered by this vision, for the young man, who now insisted on being called Malsum which means "powerful wolf" in their tongue, declared that his vision spoke of uniting the nations by force. The old shaman of this boy's village was also troubled by these conflicting visions and he sent the young man away. The young man came to live among the Onondaga people, where they accepted him and believed his vision. Soon the men were following him, but no women chose him to lead. Our Ayen here, went as a young man with his father to hear the words of Malsum, and they too followed him. Ayen's skillful mind soon came to the attention of Malsum and he became a warchief. And then, he became the warchief of all the Haudenoshonee.

Be it by might, or magic, Malsum defeated all those who stood before him. Soon the five nations of the sunset lakes followed him. They were united and now they have been called by Malsum to stand as one against the threat from the east. They have been called to fight the ones they call the "pale ones" as if the color of their skin makes them less than human."

For several moments it was silent, save for the crackling of the fire.

Drawing a deep breath, Enat spoke softly, "Thank you, Waneek, for sharing the story."

"It is an unfinished story and may not be true. I hesitate to share it around the sacred lodge fire lest it be false. Yet you have asked and I have tried to be true."

Ayen cleared his throat. All eyes turned to him. He looked around the circle of men and women gathered around the fire. Again he cleared his throat. Then he focused his eyes upon the fire and he began.

"Much of what my aunt says is true. But portions are missing. When my father and I traveled to Onondaga to hear the words of Malsum, I was already a leader of war parties. I was no child under my father's protection. My mother, Waneek's sister, had died of a disease thought to have been brought to our land by the people of the east. I had two young sisters. They too became ill with fever and died."

Enat softly murmured, "I'm so sorry."

Ayen nodded in acceptance, and went on, "Malsum spoke words filled with power. He called on us to make our world stronger and better by joining together to rid ourselves of the pale ones that would bring sicknesses upon on us and would steal our land. I may not have agreed with all he did to bring the five nations together, but in the end they answered his call and now they answer to him. He calls us now to defend our lands and move against the people to the east. We follow as he commands."

In a soft voice, so as not to break his command of the moment, Enat said, "You mentioned your father, what became of him?"

Though he held his gaze upon the flickering fire he heard her query and responded, "I was leading a war party in subduing the final Oneida resistance and my father was with Malsum as they fought the Hurons to the north. Father fell in battle."

Waneek spoke softly, "I have been told that he may have fallen at the hand of one he trusted."

Ayen lifted his eyes from the fire, and looking at her he said, "That has never been proven to be true."

Looking back at him and holding his gaze, she said, "Nor has it ever been proven to be false."

For a moment longer he held her gaze, then he lowered his eyes again to the fire. There was a long pause before he spoke again.

"In a few short months, Malsum will be sending the men of the Seneca, Cayuga, Onondaga, and the Oneida, eastward to us. We are to join them to counter the forces that are gathering against us at New Alba."

Enat said, "Surely you don't think that they are coming to attack you in your homeland. They would not come to conquer you."

"Yet, they are coming. Already your High King has sent his warriors to where the great rivers join. He is building a new city on the Mahakentuck just south of the Blue Mountains and seeks to control the entire valley. And yet you say he has no designs on our land?"

Waneek spoke up, "How do you know this to be true? Perhaps there are other reasons."

Ayen looked at her with a curious eye, "Malsum has told me this. And what other reasons might there be?"

"Perhaps this high king has a friend who has been taken from him, and he wants her back. Or perhaps he is only defending his people. After all, his people have been attacked."

Before Ayen could respond, Enat spoke as she shook her head, "I can't believe he wishes ill to you or your people. I know Skoth. He was like a brother to me when we were growing up. He would never seek to hurt your people. I know he wants all people to live in peace."

Ayen responded, "So you say. But he gathers his forces. He prepares for war."

"But that is because you make war on him."

Ayen took a moment and then looked into Enat's eyes, "I share the details of my vision quest with none, but know that I too desire peace. However, peace often does not come without a struggle. As a loon's necklace is both black and white, so life is filled with war and peace. If I want peace, I must be willing to fight for it. I must wrestle against evil for it."

Waneek, the wise woman, aunt of the great warrior, then said, "But to do so, you must discern the evil you need to confront. Evil can be a trickster."

Ayen said nothing in response, but looked deep into the fire. No one else spoke. Silently, one by one, they left and went to their sleeping pallets for the night. Finally, only Ayen remained, and still his gaze remained locked upon the glowing embers of the fire.

Chapter 37 – Refugees

Winter snowstorms came and went, and the village life settled into its winter routine. Then one day in early February, as another snowstorm was descending upon them, the daily routine of life was broken by the sight of a group of travellers from the west struggling through the falling snow.

From the height of the Mohak castle, for it did look like a castle with a high palisade of logs and earthworks ringing a high hill overlooking the river, one could see a dozen men trudging along the river road. They sent two of their party up the path to the gate of the castle where they were met by the guard. After a brief conversation, one of the guards ran to get Ayen. When he arrived, there was another brief conversation and the travellers motioned to the rest of their party to come up the hill to the gate.

One by one, the men were allowed through the gate. As they entered they surrendered their weapons and were taken to the central longhouse where Ayen and Waneek's clan lived. There they shed their heavy winter garments and it became obvious to all that these people were Celts. There were ten men and two women. The men were Celtic, or mixed blood, and claimed to be traders, and said that the women were their Seneca wives.

When asked why traders would be travelling in such weather, without any goods, and with their wives, they told their tale.

They had been forced to leave, and to leave immediately with only what they could carry on their backs. All their pack animals and possessions, indeed, even their very homes for they lived among the Haudenoshonee, had been taken from them. Malsum had decreed that they must leave and that they could take only what they could carry on their backs. They had been traveling for weeks through the cold and snow. Occasionally a few locals would have mercy on them and share provisions with them, but when they heard that Malsum had evicted them, they were leery of providing any but the most minimal of help to the refugees.

This obvious show of poor hospitality ran counter to the traditional values of her people, and Waneek insisted that there would be no lack of hospitality in the village of Ayenwatha, or in her longhouse. Food was prepared and shared with the refugees.

After they had eaten and settled in, for Waneek and Ayen both insisted that they not leave until after the storm had passed, they shared more news of what was happening in the western lands of the Haudenoshonee people.

Malsum had declared that he had received another vision from the Great Spirit, and in that vision it had been revealed to him that they must remove all of the pale ones from their land, even those who had come to live with them and to share in their society. Some of their fellow traders had been killed and their possessions were taken from them. The men, and their wives, of this group had quickly decided that flight was better than death. There were moments where they had feared for their lives, but although none would help them in their departure, neither did any openly seek to kill them.

Their moment of greatest danger came when their flight took them past Onondaga, the capital of the Haudenoshonee nation. They feared to enter the palisaded capital city, so they detoured through the hunting grounds to the south of it. The going was difficult, for the snow had fallen heavily there, and they walked single file taking turns to break a trail. For a couple of miles when they were nearest to the city, they felt a presence near to them and occasionally saw a large crow circling overhead and then perching high above them, as though watching them. When night came, they had passed the city and felt it safe enough to light a fire for warmth.

They huddled around the fire in the darkness of that evening, heating water for a bark tea and nibbling on what few morsels of food they carried with them. Out of the darkness came an old man. He didn't look very threatening as he shambled through the snow leaning heavily on a staff. They could see no weapons on him. At first his words were simple as he declared he had seen their fire in the darkness and asked if he could he warm himself at it for a time.

They were wary of him and shared but little information with him. They did share that they were traders and were just passing through, but nothing else. He cagily revealed nothing about himself, for whenever they asked him a question about who he was or why he was out and about at such a time, he shifted the conversation elsewhere. After about an hour, the old man excused himself and trundled off through the woods. His presence had been enough to trouble them, and they kept someone on watch all night. Nothing happened. But in the morning they briefly followed his tracks and found that after several hundred paces the human tracks disappeared and then there was a set of wolf tracks in the snow heading toward Onondaga.

At that description, one of the listeners in the longhouse hissed, "Limikkin!"

The narrator, leader of the refugees, nodded and said, "So, we too believe. We made haste that day and traveled as fast as we could, but we were already weak from our lack of food, the cold, and the exertion of the travel. We lost two of our party that day - Ole Snowshoes and his wife, Nannoah. They were frail and weak when we left, but we didn't dare leave them when we fled our homes. The hardship of the escape, or perhaps it was the work of the limikkin, killed them."

Ayen sighed a noticeable sigh and the narrator paused and looked at him. Ayen said, "I knew Ole well. That trader had the biggest feet I've ever seen. We joked about how he didn't even need snowshoes to walk through the snow. Why, he and his wife, wouldn't hurt anyone. Why did they flee?"

"We didn't dare leave them. They knew that they would be killed as soon as we left."

Again there was a sigh from Ayen, and then he said, "Go on."

"The ground was too hard to dig a proper grave, but we covered them with rocks the best we could. We had to keep traveling."

"Did you see the limikkin again?"

"No. At least we think not. Some of us felt at times that we were being watched," as he said this several of his companions nodded, "but it never revealed itself again. If it has been following us, then you should know that you may be being watched."

Ayen said, "I fear not this limikkin. But if it is who I think it is, then you are wise to be wary of it."

"We thank you for taking us in during this storm, and for the hearty food you have given us. Without your hospitality, this storm may have finished us off. With your permission, we'll stay until the storm breaks and then be on our way."

"Where do you intend to go?"

"We're headed to New Alba. We reckon MacGregor will take us in. Then we'll have to see what happens. Most of us here love this land and you folks. Why some of us even have family here," he nodded toward the two Seneca women, "if it weren't for Malsum, we'd want to stay. But it's clear enough he won't have us."

Ayen nodded, "You may stay until the storm ends. You have our hospitality. Before you leave, I may have a message to send with you. For now, sleep and rest."

Ayen then thanked Waneek and the people of his

longhouse for providing the food and shelter for their guests during the storm. His next action was to pull one of his men to the side and quietly tell him to take the message to all the longhouses of the castle that he wanted to meet with the leaders of his war parties in the morning.

The morning meeting didn't last long. When the men came away from their deliberations they had set jaws and faces etched with determination. Ayen went to talk to the leader of the Celtic traders. The man's eyes widened at what Ayen told him to tell the leaders of Eirgalon, but he promised to faithfully relay the message.

Chapter 38 – Tara

The birth of Brigit at Tara was followed by a typical February snowstorm that kept people inside, or at least close to their dwellings, for a couple of days. But it was then followed by above temperature days and clear skies, which allowed the sun with its growing strength to melt some of the winter snow. The men and women started to think about the spring even though true spring was still days, or perhaps weeks, away.

Throughout the winter, Skoth had been discussing with Erik the spring military campaign. As soon as the ice on the river broke, they could expect that longships from the coastal kingdoms of Eirgalon would begin arriving. They also expected that if the weather stayed moderate, some contingents from the inland northern areas would be arriving, including the Wabanaki forces led by Tkaden. The question that troubled Skoth was whether or not the Haudenoshonee would launch an attack first. Certainly the Mohawk valley was known for winters of heavy snow and sometimes bitter cold, and certainly the river would open up later than the Mahakentuck, but would that deter them from planning an attack and engaging Skoth's forces before the reinforcements arrived?

Skoth had been in communication with Drottin Karl who had established a base in the hills west of New Alba where the Mohak River looped to the north before returning to the east and joining with the Mahakentuck. Karl called this base, Nealsfort in memory of their childhood friend. It was about fifteen miles, as the crow flies, from the nearest Mohak settlement, Skenektedy, to the west. Karl had made a point of developing a good relationship with Chief MacGregor of New Alba. He wanted to make sure that MacGregor didn't feel his authority of the area threatened, but felt that the men of the High King were here to help them defend their settlement.

Karl had asked if there had been any word of Enat, and Skoth had to inform him that there was nothing new. The last Skoth knew was that she was in the hands of the Mohak war chief Ayenwatha. But that was months ago, and almost anything could have happened to her in that time.

Although Leesha and Teite had spent the days since Brigit's birth doting on the little girl and her mother, they also had been pestering Skoth to allow them to travel up the ice-covered river to New Alba. They were anxious to pursue any leads about the loon's necklace. Skoth was adamant that they not leave yet, and that they certainly wouldn't be leaving without a large force of warriors to protect them. He couldn't help but think that anytime one or more of the three sisters ventured off on some mission, they ended up in trouble! Since all indications now pointed to the fact that Ayenwatha (He Who Makes Rivers) was somehow connected to the necklace, he didn't want to risk them going anywhere near him.

One day, the sisters persuaded Evlin to ask Anoka, the Mohak warrior from Ayen's village that had pledged his loyalty to Evlin, about the necklace. If there was some connection between Ayen and the necklace, the women thought he might know what that was.

The four women (Evlin, the sisters, and Maeve) sat in a circle in the family's private quarters with Anoka. Evlin nursed her child as they talked. When asked about the necklace, they were startled by his response. His eyes went wide and a surprised expression flashed across his face. He was silent for several moments, obviously thinking his answer through before he replied.

"I have given my loyalty to Evlin, and now to Brigit, but the knowledge you ask of me is knowledge I can not share. It is not my place to speak of it."

199

Teite, the one who had first befriended Anoka when he was taken as their prisoner, asked, "Do you say this out of fear, or out of loyalty?"

"To do so would be against the honor of my people."

Evlin asked, "Is there anything at all that you can tell us about this without dishonor?"

Again he thought for a time and then replied, "All I can say is that these are matters for Ayen to discuss with you, should he choose. Perhaps the time will come when you can ask him."

Evlin spoke again, "Thank you, Anoka, for answering as you are able. Should the time ever come when there is more you can say to us, all I ask is that you come and speak to me."

Anoka nodded at that and got up to leave, but before he could leave, Maeve asked, "Anoka, one more question. Is Ayen a good man?"

This time Anoka did not hesitate, "He is a man of honor and loyalty. He is a warrior and he is a friend. He has a good heart, and he is very good at what he does."

After he had departed, Maeve turned to the younger women and said, "There is your answer. His measured responses and his respect for Ayen tell us that there is indeed a connection between Ayenwatha and the loon's necklace. What that means for us . . . well, only time will tell."

Chapter 39 – Nealsfort

It was near the end of February when the refugees from the western Haudenoshonee lands finally stumbled out of the woods and into sight of Nealsfort. Karl's men were on alert and it was a couple of these men on patrol that had encountered them a mile away and was now leading them to the fort on the hill.

As soon as a lookout had spotted them, Karl had been called for and he greeted them at the gate. Their appearance was bedraggled but the relief on their faces was obvious. The respite and sustenance at Ayen's castle had briefly replenished their strength and they had been sent on their way with extra food to help them finish their trip. However, travel through the snow, even the melting spring snows, is an arduous endeavor. They were exhausted.

Almost immediately after their greetings, the refugee leader told Karl that the Mohak leader, Ayen, had sent a message he was to deliver to the leaders of Eirgalon.

Karl told him, "I am Drottin Karl, chief military leader of High King Skoth. You may share the message with me."

The man wasted no time in telling him the message.

"Ayen says to tell the leaders of Eirgalon that he wishes to speak with them, that he is preparing to fight to defend his land and that within a few weeks more than a thousand warriors of the other Haudenoshonee nations will arrive in Mohak lands to move eastward against you. He wants you to know that he is a man of peace as well as a man of war. Before he fights with you, he would talk with you."

Karl asked, "And what would he talk about? Was there anything more specific about what he wants to say?"

"No. But he was adamant with me that he wanted to talk before he fought."

"Do you think it is some sort of trap?"

"Ach, no! I've lived among these folks my whole life. While I haven't actually lived in Mohak territory, I lived further to the west, I have traded throughout these lands. Ayen is respected. His words are true. Mind you he is a fearsome warrior, and I'm sure he uses warrior's tricks, but if says he wants to talk, then I'd lay my life on it that he does. As a matter of fact, I guess I could say I already owe him my life. If his people hadn't given us shelter and food during that last storm, I think we may well have perished."

Karl nodded in understanding, "Oh, I know about his warrior tricks. He is a smart leader of men. And he is a worthy opponent. Is there anything else?"

"Aye, there are words specifically for High King Skoth."

"You can tell me. I'm the closest friend he has. I will get word to him."

The man looked him over carefully and said, "I'm trusting that you'll share this information with him as soon as possible."

"I promise. As quickly as I can."

"Ayen said to tell King Skoth that 'Enat is with me.' Those are his exact words. And I know it's true. I saw her there in the longhouse."

"What? You saw Enat? Was she okay?"

"Aye, she looked hale and hearty. They were treating her as one of their own."

"Did she speak to you?"

"No. She said nothing around us. I noticed her with the fair skin when we stayed in the longhouse. But she said nothing. I heard them call her 'Enat' but thought little of it. I choose to live with the Seneca people and simply thought that she was a Celt that for some reason had come to live with the Mohak. Nothing wrong with that in my book. Until now, that is, since Malsum kicked us out."

"No, there's nothing wrong with it. But you say she said nothing to you. She didn't try to get you a message?"

"Not to me. And iffen I might ask, just who is this Enat that mighty Chief Ayen would send a private message to High King Skoth about?"

Karl set his jaw as he said, "She's none other than the daughter of King Unaine of Fadis Innis and a close friend of High King Skoth. She was abducted nearly a year ago. I promise you, I will get this news to the High King."

Chapter 40 - History of the Necklace

The warm days of the end of February and the beginning of March brought a consistent snowmelt to the Mohak valley. Ayen knew that in a few short days warriors of the Seneca, Cayuga, Onondaga, and Oneida would begin arriving in Mohak territory to begin their campaign to the east. He was still unsure of what the outcome might be, but he had resolved that should peace and protection be available for his land and people, then he would strive to limit the bloodshed. However, he was also resolved that if war were to descend upon them, then he would use his utmost skill to lead his people to victory.

Ayen wanted to have a private conversation with Enat before that time arrived and so it was, that on an early March day, he asked Enat to walk with him. Ayen grabbed a pouch that he slung over his shoulder alongside his bow. He also had his long knife at his side and carried a stout walking staff. He did not carry his war club with him, but he did carry a throwing tomahawk.

They walked together from the castle of Tionnontoguen to the river. At the river's edge, they could see where the melt waters were running in the river, but that the ice cover of the river had not yet completely broken. They felt comfortable in the warmth of the sun and found a comfortable rock to sit on.

They made small talk for several minutes before Ayen pulled his pouch from his shoulder and held it on his lap.

He said, "Enat, daughter of Jeni and of King Unaine, I have something I wish to show you."

He then pulled from his carrying pouch a smaller decorated leather bag. Then from the small bag he pulled out a black and white necklace fashioned in an intricate style after the manner of his people. He turned it over in his hands with a faraway look on his face. Then he looked up to meet Enat's eyes and told her the story.

"This necklace was entrusted to my mother, and before that to her mother. It has been passed down in my mother's family in the Bear Clan of the Mohak people for generations. Upon my mother's death of the strange sickness it would have been entrusted to one of my twin sisters, but they too died of that illness."

When he paused, she wasn't sure what to say, so she ventured, "I'm sorry. It is a beautiful necklace."

He looked at the necklace and said, "It is said to be a necklace of great power in the hands of the right person."

Enat's eyes widened slightly as she said, "And you wonder if you should seek to use its power?"

Ayen shook his head. "No. It is not for me to use. I have never experienced the wielding of its power, and I know not even what its power may be. Legends say it can only be used by a woman."

"Ahh. I see. Or I think I'm starting to understand. When your mother died, and then your sisters also, their line died out."

Ayen nodded his head in agreement. A spark of an idea crossed Enat's mind, and she continued.

"But what of your Aunt, Waneek. She is your mother's sister, and she is a woman of great power. Perhaps she can use it?"

Ayen said, "I have thought of that, and I have spoken of such to her, but she says not. She says that the necklace will find its true owner, but that she is not it. It will not pass to her."

"Ayen, you know I respect you. Perhaps you even suspect I have other feelings toward you as well, but I don't understand why you are telling me this. You have fought against my people. Some might call me your enemy, though I know I am not. Why would you share such important information with me?"

He removed one of his hands from the necklace and placed that hand over her hands, which she had been holding on her lap.

"Enat, I can see those feelings, and I share them. Even though we are a man and a woman from different clans and cultures, I have these feelings too. You are a woman I could make a life with if we lived in a time of peace. But now is a time of conflict. I am sharing this information because I know not what may happen to me in the days and weeks to come. There is a promise in the legends of our people that the owner of the loon's necklace will be one who brings peace and prosperity to our people. If evil befalls me and defeats me, I want you to know this."

"Oh, Ayen. I know the goodness in your heart. I would help you in any manner that I am able. What more can I do for you?"

"I am going to return you to your people. I suspect Malsum has other plans for you. And he is coming soon. But he shall not get his hands on you. Should it cost me my life, I promise you that you will be delivered from him. What I ask of you, is that when you return to your people, you talk with your friend Evlin, the Bear-Witch of the Bear Clan of the Wabanaki who has escaped his grasp. Tell her of the loon's necklace. Ask her aid. Perhaps she can wield the necklace for peace, or perhaps she will know to whom it shall be passed."

"Yes, Ayen. I promise I will do it."

He smiled, and then a sense of awkwardness stole over him and he felt his hand upon hers. He went to lift it, but she turned her hand and held his.

Then to his surprise and delight she said, "Now let's put that necklace away, and let's be doing something about

---

those feelings we've said we share."

Within moments the necklace was back in its bag and back into the shoulder pouch. Their lips touched in their first kiss and time melted away. Hours later they walked back through the gate of the castle.

As they passed the gate, she smiled and turning to him and in a teasing manner said, "Don't think we're finished with this!"

He flashed a grin back and said, "I hope that it is just beginning."

Chapter 41 - Message to the King

Karl immediately sent a messenger to Skoth relaying the message from Ayen of the Mohak. He also stressed the aspect of the huge number of warriors being sent their way. Karl was well aware that this could be a feint by Ayen to draw the Celts to the Mohak valley while he would send a force to the west of the Blue Mountains and then south and east, but it didn't seem likely that he would send a large force to do that and to leave his homeland weakly defended. Several times Karl made the trip to New Alba and the neighboring villages on recruiting missions as he enlarged the force of the men guarding what he considered the northwestern western edge of Tara and of Eirgalon.

He wished he could have experienced the scene at the King's Hall in Tara when his messenger relayed the message from Ayen. He wouldn't have been disappointed. Skoth was outside working with several of his men felling some large pine trees to add to the construction efforts when the messenger arrived. As soon as the messenger shared his news, Skoth grabbed his cloak and staff that he had laid to the side while working, and hurried the man back to the women who were at the Great Hall.

The women were understandably excited and the sisters insisted that arrangements be made immediately that they could head north to New Alba and then Nealsfort, that they might meet Enat.

Skoth had to hold them back from making immediate plans, but promised that more men would soon be moving north and that they would be able to go with them. He insisted that under no circumstances would they be allowed to go off on their own, knowing full well that they would do whatever they wished. They knew it too. But they humored him and said they would travel with his men.

He wondered what they thought Ayen meant by wanting to talk. He wished Erik was here to give his reaction to it, but Erik was off on a recruiting mission to the eastern side of the river and wouldn't be returning for a day or more.

Skoth asked for the women's thoughts on Ayen's statement about being a man of peace and wanting to talk before making war. He found they were of mixed opinions.

Maeve shared her opinion that it was often an honorable act among the Wabanaki and Mohak to see if the other side wanted to concede, or make amends, before taking action, and that Ayen might be giving Skoth the opportunity to "save face" and retreat without bloodshed. That, however, would be conceding that the Celts had no legitimate right to be in Eirgalon.

Leesha commented that, "The request to 'talk' may be a cover to get a chance to return Enat to us."

Which prompted Teite to reply, "But why would Ayen give up a bargaining chip in the disagreement with us? He seems far too smart a man to give something away."

That prompted Gela, the Lenape wise woman who was still tending the new mother, to add, "I wouldn't be trusting any of those Haudenoshonee. For generations they have sent war parties into our lands. We Lenape know them. This is most likely a ruse on their part."

Maeve said, "Perhaps, but by all accounts, Ayenwatha is an honorable man. He may be wise in the ways of making war, but he is also honorable. I don't know that he would be party to deceive us by faking deliberations. That would bring dishonor upon him."

Evlin had said nothing up to this point but now she spoke. "Let's not forget that it is Malsum that is behind all of this. Whatever you may think of Ayen, Malsum is not to be trusted. There is also the shapeshifter to be wary of. That limikkin Senadondo is evil incarnate. I don't know if there are any more of his ilk and perhaps it was only Gakko and he that were in Malsum's power, but there may or may not be more of them. Beware appearances."

This dialog went on for some time as they thoroughly discussed the situation. Skoth said nothing during this conversation, he just sat back and listened to them bring up all of the possibilities and potentialities. They would go over and over them, adding a nuance here and a variation there. He also observed (to himself, or course, since he was smart enough not to voice this out loud) that women tend to discuss issues differently than men. Men frequently make their points and then sit back and think about it, while women like to keep talking and talking about it. It was as if they were doing their thinking out loud with each other, while men would hear the information, but then think it through on an individual basis. There were obvious advantages and disadvantages to each way of thinking through an issue. In this case, he had to admit he appreciated hearing the ladies discuss the issue since they did come up with a few considerations that he had not.

Finally, he excused himself for the moment, saying he had to check on the progress of some of the work outside. As he left, he was sure of one matter. The situation was quickly coming to a head. During these winter months, he may have been setting the board in preparation for action, but he had no doubt his opponent had been doing the same. The big question that was rolling around in his mind had been triggered by what Evlin had said. He wondered who had been setting the board - was it Ayen, or was it Malsum? And a second question was - does it make a difference?

Chapter 42 - Shaman from the East

The warm days of early March caused the ice on the Mahakentuck to let loose and flow from New Alba southward on the seventh day of March. The next day, two different groups of men crossed the river to Tara from the east. Erik brought a shipload of recruits from the settlements directly across the river from Tara, and then a couple of hours later a boat of Wabanaki men came down the river, having departed from a place on the eastern bank several miles to the north.

After Erik reported to Skoth about the scouting and recruiting mission to the eastern settlements of Tara, Skoth then updated Erik with the news of the communication from Ayen. Erik allowed that talking with the renowned warrior might be beneficial, but he warned against trickery and cautioned Skoth that "he better have his wits about him" when he did.

They were sitting at a table in the Great Hall when a messenger came in saying a canoe of Wabanaki were landing on the beach. Skoth directed the messenger to go and escort the men back to the Great Hall where he would greet them. Then Skoth poked his head into the family quarters and asked Leesha and Maeve to join him. Evlin was nursing Brigit and said she would be looking in on them in a few minutes.

The group of three men followed the messenger into the Great Hall. Leading the men was the old shaman of the Wabanaki whom they all recognized. It was Dakatomi. Erik quickly glanced around the room to make sure that the guards were alert and that the visitors had made no movement to attack. He was going to take no chances with that old shaman in the room. He had tried to harm Skoth a couple of times in the past; and if Erik were any judge of character, he would try to do so again.

Skoth motioned for the men to come across the room and join them at the table. Dakatomi came forward and sat, but the other two remained by the door. It was obvious that Dakatomi was in charge and they were his followers. Dakatomi's eyes darted about the room and quickly took in the presence of Leesha and Maeve. He tried to act nonplussed but to a keen observer there were telltale signs of his nervousness and discomfort.

Skoth started the conversation. "Welcome, Master Dakatomi, to our humble hall of Tara. I believe you know my companions," he motioned with his hands to Leesha, Maeve, and Erik, and then continued, "may I ask what circumstances bring you to our home?"

Dakatomi answered, "Thank you, King Skoth . . ."

He was interrupted by Erik clearing his throat and saying, "That would be High King Skoth. Is he not your High King?"

"Of course. Of course," stammered Dakatomi, "he is the High King of Eirgalon. Whatever I may have thought of that happening. He is the High King."

"Aye. That he is, no thanks to you."

Skoth knew how much Erik liked getting under the skin of certain people, including himself at times, but how he especially enjoyed provoking the old shaman from Tkaden's hometown. Skoth deemed enough had been said to throw Dakatomi a little bit off guard, so he re-entered the conversation by directing his first comments to Erik.

"Now, now, that's enough. Master Dakatomi is a distinguished visitor, and I welcome him to Tara." Then turning to Dakatomi, he politely continued, "You are welcome here, Master Dakatomi. To what do we owe the pleasure of your company?"

Dakatomi recovered his composure and answered, "I

am here to offer you my services. A young, inexperienced chief like you might need some advice from a more experienced man from time to time. I'm here to offer you that help."

Unbeknownst to the men and women in the Great Hall, Evlin had been silently observing from the doorway to the family quarters during this conversation. She stepped forward, and as she walked to Skoth's side, she said, "What a wonderful offer, Master Shaman. My father always said that the Wabanaki shaman were some of the wisest folk around. Of course, he said that about the Wabanaki wise women as well." She nodded at Maeve, and went on, "Perhaps our High King, young and inexperienced as he may be, will find a use for your unique skills."

Dakatomi swallowed deeply. He wasn't surprised to see Evlin. He had known of her escape from the clutches of Malsum's minions and had heard of her reunion with Skoth. However, he was nervous about her presence. She was a woman of obvious power and insight. She would be hard to deceive. The other two women he had dealt with back in Wausacom. They were suspicious of him, but he felt he could handle them. Evlin, with her powers of a bear-witch, was another matter.

"I would be most honored if he would. It is not easy for an old man, like myself, to travel during these months of harsh winter. Yet I came because as I heard our young Wabanaki men were being summoned by the new High King to come and offer their lives in the protection of their lands from the wiles of the fearsome Malsum, so I thought that I should offer my services as well. I may not be a strong warrior, but I do have certain other skills."

Skoth replied, "Oh, I am well aware of that Master Shaman. I will consider what you have offered. I'd love to offer you a place to stay, but as you can see, our little town of Tara is packed to the gills. Perhaps you can find a place in one of the barracks, or perhaps across the Wissawkin River in Euanglen."

One could sense a feeling of relief from Dakatomi as he said, "Thank you. But if it is alright with you, my assistants and I will find a place to pitch a tent and stay here in Tara."

"Won't that be too harsh and cold on your old bones? It is still below freezing many nights."

"Oh, I'll manage. Just let me know how I can be of help to you."

After Dakatomi and his men left, the rest of them discussed what his appearance and offer of help might mean. The unanimous consensus was that he was not to be trusted. Evlin wondered aloud if he might be here to spy on them and might have some clandestine manner of reporting to Malsum. They all agreed that it would be wise to keep a careful watch on him, though they weren't sure of how that might be done. Leesha offered that she might well have some ways to eavesdrop on him, but that it would still be good to have someone around him. Dakatomi's helpers were to be distrusted as much as he was. No doubt they were men who would do his bidding; and if they were with him, they probably were in league with him. Maeve wondered if she might be able to convince her old friend, the horse handler from Wausacom who had accompanied her and Leesha on their trip to Tara, to befriend Dakatomi and keep an eye on him for them. She promised to check into that possibility.

Erik summed it up by saying, "There's an old Celtic saying that one should keep his friends close - and his enemies closer."

Chapter 43 – Northward

A few days later a messenger came down the river. Tkaden had brought a force of men to the eastern bank of the Mahakentuck. The messenger's query was what orders the High King had for these men. Skoth had hoped and planned for the early arrival of Tkaden and his men, and he sent immediate word back that Tkaden was to take his men west to Karl and assist him in setting out a string of defensive advance positions that would note the arrival of the Haudenoshonee host. The positions were not to be held at any cost, but rather to identify the arrival of enemy warriors, blunt a fast-moving enemy advance, but falling back to positions on the Alban plain west of New Alba.

The Celtic longships then began to arrive. Almost immediately these men were directed to head up the river and fortify the area around New Alba.

One of the first longships to make port was that of Gunnar from New Caledonia. He exchanged warm greetings with Teite. When Teite and Leesha again confronted Skoth about their desire to proceed to New Alba, he agreed to let them go with Gunnar. They did have to promise that they wouldn't go off on their own and Skoth made a point of talking with Gunnar privately and cautioning him to watch over them.

Some of the earliest longships dropped off most of their men at New Alba, where Karl took command of them, and then the ships returned to Tara to ferry northward some of the force that Skoth and Erik had recruited during the winter months.

The once bustling new town of Tara was beginning to

thin out a bit as many of the warriors went north. Gela, the wise woman of the Lenape, also said that it was time for her to return to her village of Esepus. Her departure, and that of Teite and Leesha, had left a void in the life of the Great Hall of Tara, but that was short-lived for even Evlin would soon be leaving with Brigit and Maeve as they traveled north with Skoth to New Alba.

King Duncan and his wife, Lil, stopped briefly on their way to New Alba. Lil was the daughter of Chief MacGregor of New Alba and was anxious to see her family. Evlin had some private words with Lil and arranged to have Dakatomi and his men, including Maeve's horse handler, taken with them. She had asked the old shaman to use his skills by scouting around to see if he could find out any news or strategy of the enemy.

Turla arrived from Heilsand with a couple of longships and with Erik's nephew, Finn, who had finished his apprenticeship as a shipwright and who had come to offer his services to the High King. Skoth was pleased for there were some fine stands of timber in the kingdom of Tara that would be excellent resources for shipbuilding, and he was in need of men to do the construction. Skoth immediately commissioned him to begin work on setting up a construction shipyard and gave him the authority to employ workers on the king's behalf.

One of the longships that Turla brought was newly constructed and was presented to High King Skoth as a gift from the people of Heilsand. King Tyg of Heilsand had named it "Peacemaker" before it sailed, but said that High King Skoth was free to re-christen it at his pleasure. Both Skoth and Evlin felt that it was a fitting name as it named the hope in their hearts for Eirgalon, so they decided to leave it so named.

By the spring equinox, most of the men and material that were heading north to be deployed under Karl's command had passed Tara. Skoth knew it was time to take leave of what had become his home and to join his army.

Evlin had arranged the household entourage that she wished to accompany her. Skoth had known that there would be no arguing with her about her going north with him, so he had simply asked that she consider who she wanted to go with her. Though she was taking Brigit, she wanted to travel light. Maeve would accompany her, as would her loyal Mohak man, Anoka. Anoka would also have with him Kenda and Tekaya, the Oneida warriors. Even though they were going forward to a confrontation with the Haudenoshonee, she had no doubts about their loyalty to her and to Brigit. In the few short weeks of that baby's life, she had somehow worked her magic on those men, and they would die before they would let harm come to her.

As they left the Great Hall in the care of its staff, Skoth said to Evlin, "Are you sure that you have enough men to guard you?"

She laughed at him and with a twinkle in her eye that reminded him of the first time he saw those eyes peering over a fallen tree in the forest, and she said, "It is enough. Don't forget I can well enough take care of myself. And we will have a whole army of warriors around us, as well as Erik, who never wants to be too far away."

Skoth returned the laugh, "That's true enough. The powers that be will have a battle on their hands if they tangle with you, my love."

Skoth hesitated a moment and then asked a question.

"What do you think Dakatomi is up to by now?"

"By now he has arrived in the New Alba area and I suppose he is out and about, sneaking around. That's what he is good at. I hope Tkaden and Karl weren't too put out by his arrival. I know Erik didn't really approve of me sending him off on his own, but I think with Maeve's man with him we may learn more about what is going on than if Dakatomi was just lurking about around us."

"You are probably right about that. But I can just about imagine Karl's face when Dakatomi showed up. As serious as this is, that would have been worth seeing."

He smiled at her as she held the young Brigit nestled in her arms. Those bright blue eyes framed with dark curly hair beamed up at him. For a moment the troubles of the day melted away and Skoth felt contentment. But then the reality of their lives re-entered his consciousness. With strong hearts and firm determination, they took leave of their home and walked to board the *Peacemaker* as they moved forward on their quest to make a peaceful and prosperous future for Eirgalon.

Chapter 44 - Moving Eastward

Small contingents from the western lands of Malsum's Haudenoshonee League began trickling into Ayen's homeland and as they did, he immediately had his loyal followers guide them east to the lands between Skenektedy and the newly fortified Eirgalon post of Nealsfort. They were to camp there and to scout, but to wait for further orders. Ayen sent groups of his own warriors east to organize the defensive redoubts in case the warriors of Eirgalon should spring a surprise attack.

One day, when the spring equinox was nearly upon them, Ayen received word that the main body of the western warriors would be arriving in a day. He went to Waneek and had a private conversation with her and then took Enat aside to speak to her.

"Enat, you will be traveling with me. We leave in two hours time, following the road to Skenektedy. Bundle up what you need and can carry with you. I don't know that you will be returning here, for I intend to deliver you to your people. I hope you are able to return in more peaceful times, but I make no promises as to what the future brings. Waneek goes with us. I know you trust her. Continue to trust her."

"But aren't you going to wait for Malsum and his host?"

"No. He commands the Haudenoshonee, but I trust him not with you. I am leaving orders with the guard of our Tionnontoguen castle that his host is not to stop here, but they are to follow me. I want them not in this town."

"But why? I thought you were the warchief and commanded these men from the western nations?"

"I am. And I do. But I know not the true loyalty of those men. Are they loyal to me and my commands, or does their loyalty to Malsum and his ways transcend my orders as Warchief?"

"And do you question my safety among them?"

"I do. For as I have told you, Senadondo escaped when Evlin was freed, but I saw ill intentions in Malsum's heart concerning her, and you as well. I will not risk you falling into his hands."

"But he is still the leader of your people. And you are loyal to him."

Ayen hesitated, carefully considering his answer. "I follow him, but above all, a man must be faithful to his vision quest. And remember, you have a mission for me, and for our people."

She took his hands and facing him, looked deep into his eyes.

"Ayen, I have come to know you as a good and honorable man. I trust you. Remember your vision. Surrender it not! You are coming to know what you want from life, and I am coming to know what I want as well. I have my own dreams for the future. The only thing that will keep us from those dreams is the fear of failure. You will not fail in what you seek. I will not fail in doing what I intend to do."

Ayen nodded and then to her surprise, for while they were distant enough from others so that the others could see them but not hear them, he took her into his arms and embraced her. There was no hiding his passion for her. Waneek was observing them from a distance. When she saw the embrace, she smiled for them. They were people of different backgrounds, but they were right for each other. She said a silent prayer that they would live through the days to come and that they would bring joy to each other.

When Ayen released her, she blushed and said,

"Whew, that was a bear hug if ever I've had such!"

He smiled and teased, "It seems to me that you gave as good as you got!"

She blushed some more and said, "Tis a wonder you could tell, you were squeezing me so hard. But there is one small gift I would give you before we leave this place."

A curious look crossed his face as he saw her reach into the shoulder bag she usually carried with her. She pulled a small leather pouch from her bag. Holding it in her hand, she looked it over carefully. She had spent the last several days working on it whenever she had some free time. It was carefully fringed and had a beadwork triquetra symbol on it. It had a leather thong so that it could be worn around the neck. She reached up and placed it over his neck as she told him about it.

"This little pouch may not seem like much to you, but it is made in love and it carries my medicine within it. You can see beaded upon it one of the ancient symbols of my people: the triquetra. There is power in this symbol. I have learned the lore of the land at the hands of people like Fearglas, Evlin, and the Women's Circle of my land, as well as your aunt Waneek. They have taught me some of their medicine and I have infused this pouch with it for your protection. It has Waneek's touch upon it as well. You need not open the pouch, but know that in it are items of this creation and of the life of men. There are the seeds of the three sisters: corn, squash, and beans. There is a bear claw, and there is a small white moonstone. And lastly, there is a small button from my blouse that was crafted at the hand of the master druid of my people, Theofinn."

"Enat. I don't know what to say."

"Say nothing. Just know that the power of our people, yours and mine, protects you."

"Even if it comes to war with your people?"

"Even then! Though I pray that will not happen."

"Enat, I have nothing to give you . . ." he started to say, but she silenced him by raising her hand and gently touched her fingertips to his mouth. Then she lowered her hand and placed it on his chest.

"You have given me more than you realize," she said as she held her hand there for a long moment.

In the distance, they heard the sounding of a drum. It was the communication drummer of Tionnontoguen calling the warriors to assemble in preparation to depart. They took one last longing look at each other and went their separate ways to make their final preparations.

Chapter 45 - Karl and the Sisters

Drottin Karl, the War Chief of High King Skoth's forces, was in New Alba meeting with Chief MacGregor when King Duncan of Glesga and his entourage, which now included Dakatomi and his men, arrived at the city wharf. Their ship had to anchor briefly in the river, waiting while one of the other longships, which had discharged its warriors at the small wharf of the outpost, cast off its ropes and vacated the space. This gave ample time for Karl to be notified of Duncan's arrival and for him to make his way to the wharf.

Karl wasted no time for small talk with King Duncan. He simply made formal greetings and then told them to follow one of his men to where they could camp for the night before moving out to the plain of Alba where the forces were organizing. He did request that Lil would accompany him back to the chief's hall where Teite and Leesha had been provided lodging when they arrived. New Alba was not a large city; and before the military buildup it had simply been a fortified trading outpost. Now it was filled with the movement of men and goods as they prepared for the coming conflict with the Haudenoshonee.

Karl had developed a quick eye for noticing relationships between people and to him it was obvious that while Lil was anxious to see her father, Duncan was just as anxious to see her go. It was almost as if he wanted to be rid of her. The other intriguing item to him was the departure of Dakatomi and his Wabanaki men from the ship. The warriors from Glesga were none too disappointed to be rid of them. While Karl was, at first, taken by surprise in seeing them with Duncan, he had been notified by messenger from Skoth that they were at Tara. He had expected that sooner or later they would show up in New Alba.

Dakatomi had no words for Karl when he spotted him talking to King Duncan. He scurried away with his men trailing him. Karl motioned for one of his men to follow them at a distance and see where they went. Though she needed no escort, Karl walked with Lil as they proceeded to the Chief's Hall.

The Chief's Hall was within the fortified walls of the outpost. The gates were open and they entered unchallenged; for though the men on guard duty may not have recognized Lil as the daughter of their chief, they certainly did recognize Drottin Karl.

To all appearances, the hall was more akin to the common room of a large tavern than the seat of local government. There was a large hearthfire, and the room was filled with heavy wood tables and chairs. In fact, the hall was in effect used as a tavern and meals were served there daily. Chief MacGregor was actually more of a trader and businessman than he was a political leader. But since his business interests basically controlled the local area, he was the de facto leader of the area and rightly called "Chief."

Teite and Leesha were seated at a table with MacGregor when Lil and Karl entered. They immediately rose to greet them. Lil, though in her mid-twenties, ran to her father like a little child and jumped into his open arms. The outward show of love and affection brought smiles to the faces of all who saw them. Karl couldn't help but notice the tremendous difference in affection that Duncan and MacGregor had shown to Lil. Once MacGregor had set his daughter back on her feet, she turned to the women and greeted them. As they sat down for conversation around one of the tables, a serving girl from the kitchen brought them drinks to refresh themselves.

MacGregor said, "Tis sad that a crisis brings a daughter home, but still tis a pleasure to see the lassie again."

Lil teasingly responded, "Ah, now. You were happy enough to see me go off as the wife of King Duncan. Sure enough, we haven't been up the river to see you, but then again, how often have you come to pay us a visit?"

"Fair enough, my child. I've not come down the river. But you know me well enough. I have my business operations to tend to and I do admit I'm a wee bit partial to the land about here as opposed to down about the coast."

"I know that well enough, and I know ma is not one to be traveling. You couldn't drag her away from here without her fighting tooth and nail."

MacGregor gave a hearty laugh, "Aye. You know her well. But enough of this. How are you doing? I see that your husband, mighty King Duncan, didn't come with you to my humble abode."

"No. He went off with his men to prepare them for battle."

"Ah, well. Tis better he does that. He'd not find much to like about this place. Not fancy enough for his tastes, and all."

The group continued with friendly banter for several minutes when a messenger came running into the hall searching for Drottin Karl.

Breathlessly he panted out, "Drottin Karl, you have to come to Nealsfort immediately."

Karl asked, "Why? What has happened? Have the Haudenoshonee begun their attack?"

"No. Not that. But people have arrived."

"More refugees?"

"No, sir."

"Well, then, spit it out, man. Who has come to Nealsfort?"

"They said it was Enat, sir. The one you were chasing

last summer. She and a couple other folks just walked right up to our front door, as it were, and simply asked to come in."

"Didn't our scouts see them coming?"

"Not until they were well out of the woods and already near the fort."

By this point, Leesha and Teite were standing up and grabbing their cloaks.

Karl turned and looked at them and sternly said, "And where do you two think you're going?"

Leesha said, "Don't you take that voice with me! This is our sister we're talking about. Like it or not, we are going to Nealsfort. Now if you want to stay here jawing with one of your men, that is up to you. But if you want to accompany us to Nealsfort, then you better get a move on it, because be you Drottin of High King Skoth, or not. We're on our way out the door!"

Karl knew better than to argue with one of the sisters when they had their backs up, so he simply got up, and saying a brief farewell to Lil and MacGregor headed out the door with the sisters. Within moments Karl had one of his men commandeer some of the messenger service horses and they were on their way to Nealsfort.

Chapter 46 – Reunion

The men at the Nealsfort outpost made Enat, Waneek, and the one Mohak warrior with them, as comfortable as possible as they waited for the arrival of Karl or Tkaden. Messengers had been sent to both of them, for Karl was in New Alba and Tkaden was checking on some of the camps of the outlying sentries that extended through the valley south toward the Blue Mountains.

The sentries on the wall of the Nealsfort stockade had been quite taken aback when the party had appeared walking through the open prairie toward the stronghold, for there were sentries scouting through the woods to the west and they should have spotted anyone who had come from the direction of Skenektedy, the closest Mohak community.

The sentries opened the gates when they saw the horses approaching on the path from New Alba. The party on horseback rode right through the gate. Almost before they had stopped, Leesha and Teite had jumped off their mounts and were running to Enat.

The three sisters stood for a long minute in a tight embrace. Karl just stood there looking a little sheepish as he rested his eyes on Enat for the first time in almost a year. He thought to himself that she looked a little different, and then realized that with his experiences of the past year, he probably did too.

When the sisters released her, Enat stepped forward to embrace Karl. He noticed that she held him tight, but that when he leaned down to kiss her, she buried her head in his shoulder. Then she leaned back, released him, and stepped away to introduce those with her. Without a doubt, there was something different.

"Teite, Leesha, Karl. These are my friends. Waneek, who is a wise woman of the Mohak, and her son, Sagoye, a warrior who would take a message from High King Skoth back to Chief Ayenwatha."

Then she turned to Waneek and Sagoye, and in the Mohak tongue she said, "These are my sisters, Teite and Leesha. And this warrior is Karl. He is the right-hand man of King Skoth, and is a friend of my youth."

Waneek responded to Enat, also in Mohak, "Ah, so this is the young man, Karl. He is as imposing as you have said." Then she turned to the others and said, this time speaking in the Celtic tongue of Eirgalon, "Enat has spoken of all three of you. What a pleasure it is to meet you."

They were briefly startled that Waneek spoke to them in their tongue, but they quickly recovered and greeted her warmly as she went forward to hug them. The men simply nodded at each other as they kept a respectful and significant distance from each other because both could see in the other a true warrior of whom to be wary.

At this moment Tkaden came rushing into the outpost. He had left Leesha and Teite in New Alba, so he was surprised to see them at Nealsfort, and he was pleased to see Enat, but he was none too pleased to see a Mohak warrior and woman standing with them.

Again Enat made introductions, and as she did so Tkaden looked them over with an appraising and suspicious eye. Enat tried to allay his concerns, but feared she only made them worse when she said that Sagoye was Ayenwatha's cousin. That raised eyebrows for both Tkaden and Karl. Without speaking to each other, both of them resolved to keep a special watch over that one.

Leesha noticed the unspoken communication between her husband and her friend and said, "Enough of that you two. You are both suspicious enough by nature, and given the extremity of this situation, perhaps rightly so, but if Enat vouches for this man and this woman then you two better just relax and back down. A messenger she said he is intended to be. So that's what he will be. You have no need to get your hackles raised."

Tkaden knew well enough not to challenge his wife and risk her ire. She was sweet enough and had a loving heart, but when she was riled . . . well, then one might as well try to hold on to a wild bobcat as to deal with her.

Tkaden wisely responded, "Why, of course. And we really shouldn't be keeping them here. We should be taking them to New Alba to meet with Skoth. He should be arriving soon. Perhaps today, and if not today, then most likely on the morrow."

Tkaden turned to the Mohak emissaries, "On behalf of High King Skoth and also my Wabanaki brethren we welcome you. Would you be our guests and accompany us to New Alba?"

Waneek kept a solemn face, but smiled on the inside. These two young men may be warriors, but they did have some common sense about them and they were wise enough to listen to their women. Perhaps that was a good omen for the days to come.

Waneek answered for Sagoye and herself, "We would be honored to receive your hospitality. Is there anything more you would ask of us before we proceed?"

Karl responded, "Well, if it is your intention to have Sagoye here take a message back to Chief Ayenwatha we'd best be getting a move on it. Do you have any idea what that message is to be about?"

Waneek replied, "Since Sagoye will have some words from Ayen for King Skoth about where and when they might meet, I imagine it will be about that. I imagine that there may be more details to it than that, but normally these matters of war are not conducted by our women. I'll let Sagoye share the details with King Skoth. That should suffice."

Karl was surprised by her openness. He nodded and said, "That it does. Thank you."

Waneek then smiled, and said, "And one more bit of information for you. Ayen is at Skenektedy. I understand that you, Karl, have spent considerable time searching for him. Perhaps it is reassuring to you, to now know where he is."

Enat almost burst out in laughter when she saw Karl's jaw drop open.

Karl recovered quickly and regained his composure, but he couldn't help but admire the way the wise woman had put him in his place. Why it almost felt like old times back when he was growing up in Dunsheelin with Skoth and the sisters. There always was someone from the Women's Circle who would say something to keep you humble. It made him think that maybe the Mohak people weren't so different from his own.

Chapter 47 - Question of Leadership

Horns sounded at the arrival of the *Peacemaker* coming into sight of New Alba. The standard of the High King was fluttering from its mast announcing to all who was on board. The joyous shouts of the people who were assembling on the wharf seemed at odds with the reality of the impending conflict.

There was a brief welcoming ceremony at the wharf, but Skoth and his people were quickly escorted to Chief MacGregor's Hall. The group that had arrived from Nealsfort, as well as MacGregor and Lil, were waiting in the hall when Skoth and Evlin, with Brigit, entered.

Of course, her sisters had told Enat about the birth of Brigit; so when they entered the hall, she rushed forward to embrace them. Numerous hugs, greetings, and introductions were made around the room as friends, new and old, met.

After the initial greetings were accomplished and Skoth informed of Sagoye's desire to pass a private message on him, he took him into a private room off the main hall. With Sagoye's permission, he asked Anoka to join them as a translator and Erik to join them as a guard.

After nearly an hour of discussion, they came back to the gathering in the hall and Skoth quieted them and made an announcement.

"Sagoye has told me that Chief Ayenwatha desires to meet with me. Before our assembled forces clash in battle, he would talk to see if we might avoid bloodshed. I have agreed to meet with him. I am sending Sagoye back to him with a message of where and when we will meet. I wish to send someone with him to ensure safety through our lines and to ensure his safe return when he brings a message from Chief

Ayenwatha."

Tkaden stood up and said, "I will go."

Leesha added, "And I will go with him."

Skoth replied, "Wait a minute. I'm not sure I want to risk that he might hold you as a hostage."

Enat interrupted, "There is no danger of that. Ayen is a man of honor. She will be safe with him."

Skoth nodded thoughtfully, "Perhaps, but what of the limikkin? What if he is around? Could he strike her as he did to you and Evlin?"

Leesha calmly reasoned with him, "Forewarned is forearmed. I know about him, and I know what he can do. Don't forget that I am not powerless. You saw what I did at Heilsand."

"What of Malsum, himself? What if he is with Ayen? Will you be safe against him?

At this point, Waneek, wise woman of the Mohak, interrupted, "That is a good point. He is strong in the ways of magic as well as deceit. Perhaps I should return with them as well."

Sagoye interjected, "Mother, you should not. Your job is here."

Skoth wondered slightly what he meant by that, but had no time to ask before Erik joined into the conversation.

"The truth of the matter is that you either trust Ayen's word to this point, or you do not. He did release Enat to us without asking for anything in return. If we are to send anyone back with Sagoye, we draw attention to him. If we have concerns about Malsum, or Senadondo, then I think we are better off sending Sagoye by himself. It seems to me that he is a competent enough fellow. If we see him off safely through our lines, I think he could manage to get to Ayen and speak to him privately. Even if those others are about. Am I right, Waneek?"

She looked at him with a smirk of appreciation, both for his reasoning and for his compliment to her son.

"He will be able to do his mission," she said confidently, and then she added, "and should he need to return to us, he will be able to do that as well. As you have said, he is competent."

Skoth declared, "So be it. Let us waste no further time. Sagoye, you know what I have to say to Chief Ayenwatha. The sooner you be off, the better. Tkaden and Leesha will accompany you back to Nealsfort. From there you are on your own. Go swiftly and safely."

Sagoye nodded then said a few private words with Waneek and departed with Tkaden and Leesha.

After they left, Skoth turned to the rest of them, "There is still much I would like to know. Enat, you've had some time to speak with your sisters and with Evlin while I was with Sagoye, now I would like to hear of your adventures."

Skoth had expected that Karl would be near Enat, since the two of them had been sweet on each other way back to the time when they were adolescents in Dunsheelin, but he noticed that Karl was positioned several feet away from her. Maybe it was just that Enat was doting on Brigit, but maybe it was more. Enat handed Brigit back to Evlin and began her story.

"No doubt you know the story well enough up to the point where Evlin and I were separated. Those limikkin treated her harshly and I feared for her. I was more fortunate. I was placed under the charge of Waneek. She's Ayen's aunt, sister to Ayen's mother. We left the camp near Glesga and I didn't really see what happened at Inverbaile. They took me by it in a canoe. I could see the devastation, but didn't know all that happened. When we fled up river, we knew there would be pursuit. Karl and his men pursued us from the river, through the hills, and into the valley of the Wissawkin.

Finally Ayen started splitting groups of men off from his main force. I imagine it was to confuse our pursuers and so they wouldn't know which one I was with. I was in a small group with Ayen, Waneek, and a few men from his village. We went over the hills and through valleys around the western edge of the Blue Mountains and made our way to Ayen's home of Tionnontoguen. I spent the winter with them there. Waneek helped me to learn of their language and their ways."

Skoth asked, "But you never met Malsum?"

"No. Malsum was further west, in the city of Onondaga. Ayen didn't want to take me there, although he traveled there. He went to talk to Malsum and then he came back."

"Did he say why he didn't want to take you there?"

"Not exactly, but he said Malsum had no need for me and that I was safer staying with Waneek. In any case, as you know, I spent the whole winter with them. Waneek was like a mother to me." She glanced at Waneek and smiled at her, and then went on, "She is a wise woman of the Mohak and she taught me much of their ways. We can trust her."

"And you believe we can trust Ayenwatha as well?"

"I have told you he is an honorable man. He will do what is best for his people. But if he makes you a promise, yes, you can trust him."

Karl was sitting several chairs away from her as she spoke and his eyes and ears picked up on the way she spoke about Ayen. It was at that moment that the realization hit him that Ayen was likely more to her than a friend. That realization made his concentration drift away from the discussion for a few moments as he tried to sort out the feelings that were going on inside himself. If he had been more aware of his surroundings, he might have noticed that as Enat spoke of Ayen, Waneek was carefully observing Karl. She said nothing, but she noticed his introspection.

Enat, however, was oblivious to Karl's reaction. She was focused on her story and on answering the questions Skoth was asking.

Enat went on talking, "Skoth, I think you might be surprised how much the Mohak are like us. They have the same type of values and concerns, hope and dreams that we do. They want to live in peace."

"Enat, I wouldn't be at all surprised. Just as Wabanaki and Lenape people are like us and are a part of this land, I believe that the Mohak and others could be too. The question at this point seems to be, can we learn to live together? Malsum has said we cannot. It appears from what you and Sagoye say that your friend, Ayen thinks we can. Who is it who speaks for the Haudenoshonee people? Malsum, or Ayen?"

Waneek held her hand up to forestall Enat from saying more.

She said, "I know my nephew well, King Skoth. Enat speaks well enough of him, but I have known him since his birth. I give away no secrets by telling you this. Ayen is a great warrior and he is a worthy opponent, as perhaps your friend, Karl has told you," she smiled at him and pointed to him, "and I might add, he thinks quite highly of this warrior's leadership in pursuit of him. But as I was saying, Ayen is also a man of peace, who wants peace for his people. I can not speak for Malsum. You are a wise leader to ask who speaks for the Haudenoshonee. I can see why these people are so loyal to you. I think the simple answer to your question is the disconcerting answer that the one who speaks for the Haudenoshonee people is yet to be determined."

Chapter 48 – Conflict

Ayen was in Skenektedy when he bid farewell to Enat, Waneek, and Sagoye. A few short hours after they had departed, a messenger came running from the Tionnontoguen castle. Malsum had arrived there with his personal bodyguard of loyal troops. When the men that Ayen had left guarding the settlement had told Malsum to go to Skenektedy to meet with Ayen, Malsum had forced his way into the city and was executing the old men and boys that Ayen had left to guard his city.

Ayen quickly dispatched men to assemble as many of his Mohak warriors as possible and to head back to Tionnontoguen. Messengers ran down the lines of camps that had sprung up throughout the valley stretching from the Mohak River southward towards the Blue Mountains. These messengers spoke in the camps where Mohak warriors had loyalty to Ayenwatha and passed by those that were of other Haudenoshonee nations. The Mohak warriors immediately armed themselves and began moving back toward the Tionnontoguen castle. If questions were asked by others, the standard answer was that some troops were being redeployed for reasons of strategy.

The distance to Tionnontoguen (Ayen's home) to Skenektedy (the easternmost Mohak settlement) was about twenty miles as the crow flies, but for men making their way by foot around hill and dale the distance could be several miles more.

The roads, pathways, and woodland trails of this territory were home to these Mohak men. They knew it well. Many of them traveled through the night in response to the call of Ayen. By the time the sun was breaking the horizon, Ayen was assembling his men in the woods of the hunting grounds a mere mile south of the palisaded log fortress on the hill.

Ayen gave the order and they began to advance toward the castle. In the light of day, they could see a smoke plume rising from it. As they left the woods, they stepped upon the fields that surrounded the settlement. It was too early in the year for the fields to be planted and they were yet be tilled, but they could see that what was newly grown on the fields was the army of men that Malsum had brought with him. Banners of Onondaga, Cayuga, and Seneca flew from various standards, but the dominant sigil was Malsum's personal symbol of the coiled snake. It was a traditional symbol of the power of a shaman, but to Ayen and his men it felt sinister and evil for on this day it symbolized a serpent's attack upon their people.

Their emergence from the woods was immediately noticed by the warriors in front of the city. Those warriors rushed to assemble in lines before them, but held their place in front of the palisades. Ayen's men had advanced nearly halfway across the open fields when a delegation of a dozen men exited the gates of the castle and proceeded toward them. Ayen recognized the man leading the delegation. It was Malsum.

Ayen raised his arm in a motion that ordered his men to stop. The men in front held their position, but more men continued to come out of the woods. The men who had the farthest to travel were still arriving, and as they did so, they joined Ayen's growing numbers. Soon the number of his men would outnumber Malsum's men before the palisades. But who knew how many men he might have inside the walls.

Ayen stepped out from his men, and walked forward alone. When he did so, Malsum ordered his escorts to stop as well, and he proceeded alone carrying nothing but his staff. They met midway between the opposing forces. They stood facing each, with a distance of several feet between them.

"Brother, you disappoint me. Why have you closed

your heart and home to me?" asked Malsum.

"Brother? You have entered my castle by force of arms. By the looks of the smoke rising from it, you have plundered it. It is you who has turned from me and the way of peace. You are no brother to me."

"I am cleansing this place of the stench that has come upon it. You have allowed a pale woman to live here among you this winter. Her presence has poisoned it. Perhaps it has poisoned you as well. Turn her over to me now. We can begin anew. We shall purify what she has defiled. Give me the necklace as well. You can make amends."

"You shall never have her. She has already returned to her people. And you shall never have the loon's necklace. It has been taken from here."

Anger flashed across Malsum's face and the muscles of his jaw clenched. He gazed over the growing crowd of warriors behind Ayen.

Malsum spat out his words, "Even now, the battle with the pale ones to the west has begun. I sent Senadondo with orders to strike. Our warriors fight and die. Yet you have come here. Are you such a coward? You are no war chief of the Haudenoshonee to stand here while our foe has been engaged in battle. I loved you like a brother, yet you have disgraced me. Throw down your war club and leave me."

For several moments, Ayen stood unmoving, as if turned to stone. Then, with a voice that cut the silence like a sharpened dagger cutting leather, he spoke.

"I reject you, false shaman." Then, raising his voice so that it echoed through the silent ranks of men around them, he shouted, "Men of the Haudenoshonee, I declare this man to be a false prophet and will not follow him. He is a traitor to the way of peace and unity. Reject him and follow me!"

Malsum's face contorted into a snarl, and he lifted his staff and pointed it at Ayen. With a shouted curse that was in a language unintelligible to anyone nearby, a beam of light burst from the end of the staff to strike Ayen in the chest.

For a moment Ayen staggered backward. Then he steadied himself and looked down at his chest to where the flare had struck him. There were holes through his outer and inner garments. Lying exposed upon his chest was the pouch that Enat had given him. It was unblemished. He gave a small smile, and then lifting his arms high, with his war club in his right hand, he roared his Mohak battle cry. His men rushed forward.

Malsum quickly retreated to his men, fled through them and disappeared through the gates of the castle palisade. When many of the Haudenoshonee men down the lines saw Malsum fail to harm Ayen, they doubted. They refused to fight. However, the men in the center, Malsum's strongest followers, covered his retreat and fought with fierce loyalty. There was bloodshed and many casualties and it was several minutes before Ayen's men gained access to the palisade gates and entered the castle. In their flight, Malsum and his personal guard had not even attempted to close the gate. The women of the city told them that Malsum had led his men scurrying out the far gate on the opposite side of the city and fled down the hill toward the river.

Ayen wasted no time surveying the remnants of the settlement. He could see that his family's lodge and several others had been burnt to the ground. Quickly he led his men through the city to the far gate. When he reached the riverside gate of the castle, he could seen that Malsum and his men had taken the canoes they needed to cross the river to the north side and had released the other canoes to be carried downstream by the spring floodwaters. Immediate pursuit was out of the question.

As much as Ayen wanted to help the people of his settlement deal with the atrocities that had been visited upon them by Malsum's brief occupation, he knew he had responsibilities beyond them. Somewhere to the east,

Senadondo had begun Malsum's mischief and now, no doubt men of the Mohak and Haudenoshonee were dying, as were men of Eirgalon. He didn't know yet what was to be done about it, but he knew that it was his duty to try.

Ayen took a few moments to speak with some of the wise women of the settlement. He gave them words of encouragement and a promise to return. Then he left the castle and in the fields outside he organized his men and gave his orders. Some of his men would stay here to guard against Malsum's return. The rest, including the Onondaga, Seneca, and Cayuga who now followed him, turned and headed east.

Chapter 49 - Senadondo's Tricks

Upon his arrival at New Alba, King Duncan of Glesga and his men had been directed to the southern flank of the Eirgalon outposts. They were virtually in the shadow of the high bluffs that towered over that portion of the valley. They considered their outpost to be the southern anchor of the line against the Haudenoshonee. The Wabanaki scouting parties and observers on the bluffs had revealed that their enemies were continuing to gather forces. It was with high spirits and anticipation that they arrived at their post. King Duncan and his men were eager to get into battle that they might avenge the Haudenoshonee attack on Inverbaile the previous summer.

Other recent arrivals in New Alba were Dakatomi and his men. They had arrived in New Alba as passengers on Duncan's longship, but gladly parted ways with them as soon as the ship docked. They made their way westward to where both Eirgalon and Haudenoshonee forces were gathering in preparation for battle.

Walking for several miles and avoiding contact with others as much as they could, Dakatomi's party had set up their camp for the night in a secluded spot in the woods. They made a small fire and nibbled on some of the traveling food they carried with them. Dakatomi was sitting at the fire with them and fiddling with a medallion in his hands when they heard someone approaching them. They quickly drew their weapons as a small, wiry man came into view.

Dakatomi said, "Put down your weapons, men. It is my friend, Senadondo."

One of the men, the horse-handler of Maeve's journey, whispered, "How could he have found us?"

Dakatomi took the medallion he had been holding in his hands and slipped it into his pockets. "We have our ways."

Senadondo walked up to the fire and then pointed to the horse handler and gave an order.

"Tie him up. He is a spy."

The others grabbed him and soon had him subdued and bound.

Senadondo gave them brief orders about what to do in the morning. They would be "fleeing" into a Wabanaki camp near Duncan's with word that the Haudenoshonee were attacking. Their mission was to get the Wabanaki to rush into battle, as well as to get them to send messengers up and down the line with orders to attack. Senadondo said that he would be working from the Haudenoshonee side taking similar action.

Dakatomi was a little puzzled by the orders and asked Senadondo, "Why are we warning the Wabanaki? Wouldn't it be better to catch them unaware?"

Senadondo spoke dismissively to him, "That's not a question you need to worry about. Just do your part. It may not be as easy as you think. There are people on both sides who long for peace. They must be made to think that the other side is attacking so they will rise to action. Malsum wants this war begun. It is our task to trigger it."

Dakatomi nodded and replied, "We will do our part."

"Good! Perhaps Malsum will reward your loyalty. After you sound the alarm, you are to return to New Alba. I will meet you there. We have another job to do there. Now, I must be moving on. You have no use for him," he pointed at the bound man, "untie his feet but leave his hands tied. I'll take him with me."

"Won't he get in your way, or slow you down?"

Senadondo grinned as he replied, "Not for long."

Senadondo then led the man away into the darkness. Several minutes later they heard a blood-curdling scream and then silence.

When Senadondo appeared at the Haudenoshonee camp opposite the southern outpost of King Duncan before dawn, few men were surprised. They knew him to be a close confidant of Malsum and they knew he had special powers. Any orders from him were sure to come from Malsum.

Senadondo told them that he had come with word from Malsum that the battle had begun to the north as the pale ones had attacked near the Mohak River and were moving toward the Skenektedy castle. They were to prepare themselves immediately and move to attack the southern flank. He would stay long enough, to see the battle engaged, and then move north to command other forces.

When Senadondo was asked by the warriors why the Mohak men among them had pulled back the previous day and headed to the northwest, a flicker of momentary puzzlement crossed his face. He recovered by telling them that they were just being redeployed in order to help protect their homeland, but he wondered what had happened. When he had left Malsum at Tionnontoguen, it was Malsum's plan to make sure the Mohak forces were engaged in battle with the pales ones. He wondered why they would be retreating before the battle commenced. However, he had no time to worry about such matters. His task was to get the war started on the southern flank and then to speed to the north and trigger it there as well.

Outlying scouts alerted the sentries of the Eirgalon camp when they spotted the approaching host. They blew their battle horns in warning and Duncan's warriors quickly armed themselves and prepared for battle. Soon they were rushing out of camp toward the attackers. Within minutes the first arrows flew and then the swords clashed. The battle had begun.

Senadondo left the warriors fighting as he made his

243

way away from them. In short order, he had used his limikkin powers to transform himself into a crow and was winging his way to the north. One spark of battle had been ignited, but there were more sparks to strike and flames to fan.

Chapter 50 - Northern Fires

As the battle flared in the south, across the valley to the north, Tkaden and Karl looked at the rising sun from the parapets of the log palisade at Nealsfort. The day was dawning clear and pleasant, but they both wondered what kind of day this would turn out to be. Tkaden and Leesha had escorted Sagoye this far on the day past, and Sagoye had gone on to meet with Ayen. Drottin Karl had joined them later in the evening after discussing more strategy with Skoth and Erik.

Skoth had ordered messengers to head to the front lines early in the morning, with orders for the furthest scouts and outposts to pull back to the secondary fortified positions. He didn't want there to be any accidental engagements that provoked battle before he had a chance to meet with Ayenwatha. It was to be in the open field before Nealsfort that they would meet. By pulling his warriors back, he hoped to communicate his positive intentions as well as prevent unintentional conflict.

They had already stepped down from the wall when the lone crow circled over Nealsfort and then wheeled to the west and settled into the trees beyond the open field. As men from the outlying positions walked beneath the trees and made their way to the fort, the crow cawed and then took flight again heading in the direction of the Haudenoshonee forces.

Minutes later Senadondo took human form and made his way into the main camp of his warriors. He was immediately recognized and escorted to the campfire where the leaders of the war parties were meeting.

After perfunctory greetings, Senadondo asked, "What

is going on? Why are the pale ones withdrawing?"

The leaders gave him looks of incredulity. They knew him as Malsum's pet limikkin with unusual powers, but the news of a retreat by the pale ones was incomprehensible.

One of them, a man of the Oneida said, "Who says they retreat? It is the Mohak men who have retreated."

Now it was Senadondo's turn to be stunned. "What? Explain that!"

"Yesterday a young Mohak messenger from Tionnontoguen arrived. Within minutes Chief Ayenwatha had gathered his Mohak men and headed back to Tionnontoguen. He gave us orders to stay here and do nothing until he returned. A few hours later his young cousin, Sagoye, came looking for him. Then he also headed west."

Senadondo gave a snarl and said, "So he deserted you here! Some war chief he is. Well, I tell you to pick up your weapons. We go to attack!"

The men hesitated and looked at each other. Then the man who spoke earlier, the Oneida war chief, said, "I know you have the favor of Malsum, but Ayenwatha is the Warchief of all the Haudenoshonee, not just the Mohak. He has given us directions. We can wait for him to speak again. If it is true, as you say, that the pales ones retreat, then we are in no danger here. We will wait."

"I have direct orders from Malsum that we are to attack."

"You would have us go against the commands of our Warchief?"

"I would have you obey the orders of the mighty prophet Malsum. No doubt, Ayen was unsure of himself and went to find counsel at Malsum's knee. You are the ones in command here. And now you have been directed forward by Malsum."

Back and forth they argued for several minutes.

Finally, divided in thought, they allowed the persuasions of Senadondo to divide them in action. Some of them, like the Oneida leader, still refused to follow Senadondo's commands, but others agreed. They gave directions to their men and shortly thereafter, a contingent of warriors followed Senadondo as he directed them toward the outpost of Nealsfort.

They passed the remains of the Eirgalon outlying camps and sentry posts as they went forward. Soon they were standing just within the edge of the woods across the open field of Nealsfort. Senadondo mulled over in his mind what action he might take now that could trigger this situation into conflict. He did not have enough men with him to launch a full frontal attack on the fort, and if he marched the men across the open plain to bypass the fort and engage in battle with those camped beyond the fort, then they would see how few in number his men were and also would easily overwhelm them. Somehow he must draw them out so he could strike at them, invite their pursuit, and yet escape.

He ordered some of the men to show themselves and to proceed across the open space to a point just beyond arrow range from the fort. There they were to build a bonfire from which they might ignite flaming arrows and then step forward several paces to send them flying into the fort.

Upon seeing the Haudenoshonee activity, the sentries atop the Nealsfort wall notified Karl. Accompanied by Tkaden and Leesha, he climbed the parapet to survey the scene.

Karl wondered aloud, "What are they doing? This is not yet the time for the meeting between Ayen and Skoth?"

Tkaden said, "I don't have a good feeling about this."

"We need to find out about what is happening out there," added Leesha.

Karl stood still as he thought about it, saying nothing.

Tkaden spoke again, "You know she's right."

Karl frowned as he said, "Aye, but I'm trying to figure out how we might go about doing that without creating a problem where there might not be one. Do either of you have any ideas?"

"I think you should let Tkaden and me go out there, with a small number of our Wabanaki warriors and see if we can talk with them."

Karl slowly shook his head. "I don't know. That's putting you in harm's way. Skoth would be none too pleased if I let anything happen to you."

Tkaden responded, "She would be with me and our warriors. And we won't engage in conflict. We'll stay within arrow range of the fort, and just get close enough to them to talk. If it looks like trouble, we'll fall back here."

Leesha moved her hand to touch the handle of her wand. It was the Eostre wand willed to her by her mother that she had wielded at the Great Fire of Heilsand.

"I won't be defenseless. In addition to my husband and his men, I do have a few tricks up my sleeve."

Now Karl nodded as he said, "Aye, then. Go and do what you can. But take no unnecessary chances. And I'll have a force of men waiting on the far side of the fort to come and rush to your defense."

Tkaden and Leesha quickly scrambled down from the parapet and gathered a small group of armed warriors. With one of the warriors holding a white flag of truce upon a standard, they went out of the fort and made their way towards the group of men assembling the wood for the fire. The men saw their approach and scrambled to drop the pieces of wood they were carrying and grab their weapons.

Tkaden and Leesha's group approached to within thirty yards and then stopped. Both sides stood waiting.

There was a brief commotion at the edge of the woods,

and then a wiry man, accompanied by a couple of strong warriors, walked towards them. When he reached the front line of his men, he stopped. He squinted at them. Then he smirked, for in Leesha he could see the resemblance to Enat.

"Ah, so another one of the sisters, is it?"

Leesha responded, "So you know me. We have come expecting to meet Chief Ayenwatha, but not this soon."

Senadondo chortled in a gleeful manner, "But instead you are stuck with me. And what were you expecting to tell him?"

Leesha and Tkaden shared quick glances. They sensed there was something amiss. This man, whoever he was, spoke in a strange manner.

Leesha spoke, "We wish to talk with him. Is he here? Or do you speak for him?"

"Let me think. Is he here? Well, now, it doesn't appear he is. As for speaking for him - I do not. I speak for myself and I speak for Malsum. And who do you speak for?"

Leesha knew that there was something most definitely amiss. She was beginning to suspect who this might be standing across from her.

She said, "You haven't given us your name, but surely you have one." For she knew from what Evlin had told her, that the naming of Gakko's true name had been her demise.

"Ho, ho. You wish to know my name?"

"It would be polite to know the name of one we parley with."

His almost gleefully disdainful manner of speaking was becoming more annoying as the conversation went on, yet he continued.

"Polite has never been a term applied to me. But I think you know me. You may call me Senadondo."

A couple of the Wabanaki men nearest to Leesha and

Tkaden gave out audible hisses, which made Senadondo chortle even more.

"Do you have anything for us from Chief Ayenwatha?"

"Oh, him. Why, yes I do have something for you from him. Please wait here while I go get it."

So saying, he turned and started walking toward the trees. He stopped briefly, whispered words to the strong warriors that had been with him, and then continued on toward the trees. The men watched him till he reached the trees and then pulled arrows from their quivers, quickly drew their bows and let them fly at Tkaden and Leesha.

They had been anticipating trouble so Leesha had pulled her wand and held it before them. To all appearances nothing dramatic happened but the arrows plunged to the earth short of their intended targets. While Tkaden and Leesha hastened back to the fort, the Wabanaki warriors with them stayed behind them to cover any Haudenoshonee warriors that might rush them. A few did, but not for long. For within a few steps they were within the range of Karl's men on the parapet of the fort. The expert marksmen let none of them continue their pursuit.

When they reached the safety of the fort, they stopped and looked back. They could hear voices yelling from the woods, and then the Haudenoshonee men resumed accumulating wood for the bonfire.

A few minutes later they saw a number of men carrying bundles out toward the pile of wood.

When Karl saw a couple of men carrying a smoking satchel between them toward the pile of kindling, he surmised what they were going to do. He quickly ordered a troop of men to head out to the site and prevent them from lighting the fire. They were to fight and defeat the enemy, removing them from the open space, but they were not to pursue the attackers into the woods. The Haudenoshonee men were able to get the fire lit and a couple of flaming arrows fired at the fort before the warriors of Eirgalon with their superior numbers swept them from the field. Those couple of arrows did little damage to the fort, for men with buckets of water quickly extinguished any flames.

The flames may have been extinguished and the field of battle may have been cleared, but Senadondo was still on the loose.

Chapter 51 – Truce

High King Skoth was still in New Alba when he received reports that there were skirmishes at the southern flank near the high bluff and at Nealsfort. He sent messengers to spread the word all along the front that the forces of Eirgalon could defend themselves, but that they were not to advance or attack the opposing forces. In spite of the skirmishes, he resolved to keep his promise of meeting with Ayen near Nealsfort. However, he was worried about the activity in the south around King Duncan's command, so he dispatched Bjorn of Glesga, with reinforcements, to the southern outpost.

Early in the morning of the following day, Skoth made his way to Nealsfort. He was accompanied by Erik and a troop of their warriors. Evlin and Brigit, along with Maeve, Enat, Tiete, and Lil stayed at MacGregor's hall in New Alba.

To the west of the battle lines, Ayenwatha had sent out his messengers instructing all Haudenoshonee forces to stop any attacks, and to wait for further word from him. His contingents of Mohak men that had rushed to his support went on their way to return to the positions in the line that they had held and to spread the word of Malsum's flight and of Ayenwatha's ascendency.

Sagoye had followed Ayenwatha's route back to Tionnontoguen and had shared Skoth's response to Ayen's call for a meeting. As they made their way back east to Skenektedy and then to Nealsfort, Sagoye confided to Ayenwatha all that he had seen and heard of High King Skoth and his people.

It was late afternoon when Sagoye trudged out of the woods near Nealsfort. He carried a spear to which was tied a large white cloth. He waved it high above himself as he cautiously walked forward. He could see the signs of battle from the previous day upon the field. Stopping by the now scattered pieces of kindling and wood, he thrust his spear into the ground. He waited patiently as the white flag fluttered in the soft breeze of the spring day.

Meanwhile, in the fort, Erik insisted that he be the one to greet Sagoye. He would give the word whether to proceed, or not. Skoth accepted the demand of his senior advisor and from the open gate he watched Erik walk across the open field. Erik walked with a staff rather than a spear, but he had also tied a white cloth about it. Just as Sagoye carried a war club, Erik also carried a weapon on him, his trusty sword. Both of them knew that although this may be a meeting of leaders under truce, the situation could turn nasty in a hurry.

Erik stopped several paces from Sagoye and pushed his staff into the soft spring soil.

Erik spoke first, "You're back. Is Chief Ayenwatha with you?"

Sagoye replied, "He is here. Is High King Skoth with you?"

"Aye, that he is. Just he and Chief Ayenwatha will come out to us to meet alone, is this not so?

"It is so. Are you agreed to signal for them?"

"Aye. Let's get this started."

With that being said, both of them motioned for their leaders to come and join them on the field of truce.

From the woods walked Ayen. He had replaced his undergarment to cover the pouch from Enat and to hold it tight against his skin, but he proudly wore the leather outer garment that was scorched by the flame of Malsum's attack. He carried his war club and long knife at his waist and strode forward with his hand upon a short spear he used as a walking staff.

253

From the fort walked Skoth. He wore no helm or crown. He wore simple functional garments. The only sign of his position was the king rune hanging from a chain around his neck. It was the rune fashioned by the druid, Theofinn, and bestowed on him by King Unaine at the meeting where he was given the quest. Beneath his garments he wore the iron rune that had been fashioned for him by the blacksmith of Glenoak early in his quest. That rune was to protect him from malevolent spirits. He carried his sword in a scabbard at his waist and walked with the staff that had been carved for him by Fearglas.

Each one came to stand next to their advance man as they sized up the other. Both were young and full of the strength of youth, though Ayen was some ten years senior in age to Skoth. Cautiously, the men stepped forward until they stood only a couple of paces apart.

Standing behind him, Erik was proud of the way his young king waited. Learning patience had been a difficult experience for Skoth when he was a boy, but he had learned his lessons well and he had grown into a fine man. Ayen had been the one to ask for the meeting, though Erik knew Skoth had wanted it. Since Ayen proposed it then it was proper to allow him to speak first.

After several moments Ayen spoke.

"There is much for us to say. But let me ask a simple question: Why are you here? Do you desire peace or war?"

Skoth considered for a moment how he should respond. "There is much to say in reply, but the simple answer is that I would have peace between us, and peace between our people."

Ayen kept a straight face as he said, "I have been called a great warrior, yet in truth, I am a man of peace. I have made peace for my people by fighting to bring them together. I desire peace, but I am willing to fight for it."

"Can we fight for peace without bloodshed?"

"Would you?"

Skoth nodded, "Yes. I will fight on the field of battle to defend my people. But I will fight with word and deed to achieve peace without bloodshed, if possible."

Ayen nodded in response to this and then said, "Then we have much to discuss." He hesitated, glanced at the space around them and then went on, "My man. Sagoye, and perhaps your man behind you, have traveled far to be here. Our talking may tire them more. This place seems a good place to sit and talk. Would you trust me to send my man back to the woods and tell my people that we are talking and to have them return with fire and food."

Skoth allowed a smile to cross his face as he replied, "Enat has told me that I can, and should, trust you as I would trust her. My man, he is called Erik, would tell you that he never tires, but if you would allow, may I ask him to return to the fort and bring back some of my advisors: Enat's sister and her husband, my principal war chief, and perhaps some folks with more food. I suspect that you haven't carried with you as much to eat as we have in the fort."

Ayen, without trying to give away too much satisfaction in Skoth's openness said, "That is fair. Enat told me as well, that I should trust you as I trust her."

They gave instructions to Sagoye and Erik. Leaving their white flags of truce planted in the soil, the men turned and hastened back to their respective sides to do their tasks.

After the men had departed and there were a couple of moments of silence between them, Skoth said, "It seems a little foolish to just stand here and wait. It looks like there is a fair amount of wood and kindling scattered about. I say we get to work and gather it for a nice fire."

Ayen was beginning to like this young man. He certain didn't act all high and mighty. He may be called "high king" but he put on no pretensions about it. He would treat him with respect. Time would tell how far he was to be trusted.

"That's a good idea. We may be here a long time. The sun will soon lose its heat for it is getting late in the day. We have much to talk about and we may be here for a while."

"I'm willing to talk as long as needed." They worked pulling the remnants of the previous fire into a pile and then Skoth paused and asked, "Chief Ayenwatha, if I may ask, what is the meaning of that burnt hole on the chest of your garment.?"

Ayen allowed a chuckle to escape his lips as he gave thought to what he was wearing and what he must look like to the leader of a powerful people.

"Ah, that is quite a story. It is a story to be told around a fire in the hope that it might warm the hearts of the people."

Skoth responded, "Then it is good we are building a fire. I would like to hear that story."

Soon the groups from fort and forest began walking toward them and it was time to sit down and do the serious work of forging peace.

Chapter 52 - Sacred Grove

A solitary crow circled over MacGregor's Hall and then flew west disappearing into a grove of trees. Moments later Maeve's horse handler appeared standing next to the path that wound through those trees and then headed into New Alba. He stood waiting patiently. Within moments, Dakatomi and his men came up the path. They gasped in surprise when they saw him. Dakatomi's men quickly drew their weapons.

Then the man chortled and said, "Don't you recognize your old friend Senadondo?"

The men looked uneasy, but Dakatomi just said, "I was wondering when you would show up."

Senadondo ignored that and asked, "Were you successful? Did you get them to engage in battle?"

Dakatomi hesitated and said, "We did what we could, but I fear they were too cautious. We left before we heard sounds of battle. We knew we must hurry back here to be of help. Now, what must we do?"

Senadondo growled with displeasure when he heard Dakatomi report there was no battle, but he went on to give them instructions. They were going to enter the Hall of MacGregor and kill the child of the Bear-Witch.

Dakatomi protested, "But they know me and that I opposed claiming the high kingship. I am sure they still question my loyalty. The Bear-Witch is powerful and we won't be able to get close to her."

"That's true enough. But their eyes will be on you. Not me. You will distract their attention from me. They think this humble horse-handler is a spy for them. They will welcome me with open arms and then ignore me. Your job is simple enough. Distraction. When their attention is on you - then I will strike."

Senadondo went on to give them more specific instructions and then they went on their way into the settlement.

It was a warm spring afternoon so the womenfolk were no longer inside the hall when the assassins arrived at its doors. One of the guards remembered having seen these men a couple of days previously, but so many men had come and gone, that he didn't recognize any of them by name. He simply told them that the womenfolk had gone for a walk down at the Sacred Grove.

The Sacred Grove of New Alba was a grove of mature maple trees that circled a small lake on the outskirts of the settlement. The Wabanaki people of the area had for centuries tapped most of the trees of this grove for the harvesting of the sap, which was then cooked down into a sweet syrup. Since the coming of the Celtic settlers into this area generations ago, they too had observed this practice. This late in March, after a warm spring, the tapping of the trees was drawing to a close. Most of the men of the town were occupied with the military campaign , but many of the women and youth were active in the harvest and there was considerable activity in the grove.

The grove was large as it completely circled the small lake, but there was one portion where the trees were left untapped. This was an area where there were several huge trees and where a small rock shrine had been constructed at the water's edge. It was to this area of the grove that the women had come. Evlin felt that Brigit, who carried the name of a goddess of spring and fertility in Celtic lore, should be brought to this shine during this season of the maple syruping. There was just something that felt so right in coming to this place at the time of the Maple Moon.

The dry brown leaves of the previous years lay thick

and loose upon the ground, punctuated here and there by the bright green of freshly sprouting ferns. Evlin had laid the babe on a bed of maple leaves in front of the shrine and she and Maeve were seated facing the shrine and the lake. Enat, Teite, Waneek, Lil, and Lil's mother were circling the lake in a clockwise fashion as they followed the path around it. They had just stopped at the far side of the lake and from a distance seemed in deep conversation.

The three men, Anoka, Kenda, and Tekaya, who had guarded Evlin on her captivity but who had now become her protectors, stood in the woods around the shrine, as their guards.

Evlin and Maeve had been peacefully meditating for several minutes; and if folks would observe the two of them with the babe, they would undoubtedly think of the Celtic symbolism of the three stages of a woman's life. In this moment were represented new life, full bloom, and the wisdom of elders.

Even though the grove was alive with the sound of voices and the work of the maple syrupers, their guards picked out the sound of the leaves crunching a distance away from them as Dakatomi and the others came toward them.

Anoka cleared his throat and softly called to Evlin that they had company. She glanced over her shoulder and both she and Maeve stood up, turning their backs to the shrine and Brigit.

They came in single file with Dakatomi leading the way. Anoka and his men came together to block the path toward the women and to tell Dakatomi to stop and wait, for the women were worshipping. When the men reached Anoka, they did indeed stop and wait.

Dakatomi spoke up, "We have come with news for the lady of the land. May we pass?"

Evlin responded from behind Anoka, "It is all right, Anoka. You may let him come to me."

Maeve noted that her trusted horse handler was behind the other men, so she kept her attention on Dakatomi. She had always been suspicious of him and the last year's events had made that suspicion much more pronounced. Anoka walked forward with Dakatomi while Kenda and Tekaya, the other two guards, stayed back to watch the other three men.

Dakatomi had stepped forward and stood before Evlin. He was begging to speak when his men unleashed their attack on Kenda and Tekaya. When Anoka glanced backward, that was Dakatomi's moment to slip a knife from his sleeve and to lunge forward at Evlin. The area erupted into a flurry of activity and flying leaves as Anoka wrestled the old shaman to the ground and the other two guards grappled with Dakatomi's two men.

Unnoticed in this moment of mayhem was that the form of the horse handler dissolved down to the ground and transformed itself into a large timber rattlesnake. The snake slithered through the leaves toward the shrine, and to the baby that lay on the leaves before it. While Evlin and Maeve watched the men struggling, neither heard nor noticed the rattlesnake as it approached Brigit.

The snake gave no rattled warning of its intention to strike but as it neared the baby, Senadondo in rattlesnake form couldn't help but hiss in the pleasured anticipation of his strike. Both Maeve and Evlin heard the sound and looked down in time to see the snake rear up to strike the child. But then the incredible happened.

Brigit, with her young eyes focused upon the approaching rattlesnake, had lifted her hand as if to stop it. And the snake appeared to freeze in mid-motion. Both Evlin and Maeve threw themselves on the snake, grabbing it behind the head. It writhed with incredible strength, but the innate power of the Bear-Witch overwhelmed it. Touched and held around the throat by her power, Senadondo was forced to shift back into his human form.

Anoka turned from Dakatomi's lifeless form on the

forest floor. He had wrestled the assassin's knife away and stabbed him with it. Now seeing his former commander held by Evlin, he leapt forward and plunged the knife into Senadondo's side.

Though struggling and cut by the knife Senadondo spat out, "You can't kill me, you traitor."

Then Evlin said, "But I can. I call you by your true name, Two-fang of the Black-heart. Feel again his blade as it pierces your heart and die! Anoka, stab him again and hit his heart."

Anoka did as he had been commanded.

The light in Senadondo's eyes went dim, his body went limp, and he breathed his last.

Maeve had moved away from Senadondo when Anoka had stabbed him and she now reached down to lift Brigit to her chest. Before she could touch her, Evlin shouted, "No!"

Maeve stopped in mid motion to look at her and said, "What?"

Evlin said quickly, "Loyal Anoka will stand over her and watch out for her. Before we touch her, we should purify our hands in the waters by the shrine. The filth of that limikkin may not be able to harm her, but we have touched him, and it is best we remove it from ourselves before we touch her."

So with Anoka standing over Brigit with a look of fierce determination to guard her against any evil, the two women stepped to the shore and knelt by the sacred water. Gently they washed their hands and said prayers of supplication and thanks to the guardian spirits of this sacred grove. Though the earth may have been soiled with the blood of evil hearted creatures, the grove was a place of life and peace. It was right and good to say thanks.

Now, standing and looking about as she went to pick up Brigit, Evlin saw the people who had been working in the grove running towards them. The sound and sight of the struggle had brought them running to help. But all they could help with now was the removal of the dead assassins. Kenda and Tekaya had suffered slight injuries as they had fought and killed their adversaries, but they stood proud for they knew they had played an important role in defending their charges.

Evlin picked up Brigit and nestled her to her bosom.

Maeve quietly asked, "Did you see what she did?"

Evlin smiled and replied, "So you saw it too. She is a wonder to be sure."

By this time the women from the other side of the lake had arrived. The younger women huddled around Evlin and the baby, while Lil's mother and Waneek joined Maeve in tending the injuries of Kenda and Tekaya and in giving directions for the removal of the bodies. The attackers would be burned and their ashes separated and scattered in the river.

The return to MacGregor's Hall became a procession, as news of the attack had spread among the townspeople. They all wanted to see that Evlin and Brigit were safe and healthy. Before entering the hall, Evlin stopped and gave a short speech to those who were following.

"Friends. People of Eirgalon. Thank you for showing your care and concern for us. All of us here are fine. A couple of my loyal protectors suffered some injuries, but the men sent by Malsum have failed to harm us and they have been killed. We are safe here. Please return to whatever work you were doing, and know that I appreciate your loyalty, your love, and your desire to build a peaceful land."

After a period of prolonged cheering, the people began to disperse and the women entered the hall. There Evlin and Maeve, told them the details of what had transpired at the shrine in the sacred grove.

Enat and Waneek exchange knowing glances with each

other when they heard of the power that the child had shown over the snake. Enat resolved to tell them about the necklace and share what Ayen had said about it at the earliest opportunity when Skoth was present.

Late in the evening a messenger arrived from Skoth. They were to leave New Alba early in the morning and come to Nealsfort.

Chapter 53 - Field of Peace

The conversation between Skoth and Ayen went long into the evening as they sat around the fire beneath their flags of truce. Both men were staunch advocates for their people, but neither man wanted the bloodshed and horrors of war.

At the end of their evening dialog, they had sent commands to all of their warriors and outposts with strict instructions that there was to be no fighting. Returning messengers had assured them that neither side would attack.

Bjorn of Glesga sent a message that they should not be alarmed if a large smoke plume arose from near the southern high bluff. King Duncan had charged into battle and been slain. They were building a funeral pyre at the place where he fell and would be sending him on his journey. The day looked to be clear and the smoke would rise high in his honor.

Over the bonfire of the previous evening, the leaders had proclaimed that this field in front of Nealsfort was to be honored from this day forth as a place of peace between the Eirgalonian and Haudenoshonee people. Skoth had also declared that the fort, which had bristled with weapons and warriors in the months and days leading to this moment, would no longer be a military base, but would become a place of trade and commerce between their people.

At one point in their conversation Ayen had bluntly asked, "Do you intend for the land of my people to become a part of Eirgalon, with you as its High King?"

Immediately, Skoth responded, "I seek no kingship by conquest. The people and leaders of the nations throughout the land of Eirgalon have bestowed the title and the responsibility of High King upon me."

"Ah, no kingship by conquest," pondered Ayen aloud, "that leaves the door open to other means."

Skoth smiled at that. "Aye. I'll not deny it, for I swore a solemn oath before earth and sky to serve the land and its people. Should it ever happen that your land and people seek to be a part of what we call Eirgalon, who knows?"

"Who knows, indeed."

A look of inward reflection slipped over Skoth's face as he said, "For centuries my people have called this land Eirgalon. I believe that would translate into your tongue as The Land Beyond the Sunset. Our Celtic and Viking forebearers came across the waters to this land beyond where their eyes imagined the sun to set, and so they called it Eirgalon. Perhaps that is an invitation to us to always look beyond where we are and to be open to the possibilities of what may come."

Ayen responded, "That is interesting, for my people of the Mohak nation look to the western lands of the Haudenoshonee where there are some long narrow lakes, much like the marks that the claws of a bear might make as it scratched a tree, and we call them the Sunset Lakes. For to us, that is the land where the sun sets. Perhaps our people have the same thought as yours."

Skoth mused, "If so, we may indeed share a future. And it will be a future together, not a future where one destroys the other."

"Some people have called me the Peacemaker, but perhaps that is a title best bestowed upon you and your vision."

At this Skoth laughed, "I thank you, but if your vision and people have given you the name of Peacemaker, then it belongs to you. It is rightly earned, for you have taken Malsum's War and turned it into Ayenwatha's Peace."

They had talked long into the night forging their agreement, and then ended with the promise that they would return on the morrow and bring others to help them join in the celebration of peace.

Skoth's people from the fort and camps and Ayen's people from their camps in the woods spent the morning preparing the field for their peace celebration. They brought wood for a large central fire and for several others about the field. Tents and canopies sprouted about the open field turning it into a temporary village. Men and women brought food and refreshments to be shared. Several deer and wild turkeys were set to begin roasting on spits over the fires.

By late morning, Evlin and the entourage had arrived from New Alba and shortly after that a large contingent arrived from the nearest Mohak castle of Skenektedy. Even the former Celtic traders who had fled as refugees from the western Haudenoshonee lands returned. Karl and MacGregor had encouraged them to stay in New Alba in the hope that ties would be re-established with the Haudenoshonee people.

Although the traditional story-telling time of the winter season had concluded, there would be stories aplenty to be told around the fires. Both cultures, the blended Wabanaki/Celtic culture of Eirgalon and the Haudenoshonee culture of the five nations, were story-telling cultures. Sharing their stories would be the best way to acquaint themselves with each other and to cement the newly forming alliance.

But before the feasting and celebration could commence, some formal ceremonies needed to be performed.

Skoth and Evlin, holding Brigit in her arms, stood at the front of the gathered Eirgalon host of warriors and supporters. The sisters, Erik, Karl, Maeve, and the rest stood a few steps behind their leaders but looked on with pride.

Ayen came to the fore of his gathered people. Waneek, representing the Wise Women of his people, was at his side. To the surprise of many, he made a beckoning motion to Enat, and she came to stand at his side.

Skoth spoke first, "Welcome all, to this field of peace. On behalf of the people and land of Eirgalon, I greet you in peace and friendship."

Ayenwatha spoke similar words, "Welcome to this place of peace. On behalf of the Haudenoshonee people and the land we love, I greet you in peace and friendship."

Other welcomes and introductions were made and then blankets were spread upon the ground and the people gathered close so that they might sit and hear the stories that had led up to this moment and the agreements that their leaders had made.

Erik was a wee bit discomforted when Skoth asked him to start the story telling by relating the story of the bestowal of the High King rune and the quest. Of course, Skoth enjoyed seeing his old mentor a wee bit ill at ease. However, Erik soon recovered and immersed himself into the telling of the tale.

This story was followed by Skoth telling of his winter with Fearglas, how he came to love Evlin, and then the promise he made to Fearglas to serve the land. When he finished with his tale, he turned to Ayen and asked if he would share some portions of his youthful vision quest with the assembled crowd.

Ayen stood and cleared his throat as Skoth returned to his seat by Evlin.

"Our vision quests are sacred to the lives our people. And I will not share all parts of this vision. It is a vision of war and of peace. I had thought that peace must be achieved through war and subjugation. This was also what Malsum encouraged me to believe. I saw a beast enter our land. A beast I could not defeat by myself. But if I could persuade my friends to fight with me, we could defeat such a beast. In response to this, I have brought my friends together: Mohak, Oneida, Onondaga, Cayuga, and Seneca. I brought them together so that we might confront the beast. The challenge has always been how to identify the beast. Who is the beast of my vision? Is it the pale ones from the east who might take our land from us, or is it Malsum who might take our freedom from us, or is it ourselves who might destroy ourselves as we make war on each other?"

After a short pause, he continued, "Another part of my dream included a young girl taking an old man by the hand and walking into a peaceful sunset. Perhaps the time will come when I will speak more of that, but know that all my visions have a goal of peace."

Then Ayen turned to Evlin and asked her to tell the story of her captivity. She stood and spoke of Senadondo's trickery and Gakko's evil intent. She shared the brave pursuit by Erik and his men, and she told of the sacrifice of Fearglas.

There was nary a dry eye in the crowd, for who would not give their life for their child?

A beautiful event was happening as these stories were being shared. They were tying the listeners together. Haudenoshonee and Eirgalon people were becoming part of a shared story and it was a powerful story.

Evlin ended her narrative with the birth of Brigit and as she held up her daughter for the crowd to see a palpable feeling ran through the crowd. If one was able to feel the sight of a smile, this was it.

Evlin invited Waneek to speak of Enat's year with the Mohak people, and Waneek spoke but briefly. She reminded the crowd of how Ayen's mother and sisters had died and of the grief that family and clan had felt, and then she spoke in glowing terms of how Enat's presence had graced their lodge during the past winter. With appreciation in her voice, she invited Enat to speak.

Enat shared the story of her time with the Mohak people of Tionnontoguen. She told of her growing respect for Ayen and his people. Then she spoke of her growing love for Ayen during this time, and of how she came to know him, not as a man of war, but as a man of peace.

She gave a compassionate look to Karl, who was listening with rapt attention. He gave her an understanding nod in return and she continued. She told of the tense days from when the Celtic refugees appeared at their doorstep to when Ayen sent her and Waneek away from the danger of Malsum. She thought of sharing the story of the loon's necklace, but felt that was Ayen's story to tell.

He picked up the telling of the tale, and he did speak of how he entrusted this talisman of great power to the woman he loved, for the women of his line had died and he feared to let it fall into Malsum's hands. Then he directed their attention to the hole in his outer garment and reached to the cord at his neck to draw out the amulet that Enat had given him. He continued that story, detailing how in his confrontation with Malsum outside the castle of Tionnontoguen, it had saved his life. It was hard for him to continue as he looked with great ardor upon Enat.

Skoth picked up the telling of stories by speaking of regret about the fighting that took place at the High Bluff to the South and outside of Nealsfort on this very field. He laid the blame squarely on the machinations of the loyal minion of Malsum, Senadondo. Then he told of how the limikkin's mischief continued. He looked to Evlin to speak, but it was Maeve who stood to talk.

She told of the recent events in the Sacred Grove of New Alba. Maeve left no doubt that she felt Brigit, this babe in Evlin's arms, was destined for the future of Eirgalon. She was the daughter of the Bear-Witch of the Wabanaki people and the High King. She was the granddaughter of the Green Man. With a look and a motion, this incredible child had foiled the attack of the evil Senadondo.

Ayen stood again to speak. This time Enat stood with him. He asked her to pull the loon's necklace out of her satchel so that the people might see it. She handed it to him and he began to speak.

"Hear me, people of the Mohak and Haudenoshonee lands, people of the land of Eirgalon, Celt, Wabanaki, and Lenape. I hold before you today this powerful totem of power we call The Loon's Necklace. It was given to us in trust by Gluskabi of the spirit realm. The women of my family have passed this sacred artifact down from generation to generation. They were appointed as its guardians. I know not if any of them have ever used its power, and I know not the full extent of its power. Those were secrets that died with my mother and my sisters. Perhaps the ancestors of my mother's line called upon its powers in some way to protect and strengthen my people. I know not. Even the Wise Woman Waneek, the sister of my mother, cannot tell me the full extent of its magic or history, nor can she summon its power. I hold it before you in my hands. Does anyone here dispute my right to possess this totem?"

He waited. Standing tall above the seated crowd, he turned a full circle that all might see him and that he might see them all. A hush descended upon the crowd.

Ayenwatha spoke again, "Does anyone among this gathering of people from all lands challenge my right as Peacemaker to bestow it upon whomever I choose?"

Again there was silence. None stood to challenge him.

With solemnity, Ayen lifted his voice to address the crowd, "Then I ask Evlin to stand and bring forth her daughter, Brigit."

Many eyes in the crowd widened at that summons, but none objected. Evlin stood and carried her babe forward.

Ayen continued, "The time has come to bury the war club that has been placed between our people. I have had enough of war. It is time for peace. It is a day for new beginnings. Let our people of the Sunset Lakes and your people of the Sunset Lands live in peace. Let this child be a symbol of our future. A future which stops evil in its place. I entrust this necklace to Brigit and entrust her guardians with the responsibility of protecting it for her. May all their powers be used for the good of all people, and may in time the power of the loon's necklace be revealed and used for our people."

As he finished speaking his final words and was placing the necklace around Brigit's neck, the skies were punctuated by the laughing call of a pair of loons returning to their spring nesting grounds. Ayen looked up to the sky, as did many others in the crowd, and laughed a hearty laugh when he saw the pair of loons piercing the sky like arrows.

Ayen then finished his speech with saying, "It appears to me that Gluskabi might just agree with us!"

The crowd rose and shouted in acclamation. As they were shouting, Ayen reached into the bag he carried with him and pulled out his flute. He began to play. As those around heard the sweet sound of his flute, they fell silent. Then those further away heard, and they too fell silent. Soon the entire crowd was listening in rapt attention as Ayenwatha, the Peacemaker, played the song called "The Loon's Necklace."

Chapter 54 - Mid-Summer Festival at Tara

At the end of the peace meeting at Nealsfort, High King Skoth had invited anyone that was able to come and celebrate the mid-summer celebration with them at Tara. Many of those who had traveled great distances in early spring to prepare for war had returned to their homes to live in the safety and security of the newly established peace. But some of them, especially many of the leaders, were able to make the journey to Tara. There they would celebrate with the High King of Eirgalon and his many guests.

The kings and territories of Eirgalon were generous in their gifts of appreciation and fealty to the High King. Peace throughout the land brought prosperity and there was much for which to be thankful. Trade with the Lenape people to the south and west was increasing and the trade and arrangements with the Haudenoshonee people to the west and north were returning to the level of previous years, with the certain likelihood of substantial expansion in the future. The economic Eirgalon League that Skoth had planned for was being put into place by Skoth's trade envoy, Notaku. Skoth was certain that trade and prosperity could tie the people together better than any amount of war and bloodshed.

King Unaine of Fada Innis, the long island kingdom that stretched eastward from the mouth of the Mahakentuck River, had arrived at Tara a couple of days before the midsummer celebration. The day following his arrival at Tara was a gorgeous sun-filled summer day. The sweltering afternoon heat found him enjoying the shade of a giant oak tree near the expanding-once-again Great Hall of Tara. He was having a private meeting with his young protégé, Skoth, and his old friend, Erik.

"Well, well, my young friend. It looks like you've done

271

pretty well for yourself," said Unaine as he gazed about the bustling new settlement.

Skoth smiled and looked pleased, but before he could respond, Erik chimed in.

"Yep. Sure enough, and doesn't he just look like the dog that finally caught the squirrel it's been chasing for years."

Unaine gave a hearty laugh at that, and Skoth even gave a little chuckle.

"Well, I suppose I do at that. I do feel satisfied with how events have transpired," said Skoth. He paused and then he went on, "Seriously though, overall the quest you sent me on seems to have reached a stage of completion. Eirgalon is united. We are building a society where all are included. However . . .?" he trailed off in question.

Unaine asked, "However, what?"

"We have the Loon's Necklace. If, indeed, that is the key to our future, we have it. But we don't know how to use it. And then there is still the problem of Malsum. While he may have lost his control over the Haudenoshonee, he is still out there. There have been rumors of him stirring up trouble in the Huron and Anishinaabe lands, and beyond. We still have to deal with him."

"Spoken like a true leader. One set of problems may be working to a resolution, but there are always new problems on the horizon. Good leaders can never just rest on their accomplishments in the past, but must always live in the present, and look to the future as well."

Erik chimed in, "Now don't go depressing the lad. He has done just fine, and I know he will in the future. That is, he will if he keeps his head on his shoulders and remembers the lessons his elders have taught him."

Skoth couldn't help but smile at the gentle reminder of his old mentor before he responded.

"Oh, don't worry about me forgetting. I've always got an ear to hear about cats, dogs, and any other sort of wise reflections that my elder warrior friend has a mind to share with me. Occasionally it actually does make sense."

Unaine looked at Erik and said, "I've been wondering if you will be coming back to Fadis Innis. Since I arrived here at Tara, I've been hearing some rumors that you are sort of settling in here. Have I lost my old drinking buddy, as well as my daughters, to greater Eirgalon?"

Erik hemmed and hawed for a few moments as he struggled to reply.

"I don't know how to tell you this, Chief, but I'm afraid you are right on the mark. I reckon I'm needed more here than in Dunsheelin. Not that Skoth can't manage on his own, but I have a hankering to help keep watch on that young one of his. There's something special about her. Mark my words, there's a touch of the spirit world about her."

At this very moment, Evlin exited the Great Hall, and carrying Brigit she began walking towards them.

Unaine face broke out into a genuine smile as he saw them, and he responded, "Aye. That there is, if the stories I hear about her be true. She certainly comes from an interesting lineage. But you may not be lost to me yet, old friend." Turning to Skoth he went on, "High King Skoth, It seems to me that the high seat of Eirgalon, Tara, should have its own academy. With your permission, I would bring several of old Theofinn's prize protégés here to Tara and start an academy that would rival any in the world, even that of Dunsheelin."

Skoth was stunned by the offer, but quickly responded, "Why, yes, that would be wonderful."

"With your permission, I would also give it a name such as Nealhall, in honor of your scholar friend who gave his life in your quest. Or perhaps, I should give Fearglas homage in the naming," he nodded toward the approaching mother and her child, "since we have him to thank for so much."

"Honoring Neal with a place of study would be proper, and I am planning other ways to honor the memory of Fearglas. But wait, you talk as if you personally would do this. How can that be? You are king in Dunsheelin. They need you there."

Unaine took on a reflective look as his continued, "Ah, well, there is that. But I've been thinking about that. My girls have all left the nest, so to speak. Leesha is with Tkaden in Wausacom, it looks like Enat will be making her home with Ayen, and even Teite is leaving me soon as she goes to wed Gunnar in New Caledonia. As much as I may enjoy the company of old Theofinn, I'd like to take on the challenge of forming a new academy of learning here. You did know, did you not, that I was always intended to be a druid, until my brother died and the mantle of kingship was passed on to me?"

With a quizzical look on his face Skoth responded, "I do remember hearing that. But who would be King of Fada Innis?"

"I've put a lot of thought into that. There is one man I would put forth at an alting for King of Fadis Innis, but I believe I would need your permission to do so."

The quizzical look on Skoth's face grew even more intense as he responded, "And who would that be?"

"Well, my High King, if you could see fit to release Karl from his duties as your Drottin, I would stand for him to be Chief in my stead. I think he has shown the mettle to make an excellent king for the people and land of Fada Innis."

Erik jumped back into the discussion, "Why of course he will release him. Karl has shown that he is a true leader. Folks listen to him and follow him. He'll make an excellent chief!"

By this time, Evlin and Brigit had arrived and joined the discussion. The men repeated to her what they had been talking about and she gave her words of approval as well.

Then Evlin turned her eyes on Erik and said, "As for you, my noble guardian, I will be most happy to have your insightful eyes join Anoka in watching over our young Brigit. I have a feeling she'll need plenty of watching. And I might add, since Waneek has agreed to stay with us as a sort of substitute grandmother, she will probably be pleased to have you here as well. I've seen the two of you together, and I must admit you make an interesting pair."

Erik was never the one to blush, but his face reddened a wee bit as Skoth and Unaine looked at him with raised eyebrows. After a few moments of discomfort with the attention, Erik recovered his composure and replied.

"Hmmmph, well, one could do a lot worse. She'll keep that young'un in check if anyone can. This may not be the same as Dunsheelin, but I think we can build a home here in Tara."

To which Evlin responded, "This is our home, and this is where the future begins."

Skoth put his left arm around Evlin and gently touched Brigit on her cheek with his right hand.

"We have a future to build here in Eirgalon. We may have had the Loon's Necklace bequeathed to Brigit, but we will have to help this little one figure out how to use it. May we have the wisdom and time to do so."

Unaine smiled in satisfaction at the words of the young couple. Erik was also pleased, but as he leaned back in his chair his thoughts went to some of the challenges that lay before them. If this child was anything like her parents, she would be headstrong and full of seeking adventure. She would not be an easy child to raise. And then there was also the reality that Malsum was still at large. Dangers there were aplenty in this life, but evil incarnate in the form of Malsum would be a challenge that could destroy Brigit and the future of the Eirgalon.

Then he thought, ah, well, time enough there will be to worry about and deal with the trouble of the future, now is the time to celebrate the goodness that is here. He looked again upon the young family and smiled.

The Chronicles of Eirgalon continue:
Book 3
Brigit's Bow

Prologue

By mere wisps of whispers do the gods speak,

ere so softly,

to the choices of a young woman,

and so is altered the course of human history.

In realms which lay beyond domains of humankind, exist such beings called by mortals: "the gods." Be they gods or demons in human thoughts matters little, for truth be told, to some they may be gods and to some they may be demons. Be that as it may, at times they touch the human world, and in their touching they move and turn that world into different outcomes and alternate timelines.

One of theses beings was known as Gluskabi. The people of Eirgalon viewed him as a benevolent spirit who delighted in the passion and pathos of the people of the land. It was his touching of human history that resulted in the timeline of a mixed society of people descended from the first inhabitants of the land joined to the immigrants from eastern Celtic and Nordic lands.

His alter-ego was a spirit called Lox. Lox's malevolence toward the human migrants from the east was palpable. So much so, that Lox manifested his evil intentions into the dream of a chosen one of the Haudenoshonee - Deganawida - and corrupted him to become Malsum. The Great Creator had intended Deganawida to be a great peacemaker for the people of Eirgalon, but Lox had twisted this man's vision quest to evil ways. The new High King of

Eirgalon, and the legendary Ayenwatha, leader of the Mohak, had thwarted these designs. Together they had worked to join all the people of the land - Celtic, Norse, Wabanaki, Lenape, and Haudenoshonee - into one society. They had defeated and banished Malsum.

However, while Lox was stymied; he was not destroyed. Malsum, Lox's human incarnation, now set his sights upon the bearer of the Loon's Necklace, the one who could seal into permanence the timeline Gluskabi had intended. Brigit became his target.

Born of blood, with the fire of life coursing through her veins, she had been entrusted with the power of the Loon's Necklace. Should she live and learn to use it's power, the people would grow and prosper. Should she fall to Lox, the people's future would flounder.

Become a follower of the Chronicles of Eirgalon at:

http://www.facebook.com/ChroniclesofEirgalon/

Appendix - Character List

Anoka - Mohak warrior

Ayenwatha - warchief of the Haudenoshonee

Bjorn - captain of a Glesga longship

Claire - wife of the ruler of Drogheda

Duncan - King of Glesga

Enat - daughter of Unaine of Fada Innis

Erik - warrior and advisor to Skoth

Evlin - daughter of the Fearglas, partner of Skoth

Finn, Erik's nephew

Gakko - Senadondo's mate

Gela - wise woman of the Lenape

Jake - one of Erik's men

Keith - Chief of Dundee

Kenda and Tekaya - Oneida warriors

Lil - Duncan's wife

MacGregor - leader at New Alba and father of Lil

Maeve - mother of Tkaden

McLean - ruler of Drogheda

Notaku - protégé of Keith

Rolf - one of Erik's men

Sagoye - Waneek's son, Mohak warrior

Senadondo - Haudenoshonee limikkin (shapeshifter)

Skoth - High King (Ard Ri) of Eirgalon

Talli - sachem of the Esepus village of the Lenape

Teite - daughter of Unaine of Fada Innis
Theofinn - druid master at Dunsheelin
Turla - war captain from Heilsand
Unaine - King of Fada Innis
Waneek - wise woman of the Mohak

Appendix - Map of Eirgalon

Eirgalon